Thank you for everything! Love Kali Shevlin

Battle for the Stars

Kali Shevlin

PUBLISH AMERICA

PublishAmerica
Baltimore

© 2008 by Kali Shevlin.
All rights reserved. No part of this book may be reproduced, stored in a retrieval system or transmitted in any form or by any means without the prior written permission of the publishers, except by a reviewer who may quote brief passages in a review to be printed in a newspaper, magazine or journal.

First printing

All characters in this book are fictitious, and any resemblance to real persons, living or dead, is coincidental.

PublishAmerica has allowed this work to remain exactly as the author intended, verbatim, without editorial input.

ISBN: 1-60672-658-7
PUBLISHED BY PUBLISHAMERICA, LLLP
www.publishamerica.com
Baltimore

Printed in the United States of America

Acknowledgment

This book wouldn't have been possible without the love and support of several people who I'd like to thank.

First, I would like to thank my family for believing in me and helping me out whenever I needed it. You have been great inspirations, especially my twin, Kelsey.

To my English teacher and friend, Mrs. Sue Johnson, for editing the rough draft and staying after school to help me with certain story problems.

And lastly, I would like to thank my friends; Gerald Lassaline and Jake Caporaletti, for letting me use them and their stories in this novel. They're the best online friends a girl could have.

Chapter One

Once, a long, long time ago there was nothing. The entire universe was black, empty, and lifeless. For eons the universe existed in complete silence. Everything remained exactly the same with nothing changing.

The only forms of life were the Celestial Gods, beings of pure power. They looked at the blank universe and thought of what they could do with it. The time for a change had come. Pooling their collective powers together they sent the first spark of life into the universe and waited to see what would unfold.

At first nothing happened. Then that spark started tugging on the fabrics of time and space causing life to begin. Colors flashed, sounds thundered, and pyrotechnics occurred all over the universe causing strange and new things to come to be. Soon stars, planets, asteroids, and every type of stellar phenomenon appeared in the universe in a very short amount of time.

In the center of the universe was a planet much like Earth. On this world intelligent life formed almost as soon life began. This race of beings was created from the leftover energy from the Big Bang, which created the first four Entities. Their names were Time, Nature, Wisdom, and Emotion. They became the Council of Four, the leaders of the Entity race that came to be shortly after the Council was formed.

Entities were beings of pure thought and energy bound together in one form. They could literally control the fabric of time and space making it do whatever they wanted it to do. Because of this they were beyond the ability for most races to comprehend their true forms and they seemed to be all powerful and immortal, but they were not.

Only the Celestial Gods were more powerful because they had control over life and death and they had started things. They would meet with the Entities once and while to discuses things, but other then that they remained in the heavens not interfering with their lives. They had done their part in creating the universe now it was the Entities turn to take care of things.

Every Entity had the same basic powers, but each individual represented or controlled something different. With these powers they inspired their own thing to flourish in the new universe. This became their purpose in life.

As time passed the Entity race grew into its own society. They developed their own language, customs, and culture. They built homes, started families, and started roaming the cosmos using their powers responsibly.

They named their world Entara; it meant eternity in their native tongue. They took it upon themselves to populate the universe and observe it and the people growing and developing.

For centuries they were all content. They had everything they wanted and would ever need. Everything was okay and it looked like it would stay that way for all time. The universe was growing, changing, turning into something the Entities could be proud of. New races were coming into existence, all kinds of space events occurred, and the Celestial Gods seemed pleased by their efforts. That's when they felt the presence for the first time. Something was destroying the very universe they had sworn to protect.

It was the Nameless, a huge black shrouded creature with a reddish brain. This creature was neither a he nor a she. In fact it wasn't even a true life form in the proper sense. It was more of an anti-creature. It was also created in the after effects of the Big Bang. Its one goal in life was to return the universe to a complete state of nothingness. It couldn't stand all this life because it was unable to die unless all life was silenced.

In order to fulfill this goal the anti-creature had the ability to destroy the time/space fabric. By ripping it apart life would cease to exist. Given enough time the universe would go dead again and would never be able to produce sweet life again. This could not be allowed to happen.

The Council met in the Grand Meeting Hall to decide on a course of action. They deliberated what to do for twenty years. Finally they declared war on the Nameless. It would be a strange war. There were three objectives to be carried out. The first was to repair the damage already done to the universe, the second was to protect the universe from further destruction along with Entara, and lastly to destroy the Nameless at all costs. They couldn't let the reality around them die.

Things were difficult while the war raged on. The Nameless counter attacked the Entities early attempts to contain it. It created a race of minions from dead star matter to serve it. They were called Killgonas, a word meaning "Entity Eater" in their language. They would devour the sick, injured, or pregnant for their energy then they would transmit the extra to their Master so it could grow stronger. In their natural state, they looked like pale blue, transparent, wingless dragons that could fly through the air. They could shape shift and channel enormous amounts of energy into attacks. In their human form their were only a few differences such as extra sharp nails, pointed teeth, and blue tendrils on their temples, which ran into their hairline. They were equal in power to the Entities and almost impossible to kill because they existed on all planes of existence at once.

The war lasted approximately two trillion years. In that time much damage was done, irreversible damage. Many worlds went lifeless, stars had gone dark, and the death toll was too high. The Entities had one last chance to save the entire universe and all reality from destruction that was nearing. But the cost would be dear.

All four thousand Entities combined their power together to create an anti-universe and trapped the Nameless there, sealing it within. The anti-universe was nothing but, blank, white, empty space. There was no beginning, no end, and no direction at all. No one could even begin to judge the size of this place. It would serve as the Nameless's prison for all eternity.

Then they divided the fractured universe up into a multiverse, which split all of reality into a trillion little ones, each with their own dimensions and planes of existence. This ensured the survival of all life that remained after the war.

To prevent realities from mixing and causing further damage, an energy barrier was erected. Each reality vibrated at a different frequency, and all the energy together traveled throughout the multiverse to a special door that connected to the anti-universe. Here it reinforced the seal that prevent the Nameless from escaping.

The last step was to move Entara out of normal time and space to observe the newly created multiverse and keep an eye on the anti-universe. It was a victory of sorts, but things were far from perfect.

The Killgonas, who had been merely scattered, wouldn't rest. They were determined to free their creator from its prison. They wouldn't rest until the

Nameless had completed its quest. There were at least two ways to do this.

One way was to cause the extinction of a reality. When a reality collapsed they would steal most of the energy for their Master and themselves. What little was left would travel to the next reality. Eventually it would reach the seal and weaken it because it carried the seed of extinction in it. A way had to be found to prevent this from happening. The way the Enties discovered to prevent this led to the second path, which could free the Killgonas Master.

Since Entities couldn't risk another war or direct interference with younger life forms they searched for another way to help save them. They wouldn't allow all their hard work to be for nothing.

A new way was discovered by accident. Entities could perceive a person timeline. From these they were able to determine that there was a delicate balance that could be used not only to fight the Killgonas, but also reinforce the energy barrier.

It seemed that certain people stood out from the entire population. These people had a certain glow to them that made them special. These people were known as the first generation of Crystal Carriers. They were the protectors of their realities.

Crystal Carriers where beings who's pure heart crystal had become visible for all to see. There were three colors, blue was for good, red was for neutrality, and black was for evil. They hung on gold chains and the crystals themselves were long and pointed. The crystals had amazing powers and with these the Carriers could protect their reality and communicate with the Entities that guided them.

These powers included having the power of a previous owner if the crystal was passed on to another generation or even the limited ability of an Entity, doubled a person natural power, create a protective force field and heal. Also it could be used to determine if someone was telling the truth, change outfits, teleport, and locate other Crystal Carriers in the same reality. A piece of a person soul could be preserved inside the crystal and they could manipulate energy fields. There last few powers were the ability to summon their Entity, combine crystal powers together, slow down aging, and move a person through short amounts of time and space. These powers along with a Carriers natural ability made them excellent protectors, but it also came with a great price. To be a recognized Crystal Carrier meant you were in constant danger and had tremendous responsibilities.

The Killgonas were both happy and angry when they learned about these protectors. On one hand, they couldn't harm a recognized Crystal Carrier which where the most powerful. The ancient laws of war forbid it and even they couldn't break them. On the other they could hunt down and kill unrecognized Carriers. They would use their energy to help their Master grow stronger. But it wasn't easy to find them because Crystal Carriers were watched over since before they were born by the Entities. No matter how hard they searched, they were not always successful in their hunts so their Master stayed imprisoned.

It has been nearly three eons since the Nameless was locked away. The Entity race is at peace and the multiverse has flourished greatly. The Crystal Carriers have done the job of keeping the balance between good and evil, which in turn keeps the barrier strong. They also have defended their realities from the constant threat of Killgonas making sure that the situation doesn't change. But that's all about to change.

In the war against the Nameless and its minions two of the most important Entities that ever existed were born. The twin girls are now seven eons old and their names are Star and Nova. They were the only twins to be born during the war. They were four eons when the Nameless was defeated. Now as teenagers they had one of the most important jobs in their world, to train Crystal Carriers and preserve realities. Because of who they are Star, Spirit of Justice, Entity of all Goodness, Creator of Life and Nova, Spirit of Injustice, Entity of all Evil, Representative of Death they have been chosen for a great honor. Together these two, their family and friends, and some special people would save the entire multiverse from destruction.

Chapter Two

The reality bubble glowed softly as it hovered in the center of the room inches from the floor. Images flashed across the smooth surface of the bubble and the nearby smaller bubbles pulsed in sequence with the main one.

The room itself was huge, about the size of three Distract Attorney's offices put together. The floors were covered in cream-colored tiles and a glittering rotating starry night covered the ceiling. The walls were lined with colorful tapestries dictating this particular reality's history, which consisted of exploration and space travel.

The huge engraved doors at the end of the room opened quietly and were gently closed. Light footsteps could be heard echoing across the room as a young Acolyte walked towards the center of the room. She paused in front of the bubble looking at it expectantly.

The Acolyte's name was Jasmine, and she was one of three hundred low-leveled Entities whose job it was to manage and tend to the Grand Temple's need. Being low level meant they were more in tune to the needs of Entara and weren't distracted by the problems that existed in the multiverse. The Acolytes guarded the reality bubbles that were gateways to the multiverse realities, as well as other minor duties around the Temple. They almost never left the Temple and they were always given great respect for the ancient wisdom and guiding nature.

Jasmine was six eons old, which was about thirteen in human years. Entities aged differently then other races so it was difficult to tell their actual age. She wore the traditional Temple garb, a long red robe with orange trim, gold sandals, and a black veil with bronze hangings. She was in her corporal form since all Entities recognized one another in their natural state it was just easier to converse in these forms.

In this form she was six feet tall and weighed about one hundred and fifty pounds. She had light green skin, pointed ears, and long red hair. She clasped her hands behind her back as she waited patiently for the user of the room to return.

She didn't have to wait very long. All members of the Entity race were both linear and non-linear creatures. This meant simply that the passage of time and how they viewed it was different depending on how they looked at it. What was twenty years for humans could be viewed as twenty seconds to them. It just depended on ones perspective.

Jasmine had been waiting for about ten minutes when a teenage girl emerged from the bubble. Frowning slightly she coughed to get her attention and spoke. "Welcome home, Star. I was getting a little concerned about you. You were gone longer then usual this time."

"You don't have to worry about me, Jazz. I was just enjoying the company of some friends is that so wrong? I mean its great when you're in a reality like Space Exploration and Adventure because in half of the others it's just a television show. Isn't that hilarious?" Star commented gently. She was about five seven and a hundred sixty two pounds with long, light, wavy blond hair and crystal blue eyes with tan skin. She wore a purple halter, blue jeans with purple patches, purple platform shoes, and a pair of gold star earrings and bracelet. She looked only about seventeen; her human equivalent and she gave off a purplish aura.

"I realize I was gone longer than usual, but there was a crisis I had to deal with. Besides with my job requirements and since I'm nearly graduated can't you cut me some slack?"

"You were gone for thirty minutes our time Star. You are still a student and just because of your job requirements and being a near graduate doesn't mean you can break the rules. They are imposed on us all for a reason. Your time limit is twenty five minutes and that's all," Jasmine reminded her. "I know the multiverse can be fun. Believe me sometimes I wish I could go to a reality instead of guarding them, but we all must do our duty and obey the rules."

She brought her hands up to the bubble and waved them in a circle. A light mist escaped from her fingertips and encased the bubble in a protective container. Sighing she turned to face Star.

"This isn't any easier for me then it is you. I've been working hard lately trying to keep the reality bubbles intact. These things are very fragile and could break if misused. If that happened how would we be able to keep an eye on the multiverse?"

"I know they are and I'm sure I didn't hurt them. You really think I want the only way to the multiverse destroyed? Honestly, Jazz, don't you ever wish you could leave this place? There is so much more to do on Entara then work at the Temple."

"I would love to leave this place and walk the grounds, but I can't. My mother and father need my help. As head of the Congregation they are training me to take over for them when the time comes. They have been acting strangely lately and I have been preoccupied with other duties so I haven't had a chance to dream about leaving. Really Star I'm okay you don't have to worry about me being lonely," Jasmine told her smiling with only a hint of sadness.

"Okay if you're sure. Anything else you want to talk to me about?"

"The rest of your friends left a hour ago. Nova told me to tell you she'll pick up Asteroid from the Institution today. Your parents are going to worry if you don't get home for dinner. I'll close up in here."

"Thanks, Jazz, I owe you. Bye," Star shouted as she headed out of the room to the Temple foyer.

The entire place looked like a ten story pink castle from the outside. But on the inside it was much larger and grander then anything ever imagined. Lanterns lit the halls, all types of artwork littered the halls and the floors themselves, magnificent columns held up the Temple and gorgeous jewels covered the ceiling. In every hall there were hundreds if not thousands of marble doorways. It was easy to get lost in here if the doors weren't numbered and there weren't maps to guide you.

Stepping outside the Temple was like entering a history book. All the buildings were from different eras and they came from all types of planets and realities. Entities loved combining their taste with that of other realities. There were billions of plants and animals and people walked, flew, or rode about everywhere. The enchanted sky above could show them anything their hearts desired. This was Entara Central, the capital of the world.

Most of the world's populace lived here, but there were other cities, towns, and villages on this and other continents. This place was where most of the race lived, worked, and died. Many things had changed on Entara since the war. The population had nearly doubled, there were hundreds of new cities, and the laws had been greatly altered, but mostly it was still the same paradise it had always had been.

Star smiled pleasantly as she walked through the city and towards the countryside where her home laid. She could have taken public transport or even teleported, but she preferred to walk whenever she got the chance.

Her mind was occupied by hundreds of different ideas and thoughts. She had ten new Crystal Carriers to train, her family's picnic next week, hanging out with Sporty and Faith, and her upcoming date with Animal to worry about. She was swamped for next week.

"I can't believe I have all that and school to deal with too. Mrs. Phil's class is so hard. I can't deal with her and science class. I can't believe I have to deal with all this and my responsibilities. Ah home sweet home."

Home was a huge three story, forty-five room purple stoned mansion with a pink roof and flags complete with a patio, pool, rose garden and front lawn the size of a football field. The entire place was a combination of Victorian Classic meets Twenty-First Century. This home was typical for a family of her status.

Entering the house, the first thing Star heard was a voice shout, "Watch out!" A miniature asteroid belt came whirling through the air and heading straight for her head at three light years per hour.

"Ahh!" she screamed using her telekinesis to stop the runaway belt. The belt stopped inches from her face. Brushing back a strand of loose hair she yelled at the top of her lungs, "Asteroid! You lost another belt. Could you come down here and get it please?"

A boy about five came racing down the grand staircase into the front hall which resembled a four star hotel. Panting hard he said, "I'm sorry, sis really. I got distracted and this one got away. I got it now see," he said standing up and grabbing the belt and putting it away in his pocket. The noise had brought the rest of the family, so Star could examine each one of them.

Asteroid was short, light skinned, with short dark brown hair and crystal blue eyes. He wore a blue t-shirt and shorts with sneakers. He controlled asteroids, meteors, meteoroids, and meteorites. He was shy, curious, excitable child who loved to play and have fun. He resented being the baby of the family.

Her mother, Sun, was tall and thin with her long blond hair kept up in a bun with blue eyes and tan skin. She wore a long, flowing, and pale yellow gown. Sun controlled stars and suns. She was a kind, warm hearted, gentle person. But when pushed came to shove she could be bit of a hot head and was over protective at times.

Moon, was slightly taller and broader then the rest of the family. With his short brown hair and gray eyes he looked quite dashing in his silver three-piece suit. He was in charge of moons and planets. He was serious, calm, yet a fair person. Both he and his wife were twelve eons old which made them about forty-five in human years.

The last member of the family was leaning against railing, annoyed at being left out. Nova was identical to Star except for her colors. She had black hair not blond, her earrings were six pointed red stars and a gold bracelet, and her clothing consisted of red halter, black jeans with red patches, and red platform shoes.

"You're late. I waited twenty minutes for you, but you never showed up. I had to pick up our little brother alone. I'm getting a little tired that you're dumping your duties on me."

"I'm sorry, sis, and I am sorry Asteroid. I never should have let myself get carried away with my duties. Do you need help with your homework? Maybe I could show you some new techniques for creating proper belts," Star offered. She really felt bad for letting him down.

"Maybe another time, dear. You have your own homework to do. Just because you're a working girl is no need to neglect your studies. I don't care if it's your first or last eon of school, family and studies are first," Sun told her daughter. She bent down and scooped up her son and headed for the dinning room to finish dinner. Nova followed her angrily.

Star muttered angrily under her breath. She had more important things to do than worry about philosophical issues, energy management, and her own unique talents. She just wanted to have some fun in realties.

Her father heard her and laughed. He hugged her tightly and whispered gently into her ear, "Don't argue with your mother. She's only looking out for your best interest. Your final year in school is as crucial as your brother's. All three of you need to perform perfectly at your midterms or you risk regression. I don't think you want that do you?" He looked at her gently as he brushed back her hair. He kissed her on the forehead, "Well, do you my little angel?"

Star looked up at him wide eyed and shuddered in horror. "Of course I don't! That would be the worse."

Regression was a very serious thing. All Entities were born with the same basic powers which they needed to master before they entered school. In school they learned how to control their powers and protect the multiverse, but it was the exams that counted the most; they decided one's fate.

Before entering school and during the exams the teachers and Council would evaluate a person's control to make sure no one got out of hand. If they felt the person wasn't up to the standards, they took away some of their powers and privileges until they were ready to handle them. Adults only occasionally had to be retested. It rarely happened, but it was still greatly feared.

"Father, please don't go there. You don't have to worry about Nova, Asteroid, or me. We're not going to be regressed. I promised you that my last year would be the best ever. I always keep my word. Now lets go have dinner shall we?"

Dinner was a simple meal of sloppy joes, potato chips, applesauce, and milk for the kids while the adults shared some crimson flower wine. Conversation revolved around Sun's new binary star system she had recently created and Moon's hope for the creation of a habitual planet. Asteroid babbled on and on about the upcoming galaxy ball tryouts at school. Nova just sat silently rolling her eyes. She seemed to be a million miles away.

"May I be excused please? I have a list of candidates for the Spirit Club I need to look over."

"All right, but finish your homework first before you go to bed," Sun told her.

Nodding her head, Nova pushed herself away from the table and marched upstairs to her room not even glancing back at her family. She didn't mean to be rude, it was just her powers and the things she represented showing their colors.

Star glanced up from her meal, filled with curiosity. Why had her sister been so abrupt? She had been acting especially tense today, more so then usual. Time to see what was up. "May I be excused as well?" she asked her mother. She didn't wait for an answerer; she just got up and left the room.

The instant she was out of the room she though herself outside Nova's room. She hesitated a moment before knocking on the large door. She steadied herself for whatever mood Nova was in.

"Nova, please talk to me."

The door opened a bit and Nova stuck her head out. "What is it? I'm busy Star."

"You seem to be a bit out of it tonight. You're a lot angrier then usual and I'm wonder if you're okay. If I did anything to upset you please will you tell me," Star asked concerned.

"I'm fine really, Star. I just have a lot on my mind and things that need to be taken care of. I promise you that there's nothing wrong okay. Look, I have to get back to work right now so if you don't mind I like to be alone," Nova told her tiredly before she slammed the door shut in her face.

Stunned and hurt by her twin's actions and the way she was treating her. It upset her a lot. She transported herself into her own room.

Her room was huge, like the size of a penthouse suite with room to spare. There were Persian carpets, Ming tapestries, crystal chandeliers with a fountain and reflecting pool to the right of the door and a Zen garden to the left. Art from every era and from a dozen worlds covered the walls. On several shelves were collections of figurines, books, stuffed animals, and treasured items lined along the wall and on a couple of tables.

Her most prized possessions were kept in a locked viewing case behind glass and protected by the best security money could buy. No one was going to take her treasures. These treasures came from realities she had visited and help out in although she never appeared in any viewings or writings about them. There were holoprograms from the space travel realities. On another shelf contained treasures from the animate comic realities were a bunch of oddly shaped boomerangs, freeze disks, and pictures of heroes. Her latest items came from a reality based of a cartoon about ghost hunting teenagers. It was silver metallic thermos that was used to catch ghost. Each of these things was an irreplaceable treasure that she wouldn't part with it if her life depended on it.

Star levitated to her canopy Queen Sized bed and settled down amongst the silk pillows and satin sheets. She sighed loudly. She liked a lot of the stuff in this room, but it mostly reflected her family's wealth. She would have preferred a normal teen room, but this was okay.

"Ah, no place like home. I guess I should start on my homework. God, I hate schoolwork. Computer, I would like some music, preferably animated movie soundtracks. Surprise me with a mixed selection. Start now please." The room was suddenly filled with songs from different soundtracks. Smiling she settled down and began working on her homework for Mrs. Phil's class.

It took about an hour and half, but she finally finished all her homework. Glancing out her windows she saw the enchanted sky was darkening. She wished for the hundredth time they had a real sky. It was one of the prices her people had to pay for existing outside normal time and space.

"How I wish that Entara was more like the realities we help nurture. Then maybe I could act more like who I want to be. Why can't I be as confident and happy at home here as I am when I'm in the realities helping people?" Closing her eyes she went to bed and dreamed sweet dreams about a life full of excitement and adventure.

Downstairs her parents continue their discussion about their children. Things had been very tense around home lately. Fights had broken out between family members and the children were starting to distant themselves from their parents. It was very unnerving for a close-knit family such as themselves.

"I just don't understand it Moon. Nova has become so distant lately and Star spends all her time in the multiverse realities. Asteroid wants to spend time with friends or trying out for school teams. Sometimes I feel I don't know my own kids," Sun told her husband as she cleaned the music room. She always cleaned the house from top to bottom when she was nervous or upset.

"Sun, there growing up. There no longer little kids anymore. The girls are seventeen in human years and our little boy is ten going on eleven. Its only natural that they want to explore their world and find their own place in it," Moon told her. He walked up beside her and gave her kiss on the check to reassure her.

"I hope your right. I just hope they don't grow up to fast or I might lose them forever," Sun told him.

"I'm sure things will be fine. We just have to wait and see what develops. That's the only thing any parent can do my dear."

Chapter Three

The next morning the sun was shining in a lilac colored sky. Two rainbows shone brightly in the morning sky. There was a gentle warm breeze wavering through the air and the morning dew sparkled on the grass. It was another wonderful day on Entara.

Star yawned loudly and rubbed the sleep out of her eyes. Rolling out of bed she went into her adjoining bathroom to take a warm shower. With a flick of her finger she turned on her T.V. to listen to the morning announcements for the entire city. There wasn't anything new that caught her interest. After grooming herself for a half hour she was finally ready to head for school. She picked up her bag and walked out her room remembering to turn the lights off.

"Come on Nova! We have to get to school early so we can meet Sporty and Faith. Asteroid, have you found your texts yet?" she called up the stairs. She tapped her foot impatiently and looked over at the grandfather clock in the corner ticking away. "Come on you two!"

"Settle down Star, your brother and sister will be down momentarily. They just need to finish getting ready. Now remember your father and I will be at work most of the day so if were not home when you get back from school don't panic," Sun told her oldest child.

"You're going into the office today? Why? I mean your new projects can't be that far along."

"Their not, but I need to use the computers to help me with some projections and your father needs to file some papers. I know we've been working hard lately, but I promise it won't be forever. Ah there you two are. Your sister was getting a little impatient waiting for you two."

"Isn't that Nova's department?" joked Asteroid. Nova elbowed him angrily. She hated it when her family joked about her individual powers. It

20

wasn't her fault she was the one chosen to represent evil, injustice, and death.

"That's enough from both of you. I warned you about fighting in my presence. Now you better hurry. I'll see you later tonight. Have a good day at school," Sun said hugging and kissing her children before ushering them out the door. She watched them go sadly. It was hard for her to watch her kids grow up and leave her behind because they'd been so close. She missed those times.

The three siblings decided to walk to school that day and enjoy the wonderful spring day. They may have complained a lot about school, but that didn't mean they didn't enjoy it. There were so many opportunities they had at school that weren't offered at home.

Star sighed inwardly glad today was only a half-day for the older students. Poor Asteroid had a full day and she knew he wasn't very happy about that in the least bit. But that didn't change how she felt. Things hadn't been easy for her these past few weeks. Lately she had grown restless at school she preferred to hang out in the realties any chance she got instead of enjoying the pleasures of Entara or even her friends and family. A life as a teenage Entity could be very frustrating at times and her duties didn't make it any easier on her.

Lost in thought she didn't even realize they had arrived at the school until Nova slapped her. Nova looked at her twin exasperated. "Quit zoning out on me, will you? I already sent Asteroid to the elementary area of the school so come on. We're supposed to meet Sporty and Faith before Ms. Phil's class, remember?"

"I'm well aware of my surroundings and of our meeting, thank you very much Nova. I didn't become top of the class by being forgetful or absent minded. I resent the fact you even think that," Star chided her, looking around her at the school taking it all in.

The Institution for Higher Learning was a wonderful school rich in history. It looked like a cross between the famous gardens, Ivy League Schools, and ancient Greek ruins. Here was the place in which every Entity could learn to safely use their powers and learn about their culture.

Leaning against a statue of the Council of Four in the courtyard were two girls. Their names were Sporty and Faith, and they were the twin's best friends in the entire world.

Faith looked Hispanic except for her long flame red hair and emerald eyes. She wore a pure white sundress and wrap around brown heels. She had a halo above her head and pair of feathery white wings on her back. She was the Entity of Faith and Religion. Out of the four friends she was the one most called upon to work with the Celestial Gods. Standing next to her was the fourth member of their group, Sporty.

Sporty was a buff African American girl with at least fifty different types of sports equipment on her. She was currently playing hacky sack. Out of the four friends other species, mostly humans, found it easier to relate to her.

Faith saw the twins and waved to them over. "Hello friends. It's good to see you two today. After yesterdays experience in the Grand Temple I have to say I'm feeling a bit of a rush. How was your experience yesterday may I ask?"

"It was beyond cool if you ask me. I didn't get to do much with my talents, but I had loads of fun. I helped a primitive race of beings develop a new way to play soccer. This time they actually used a ball instead of a rock! Talk about improvement," Sporty stated energetically. No matter what the situation she was always pumped up and ready to go. One of her more enduring qualities and she had several more.

"I worked with one of the Celestial Gods! How amazing is that? Me! A mere student working with one of the ancient creators? We worked together to bring peace to a land of dying people. It was sad to see them and knowing all I could do was to ease their suffering," Faith said sadly. She was usually more uplifting and spiritual, but when she got depressed life seem to cease around her.

"Good stories, but I've got a better one if you believe it. Mine was very potent to say the least. I helped an evil supervillian inflict harm upon an innocent. Not as much fun as your experience and obviously a lot less cheery. But that's what you get when you're me. We can't all have powers over sports/games or even religion. What about you Star? What was so fascinating yesterday that your forget your promise?" Nova asked annoyed still.

"I simply performed a small bit of service that's all. I helped exonerate one of my Crystal Carriers of a crime he didn't commit by allowing justice to be fulfilled. Or at least I advice his friends so it could happen. I mean isn't that a more accurate statement? You all know that we don't actually make anyone do what they don't want to do."

"She's right, you know. Remember Rules of Conduct 101? We may use our powers to aid, guide, influence, and manipulate a Crystal Carrier or ordinary individual, but under no circumstances may we directly interfere or control them or events surrounding them. If we did that, we totally take awake free will and mess with people's fate or destiny," Faith stated calmly. She picked up her school bag and threw it over her shoulder. She glanced at the clock tower in the distance. "Come on guys we better get going. Class starts in ten minutes and you know Ms. Phil hates for any of us to be late. If we miss a minute of class we're in for three hours detention or worse."

"Yeah, last time I was late by a minute she had me writing a fifty page paper on the reasons to be punctual. I swear that woman has it in for me," Sporty said angrily. With a snap of her fingers her hacky sack and baton vanished into her gym bag. Picking up her bag they all started to march towards class.

They reached their classroom with only five minutes to spare. The room looked like something found in a collage classroom except the walls were changing color every three minutes. The effect was supposed to sooth the student's minds. There were just fifteen kids in the class, including them. Star took her seat next to Nova and her boyfriend Animal.

Animal was very handsome by Entity standards. His long tawny colored hair and green cat eyes went well with his clothes. He wore a fish scaled jacket, feathered down shirt, amphibian skin belt and fur pants and snake boots. When he smiled it was always different no matter what his mood was. He was in charge of animals. He had a habit of rescuing extinct animals and bringing them to his private menagerie to live out their lives.

"Hi Star, it's good to see you. You look exquisite today. Got your report all done?" he whispered.

"All thirty pages of it. I found the topic easier to write about than last week's three thousand word essay on When to Help and When to Observe," she told him giggling.

Suddenly she went silent. Ms. Phil or Philosophy, her full name, appeared behind her desk. With a quick gesture she brought the class to order. Ms. Philosophy was very strict and didn't care for shenanigans in her classroom.

She was here to teach them about philosophy and that's what she was going to do. She had chosen for her corporal form a petite gray skinned woman with a big head, which her rainbow hair hid, in gray robes.

"Settle down class, please pass your reports to the front of the class, and no, I repeat, no altering your responses with your mind. May I remind you that if you're caught cheating the penalty is two weeks detention? Alright, now that we've finished our discussions on why by helping to save realities we help better ourselves grow as individuals, its time we started preparing ourselves for what will be on your upcoming midterms."

The class groaned and protested loudly. Midterms were still half a decade or five months off, depending on how you looked at it. Philosophy was one of the hardest classes that were required. They we all ready exhausted from trying to keep up with regular homework. Why did they need to start preparing now?

"That's quite enough from all of you. Midterms are nothing to joke about. For reasons that shall remain unmentioned, exams shall be moved up this year. You're having them in three months so you'd better be prepared or else you'll face regression. I'd be very disappointed in if any one of you failed and had to be regressed," Mrs. Philosophy said coolly.

"Its no use complaining it's already been decided. Don't give me those looks children. I don't make the rules I just enforce them. Now your full attention and I do mean your full attention on the board please. What we have to discuss today is very important. We are going to talk about opposites today. Why do two things that are completely different need one another to exist? Can anyone give me an example of two things that are opposites of one another?"

Several hands shot up eager to answer the question. She called on a boy who appeared to be made completely out of gemstones and jewels. "Yes Gem?"

Leaning back in his seat, he causally said, "Fire and water. There two things that are opposite of one another. We need fire for warmth and water to drink. Both are good and bad depending on how you use them, but when you combine them together they destroy each other." Gem was the Entity in charge of minerals and jewels. He was a little rough around the edges, but he had heart of pure gold, literally!

"That's a very good example of two opposites. However in your example the two things destroyed one another when they met one another. Why is that so? Faith care to explain it to the class?"

"Because neither can work in harmony with one another. They end up destroying one another. While this is true about most opposites, it's not always the case. Sometimes two things that are different can find a middle ground or become stronger when combined together," she answered swiftly.

"But how can that be true? By its own definition, opposites are two things that are nothing alike. It doesn't make any sense how they would need each other to exist or to become stronger," Sporty insisted.

"Yes, it does. If one didn't exist, how could it have an opposite to begin with? Take darkness and light. You need light in order to cause a shadow to appear. Shadows are a form of darkness," Animal pointed out.

"Further proof two unlikely objects or things can work side by side, but together? That's just not possible. Opposites can't intermix its as simple as that," Nova stated evenly. She gave a hard look daring anyone to challenge her.

"Then how do you explain us? We're beings who defy that rule. I mean we can be a liquid and a solid at the same time if we chose to be. Also we experience time both as linear creatures and non linear. So I think you're wrong," Weather, a geeky looking boy who controlled the weather, shot at her defiantly.

Ms. Philosophy let the discussion continue for an hour and a half before calling order. She was greatly impressed by her student's enthusiasm for the topic. "You have all brought up interesting points and listed several easy examples today. Right and left, up and down, and life and death are easy opposites to identify and explain. Yet, what you were unable to do was define the clear meaning of how these opposing forces come together as one. How they can cause an inhuman attraction between each other or the varying degrees they oppose one another. These questions you will need to be able to answer for yourself when the time comes."

"I advice you to look for the answers to these questions not in your textbooks, at home with your family, or even here on Entara. The answer is inside of you just waiting to be discovered. Remember these three important facts. (One) everything has an opposite no matter how insignificant it may be, (two) Opposites can't exist without one another so they seek each other out, and (three) separate they are weaker, but together they can accomplish much. It's time for you to go today. I want a ten page report on how many opposites you see in your day and what degree they are by Monday. Class dismissed," Ms. Philosophy said as the bell rang. The students gather their belongings and hurried out, racing for second period.

As the six friends walked through the halls they began to talk amongst themselves about what they had just learned. They passed several students and teachers on their way to other classrooms. On any given day the Institution was filled with over a thousand people busy learning and teaching.

"You have to admit this topic is a lot more complicated then anything else we've ever discussed in her classroom. They weren't kidding when they told us philosophy class would be hard. How do we even begin to deal with this particular subject? Also did you notice she seemed to be emphasizing this topic? I wonder why," Star asked her friends as they strolled down the corridors.

Perfumed candles lighted the corridors and the walls were made of special bluish yellow stone called sapharon. Statues and display cases could be seen everywhere. There were lockers that open by mental command and several classrooms. It was beautiful and comforting.

"Who really knows? Maybe its part of the practical exam we have to take during the exams. Nobody knows what's in those because they change every year. What I want to know is why they moved up the midterm exams in the first place. You have to admit that's strange," Gem told the girls. He began to fiddle with his gemstone watch a sign that he was nervous about this news. Usually he was solid as rock, but not now.

"Well, we shouldn't question the Council's decision. If they think that the exams should be moved up, then who are we to question them? They've never led us wrong before. Look I'll see you guys later. Faith and I have advance physics class next and I'm totally unprepared. See you later," Sporty said grabbing Faith arm and dragging her down the hallway.

"Gem and I have to get to History class. Were studying the formation of Entara's animal preserve on the southern continent and I don't want to miss that. So I'll talk to you later," Animal told Star kissing her goodbye.

"Well, see you later my lovely lady. I can't wait to hold you in my arms again. Always remember you're my precious jewel Nova," Gem declared, kissing her hand and depositing a canary diamond in her palm. With a flip of his fingers he was gone.

Star laughed at Nova's bemused expression. "You certainly have a way with the boys."

"Shut up. Boys, honestly they think they know it all. They believe that their better then us girls. How arrogant can you get? Still I have to admit Gem is a sweetheart. Why he wants to go out with Ms. Evil Girl is beyond my knowledge," she informed her sister as she pocketed the diamond.

"Hey, just because you're a bad girl at times doesn't mean you can't fall in love. Now come on, we're late for Gym class and your first in sims today," she reminded her.

When they reached the Gym class was in full swing. Several students were already in the sim rooms while other students were doing power control exercises. Instructors were barking orders out trying to keep things under control.

Sims were the most advance gym exercise there was. It was a way to practice their powers in a simulated environment similar to a reality without any danger to Entara or the multiverse. Since no one had the exact same sim, it was difficult to train or help one another for him or her.

An instructor spotted the two entering the gym and scowled. "Star! Nova! You're late and I don't have time to hear your excuses. I want both of you in the Sims right now. You two better get a perfect score or your staying after class to give me a hundred pushups understand?"

"Yes sir, we got it. We're getting into the Sims right now. Man what's bugging him?" Nova whispered. Star hushed her twin as they made their way over to the Sims. This wasn't the time to talk.

Nova got into one of the newer Sims models. Putting on a pair of VR goggles she stepped into a zero gravity chamber. Instantly she was free floating five feet in the air incased in a red sphere of thought energy. She activated her powers and the sim began.

Star stepped into an old style sim room. This one was a simple, plain white room. She readied herself for anything. Taking a deep breath waited for her Sim to begin.

Suddenly she found herself in a room full of junk with a Killgona in human form hunting her. Her heart pounded the moment she saw that creature and she almost gave away her presence before she calmed down.

Quickly thinking she transmogrified her body into an old fashion candle lamp. She waited patiently wondering, what would occur next. Suddenly, she found herself shattered into a hundred pieces. Her own conscience was scattered, and she worked furiously to reintegrate herself into one body again.

By the time she had pulled herself together her surroundings had changed again. She found herself in the middle of a gas giant planet. She began to choke and lose consciousness. Quickly, she rearranged her molecules till she was nothing, but free-floating white mists in space. She was safe, but for how long?

That's when she was returned to her normal body and dumped amidst running, panicking humans screaming for their lives. She was wondering what the problem was when she saw it. The Nameless appeared in the sky, devouring everything in sight.

"NO! I won't let you destroy this planet!" she screamed at the top of her lungs.

Her aura intensified as she called upon her full powers so she could use them in one attack. Thrusting her arms forward, she concentrated her attack on one spot. She intensified her attack reaching critical low energy levels, but she wasn't about to stop.

Right before she passed out from almost zero energy the Sim ended, and an instructor was attending her to. Nova was kneeling next to her, merging their powers together in an attempt to bring her energy levels back up.

"How many times do we have to explain to you kids? If you lose all your energy levels plus your reserves you risk death! An Entity can't exist without both thought and energy working together to bind each other," he ranted angrily.

"I'm fine, thanks for asking sir. Now if you don't mind, I need to get going to my next class. Good bye!" Star snarled as she got to her feet and stormed out of the gym. Never in her life had she been so humiliated. How dare he chastise her about the dangers of using too much power?

Her feet automatically carried her to her final class for the day, which was Time Dynamics and Reality Theories. It was her master honors class. She really enjoyed it because it gave her chance to challenge herself. She spent the next hour and half trying to understand all there was to know about multiple futures and how you could identify the correct one. The equations were very complex and there were several conflicting studies she had to read. Finally, the day for the seniors was over and the twins left to go home and get ready for their dates that were later that day.

Their dates went very smoothly. Both girls enjoyed the company of their boyfriend and had a fun time at the park. It was typical for young Entities in love to come here and have fun. They loved watching the fountains go off at different intervals and music filled the air. The best part was when they played a game of power tag and Star won.

As the boys escorted their dates home they discussed what had happened in class and what the future might be for them. They all hoped to pass their exams and not be regressed. When they reached the mansion the boys kissed their girls goodbye and they went inside to start on their homework. They went to the library to do their work.

"So how are you doing in your masters honor class Nova? Advance Equilibrium. Learning the proper balance in the multiverse is hard," Star commented offhand.

"It's a stressing subject believe me. I hate the entire math and the debates give me headaches. But no way was I taking Cooking or Art. There not my thing," Nova replied as she levitated several volumes to her table. "Don't you ever get tired of all these advanced classes? I mean how will they help us in our duties? It just doesn't make any sense to me."

"Me neither sis, but I know that one day all of this will make sense. I just hope that I can figure out what to write for Mrs. Phil's report on opposing forces. I can't help, but feel this paper is going to come in handy sooner then we think," Star foretold.

The sounds of the doors opening and things crashing told the girls that Asteroid was home and he was probably playing galaxy ball in the house again even though he wasn't suppose to.

"I'll check on baby brother. You keep working on that report. It will help me later when I have to write that thing," Nova said heading for the door.

"Thanks, you're a good sister," Star told her meaning it.

Chapter Four

In the very heart of the Great Temple, the Congregation of Acolytes had gathered together for their nightly ritual. They entered the only room that was off limits to the general public. This room had the highest security and very few outside the Congregation knew of its existence. This room was where the door of to the anti-universe was housed.

The room gave off a forbidding feeling. On the walls on special perches sat glowing orange orbs that produced energy. Each orb pulsated in sequence with a particular realities energy barrier. The very barrier that kept the multiverse divided up. The energy that streamed down from the orbs circled the Acolytes who were kneeling on prayer mats. Their prayers magnified the energy and channeled it over to an ornamented door that was covered in chains on the far wall. Once the energy was received it glowed brightly as the seal that kept it locked up was reenergized. This door was the only thing that kept the Nameless locked up in the anti-universe.

When Entara had been moved outside of normal time and space, they had to develop a way to interact with both the anti-universe and the multiverse. The best example to explain the situation was to think of the three of them like layers of a cake. The top layer was the anti-universe, the middle Entara, and the bottom layer was the multiverse.

The Temple had originally been constructed to house the portals to the multiverse, but also served to house the door to the Nameless prison. The Congregation had been charged with the task of making sure the three universes never met. If they did it would be catastrophes for everyone.

From the Temple the Entities could keep an eye on all the realities in the multiverse, but more importantly the seal that kept the anti-universe closed. If that seal ever disappeared then nothing would stand in the way of the Nameless escaping into Entara and destroying their home.

Since they were low powered and had helped construct the Temple they were more in tuned to the needs of both places. When they worked together their powers were almost equal to the Council. They had each given their solemn vow to defend the Temple and protect the contents inside from any harm.

Jasmine stood up and looked worriedly at the sealed door. She may be a child, but even she could tell that something was wrong. It took a lot of effort to trap the Nameless in the first place, because of the energy required to do so the seal needed daily reinforcement. Lately, though, they weren't having as much as an effect that they use to. "I'm worried, Mom, Dad. For almost a century now the reenergizing of the seal has been taking longer to take hold. I fear that something is amidst."

Her mom, Sapphire, placed a hand on her shoulder to comfort her worried child. She looked almost identical to her daughter except she had pale blue skin and fin shaped ears. This ancient Acolyte was in charge of preservation and sacredness. She herself was troubled, but she couldn't let that on. She knew for a fact something was wrong, but couldn't tell her daughter anything. "I know, dear. With the extinction of the more ancient realities caused by those wretched Killgonas, things aren't the same anymore. I'm not sure what to make of it."

"I don't understand it at all. We've barred the only exit to the anti-universe, weakened the Nameless greatly, constantly monitor everything in the Temple and it still is able to talk with those killers. It's not fair Mom. Why? Why can't we put an end to this?" Jasmine asked frustrated by the helplessness she felt.

"The multiverse very existence is in a constant state of danger. Those Killgonas have been spreading their chaos for three eons now and nothing we do seems to hinder them. Until a way is found to stop them from attacking non-recognized Crystal Carriers and being the leading cause in an reality destruction permanently we are at their mercy. And they know this so they exploit us any chance they get. We must keep doing our duties or the Nameless and its attack dogs will once again be able to threaten all we hold dear," Guardian, her orange colored father, told his family. As Head of the Congregation, and the Entity of protection, the weight of the situation was on his shoulders.

The three of them stared at the door quietly as everyone else filed out. They all knew that it was their sworn duty to protect Entara and the multiverse from the danger locked on the other side. This did not make their lives any easier by a long shot. If anything it made them harder.

Suddenly, the door to the chamber burst open and in rushed two Acolytes who had left only moments earlier. They were panting hard and their faces revealed their fear. "Guardian! Sapphire! You must come quickly! We've got serious trouble on our hands," one of the two said.

"A reality bubble is falling apart and its one of the more major ones! You must come quickly to help us save it before it shatters!" the other yelled frantically.

Guardian and Sapphire immediately rushed off to see if they could repair the damage before it became irreversible. Jasmine watched them go, knowing this was only the latest in several problems that had been occurring lately. "Can things get any worse?" she said out loud.

Shaking her head she headed out of the heart and headed to her room, which was housed in the upper levels of the Temple away from prying eyes. She got herself some food and lay down on her bed to think. First the lag time in energizing the seal, then there was the increased attacks by the Killgonas, and now the threat of a reality bubble collapsing what did it all mean?

Even with her limited training as an Acolyte she could sense that things weren't as they should be. How much longer could her beloved Entara remain safe she wondered as she finished her snack and fell asleep. Her dreams were filled with confusion and fear.

When she woke up later she heard voices arguing outside her bedroom door. Surprised by the noise she decided to find out what was going on. Creeping slowly towards the door and listened in on what her parents were saying. What she heard shook her to the core.

It seemed that they had only just barely managed to save the collapsing reality. But in order to do so they had to sacrifice two alternant dimensions within it to keep it running. That would have major consequences later on as the reality grew and developed. If they had to use such drastic measures once, who knew what they have to use next time. What was going on?

"I don't like this one bit Guardian. We should inform the Council immediately about today's events. This incident is only the latest of several problems we've been experiencing," Sapphire argued to her husband. Her voice had risen several volumes, as she got more upset.

"We mustn't alarm the Council just yet. If we do things could be blown out of proportion or even worse. I say we should wait for awhile before taking any action," Guardian replied tensely. His voice betrayed his fear though.

"We can't wait much longer! You and I both saw the door acting up earlier. Added to the fact that the reenergizing are starting to fail and the reality bubbles are falling apart I say we have a crises on our hands."

"I know my dear, but I still I feel we shouldn't be to hasty. Caution is advisable in situations like these."

"If you weren't the Head of the Congregation and my husband I wouldn't let this go so easily. But I feel I must accept your judgment for now even if I think your making a mistake. I wish you would reconsider. I'm going to bed now. I shall see you in the morning," she told him and with a swish of her robes she was gone.

Jasmine trembled slightly. She had never heard her parents this worried before. Nor had they argued like this in her entire life. It was a sure sign something was seriously wrong. Knowing there was nothing she could do at the moment she crawled back in bed and tried to fall back asleep.

Later that night, Guardian left the Grand Temple and headed on foot for the Grand Meeting Hall that was in the center of the city. He stuck to the shadows and made sure to stay out of sight. He didn't want to be seen. If he were to many questions would be raised.

After twenty minutes of walking he came upon his goal. The building looked a cross between a giant ziggurat pyramid with huge arches and stone benches in an elegant courtyard. Four giant metal towers were placed at the four corners and in between them was a tall brick wall. On the wall itself was a beautiful mural showing the history of the Entity race. The mural ended at the wrought iron gates. From here you could see the many plants and animals that roamed freely through the grounds. This was the home of the Council of Four.

It was very strange for an Acolyte to leave the Temple. It was even stranger for them to leave the Temple in the dead of night and not tell anyone and to even come here made this even stranger. Something was up, big time.

Guardian came to the gate and pressed his hand against the plate by the side. It read his palm and identified him. He then pressed the intercom button and spoke clearly into it, "It's me Guardian, Head of the Temple Congregation. I have to speak to the Council of Four now please. It is urgent!"

The gates swung open and a sentry escorted him inside. Together they climbed the stairs until they were just outside the Inner Sanctuary of the Council. Taking a deep breath, he knocked on the door. "Council Members, I need to speak with you of a matter of great importance. May I have permission to enter?"

"Acolyte Guardian you have permission to enter our sanctuary," a melodious voice called out. The doors opened and the sentry nodded. Guardian gathered his courage and entered the Inner Sanctuary.

The room was both simple and grand at the same time. The floors were made of clear glass with water underneath them. The walls looked like clear ice with a variety of pictures on them. A ring of hieroglyphs circled the dome, which was covered in a soft green satin and in the center of the ceiling hung a mini sun, which bathed the room in its brilliant glow.

On a raised dais in the center of the room were four people in four magnificent thrones. Going right to left they were Time, Nature, Wisdom, and Emotion. Each of these ancient Entities gave off a powerful aura despite their age. They were the Council of Four. They were the oldest of the Entities and leaders of the race.

Time sat in a glittering silver throne that had all sort of timepieces carved into it. He wore a long sparkling silver robe with a black cape. On the center of his chest was a huge clock. His black hair and eyes shone brightly against his silver skin. In his left hand he held the glittering Time Scepter, his symbol of power. He was very patient and calm never acting before thinking. His right hand lay on his wife's, Nature's, hand.

Nature's throne was a work of art. It was made out of the finest oak with all kinds of animal and plant designs etched into it. Nature herself was very beautiful. Nature wore crown of roses, tulips, and orchids in her long wavy green hair. She smiled pleasantly which went well with her ivy colored skin and moss green eyes. She wore a dress made from the leaves and grass of trees. In her right hand she held a small globe called the Nature Globe. She was passionate and serene, but unpredictable at times.

Wisdom's throne was made to look like a bunch of blue books stacked on top of one another. Wisdom himself had ice blue skin, white hair, and crystal blue eyes. His skin was scaly and his clothes were strange. A designer one-piece body suit with a vest over it. His left hand contained the Scroll of Wisdom. The man was thoughtful, logical, and wise. He loved to contemplate everyone and everything before acting.

His wife, Emotion sat on the last throne. It was magenta in color and every emotion that was ever felt was written on it. Emotion had short blue hair, a band of freckles running from her forehead down to her neck, ridges on her nose, violet eyes and cinnamon colored skin. She wore a magenta colored French style Renaissance dress with a white cloak. In her hands she held the Wand of Emotions. She was wild and reckless one minute and the next she would controlled and measured. You never knew what she would become.

The four of them looked at Guardian with apprehension. They could sense much fear emulating from him, which concerned them greatly. They wondered what could have frightened the man so bad he would come to them to talk in the dead of night.

"Acolyte Guardian, this is a surprise. Acolytes rarely leave the sanctuary of the Grand Temple and certainly not at this late hour. Tell us why you have come to speak with us. What is so important that you came to see us at the dead of night?" Time asked patiently.

"Council Members, I humbly thank you for granting me a chance to speak with you. I know that you are very busy and at this late hour you should be resting to conserve your strength. However what I have to say is of the utmost importance and I feel that you should know about it right now rather then wait till later," Guardian began. Taking a deep breath he continued with his narrative.

"As you well know, for the past century the Killgonas have been more active then ever in their activities. They are hunting down Crystal Carriers ruthlessly killing them and devouring any Entity who crosses their path. They have been personally been responsible for the death of at least ten Entities and over a dozen Carries leaving hundreds of realities with no protectors. No protectors mean the realities are vulnerable to attack. I know for a fact that at least fifty realities have collapsed into nothing because of them this past century alone."

"We are well aware of the news you have brought to us. We all know the ruthless nature of the Killgonas and their never-ending quest to free their master from its eternal prison. This increased aggression this past century could just be a sign of frustration from them. Do you have evidence to the contrary?" Nature asked rolling her globe from one hand to the other. It glowed brightly showing her the events that had just been described to her.

"Yes I do. Many of the prime realities are nearing a critical moment in their universe's life span. In three months time they will reach their peak energy output. This is good for us because we can use the energy to strengthen the seal by tenfold. But this concerns me also for several reasons. These particular realities weren't supposed to reach this level of energy output for at least another five billion years. I have reason to suspect that the Killgonas have deliberately sped up the process for their own reasons. Based on their past actions whatever their planning can't be good for anyone," Guardian replied darkly. He looked at each of them in turn trying to get his point across.

"You think that the Killgonas are acting on orders from the Nameless to manipulate the situation in the multiverses energy barrier in order to create a faster build up of energy? The only possible explanation for this would be is if they were planning on transferring the energy for themselves to the Nameless in order to free it. The Nameless was greatly weakened when we locked it up. With this much energy plus all the rest it's absorbed from them in the past it could break free. If that is the case a way must be found to prevent this from taking place. Tell me have you and your fellow Acolytes tried the usual methods to stop this terrible event from coming to pass?" Wisdom pondered out loud.

"Yes we have. The Congregation has been trying everything imaginable to prevent the crisis, but we can't contain it for much longer I fear. Even with increased renewal sessions on the seal door, it isn't enough these days. We've also attempted to reconstruct damaged realities with a bit of success as well as create new ones to replace the old ones that have died, but their not taking a firm hold. I know I must sound like a child, but nothing is working! Tonight we nearly lost another reality, middle aged one, and we were only able to save it by sacrificing two of its alternant dimensions to do so. That is never a good thing because we have no idea what the long-term consequences are. This can't continue because if it does we will lose every last one of the reality bubbles losing our connection the multiverse. If that happens we leave the multiverse vulnerable and the Killgonas are that much closer to opening up the anti-universe. You must do something," Guardian pleaded with them. He wiped the sweat off his brow and gazed at them helplessly. He looked completely exhausted from his speech.

"I'm getting a lot of mixed emotions from you. What you have told us is very disturbing. The Killgonas can't be allowed to continue their attacks on the multiverse and our people. Still I would advice caution with this situation. We don't know for certain what's going on. We can't afford a repeat of last time. I don't have to remind you what happened," Emotion advised to her fellow Council Members.

"Agreed. We need to hold Council right now in order to come up with plan. Guardian I thank thee for bringing this news to us. You have been very helpful. Your news will not be taken lightly. It would be best if you return to the Temple and keep an eye out for things. Report to us immediately if there's any change. Also don't tell anyone about this meeting, at least not yet. We don't want to start a panic," Wisdom instructed.

Guardian bowed to each of them and stood up. "Thank you for listening to me. I feel much better knowing that the future of Entara is in your safe hands. I hope you find a solution and soon. Good bye." With a swish of his robes he was gone leaving the Council of Four alone.

Pressing a hidden button on the arms of their thrones, they rotated until they were all around a small stone table that rose up from the floor. Four slots were carved on the table in front of their thrones and this is where they deposited their symbols. Their symbols were a source of great power and aided them. When all four symbols were used in tandem the entire multiverse shook from their power. The pictures on the wall disappeared and the lights dimmed. The floor beneath them splashed as the waters churned angrily. It was time for a meeting of the Council and nothing would disturb them until a solution was found.

Time called the Council to order. After organizing his thoughts he spoke, "Guardian's news was an unpleasant reminder to something we are all well aware of. These problems are only the latest we've been sensing for some time now. We all knew that it was a strong possibility that this could occur if we locked the Nameless away and we did it anyways. For the past three and half eons we have been at peace and now it's all falling apart around us," he began. He lost his composer for a moment and banged his hand against the table. "As the Supreme Ruler of Time I should have foreseen this happening! I have observed everything else that has happened these past few years why did this escape me?"

"Time, please that's enough. You know as well as I do that is next to impossible to truly know the future. Time is forever in motion always changing. What is most likely to happen doesn't always transpire. No one here is blaming you for not catching on to these disturbing events sooner. All four of us are partially responsible for the mess we are in. Remember, I was the one who kept thinking we could change the monstrous natures of our enemies, but I was wrong. Now that we know that the Killgonas are planning on trying to free their master by manipulating a energy build up we should think about how were going to handle this," Nature reprimand her husband gently.

"What you speak is very true. Even with my infinite knowledge I am unable to come up with the answer to who's to blame. Perhaps no one is. In any case we should concentrate on coming up with a plan of action to deal with the threat," Wisdom spoke up.

"I couldn't have said that better myself love. Right now I think we should decide on what action were going to take before we lose our chance to act. Firstly how should we deal with the public? The people of Entara have a right to know there's a possibility that the Nameless could break free and that our world is in danger. I vote that we make a statement to them," Emotion declared passionately.

"It would be unwise to do so. As stated earlier our people have been at peace for nearly three and half eons. To suddenly thrust them into a situation like this would surely cause widespread panic. Our utopia that has sheltered us for so long would vanish. To allow this to happen would be most illogical," Wisdom stated evenly. Time and Nature nodded their heads in agreement.

"If you three are sure then I won't argue about it. But I still feel as if we should trust the people to make a rational decision based on this information," Emotion huffed angrily.

"Your complaint is noted, but it doesn't change the fact that we are in agreement on this issue. The public will not be told of the threat for the moment. Now that is settled, we should move on to our next step in solving this crisis. Time isn't on our side when were dealing with our enemies. We need to come up with a solution that will once and for all rid us of our problems. I don't have to remind you that the steps we've taken to deal with this threat haven't been quite as effective as we hoped," Time stated.

"You're referring to our earlier motions from previous Councils over the eons. Such as limiting the use of Entities powers while here on Entara. The reinforcing the non-interference rule, training Crystal Carriers to be guardians of the realties and keeping the delicate balance between good and evil, and finally moving up the exams for the students. I assure you these steps have been quite effective Time. A lot of good has come out of it. They've also given the natural order of things a chance to create something we need desperately. A back up seal for the seal to the anti-universe," Nature revealed smiling pleasantly at her fellow members. "My colleagues have told me that the energy barrier can produce a back up seal incase the original one breaks," she said pointing to her plants, who curled around her as her source of information.

"If that's true then we must act on it quickly. I've sensed the emotional stability of our people and those in other realities. What I feel is surprising, but not all that unexpected. I can sense much bravery and other positive emotions from them, but they are very afraid of the Nameless. They have seen and heard from us what it did before and they have no wish to witness it first hand. If we could avoid a direct confrontation, I believe that would be the best thing for everyone all around. In fact I insist we do that," Emotion said evenly.

"I agree with you Emotion on this point. None of us wish to have another confrontation if it can be avoided. The question is then how to we get the back up seal and avoid getting directly involved with this?" Time asked everyone.

"In order to get the backup seal we would need to reset the energy barrier that protects the multiverse. I know of only one way this could be accomplished. If an ordinary Crystal Carrier from an ordinary reality does something extraordinary with his or her crystal an energy surge will be created. That in turn will cause a ripple effect throughout the entire multiverse, which should in theory create a new, better seal to reinforce the existing seal," Wisdom explained to them. He used his powers to show them a holographic model of the events he just described.

"There's a fatal flaw in that plan that I like to point out. In order to create this massive energy surge, it would take a hundred times the normal amount of power a single Crystal Carrier can produce. The effort alone would be enough to kill a person. Also the result of a failed energy surge could rupture the seal or worse, cause a chain reaction that would cause an explosion big enough to wipe out the entire multiverse. I bet you didn't think of that did you?" Nature retorted hotly.

"I'm well aware of this predicament. But I assume that the four of us can figure away around this problem. After all we are the Council of Four."

"Well what do you suggest then?"

"I'm open to ideas. That is the point of Council. We must listen to one another in order to come up with the best results for everyone."

"Enough you two. The hostility between you two is giving me a headache. I have an idea. What if the person we chose for this duty has an Entity working with them? Together they both should be able to control the flow of power meaning there would be less of a chance of an explosion or ruptured seal. Also if the power was to gradually increase the Carrier's body could adapt to the flow without shutting down. I also like to note their desire to do the right thing should offer a bit of protection." Emotion reasoned with them.

"This plan sounds like the only plausible one. But we need to be prepared just incase the plan fails. I recommend that we need to send a second Entity into the field to make sure things go according to plan. They can also offer their assistant if necessary." Time stated

"We should try someone new. Those with raw undeveloped talent usually have a bigger impact then those already fully trained. If we use our symbols to locate this champion we can be sure to get the best results. Now who do we send?" Nature wondered

"I suggest we select a younger Entity, a student that's about to graduate. I know you might think I've lost my mind, but logically it's the right choice. Their the ones with the most experience currently with Crystal Carriers and if they believe this is some pre exam test they'll keep it a secret," Wisdom advice

The wall that had been filled with pictures earlier came to life once more. Images and files of information on the student body appeared. At superhuman speeds the computer went through each file trying to select the best two Entities for the task.

Suddenly, the screens froze. Two files appeared on the screen displaying the image of the only twins to be born. Star and Nova, the representatives of good and evil appeared. The perfect choice for this kind of mission. The Council was a little surprised by the computers choice.

"I remember those two girls. Their Naming Ceremony was most unusual. Their parents chose to name them after objects that people associate with their preferences. They are quite powerful and were a lot of help during the war. These past few years they've helped a lot of different people," Nature remarked

"Their files are impeccable. Top of their classes at school, found and trained more Crystal Carriers then anyone else, have a high-ranking power level, and good family relations. Their psychological profiles show them to be of sound mind and very independent with a complex personality. According to this they haven't failed at any task given to them yet. They even play their own little game of chess between one another while doing their assignment. I like them. They know how to keep a balance." Wisdom said

"They do say opposites attract. If Star and Nova tracked down a pre selected Crystal Carrier and both contribute to that person's training, we could cut the time it would normally take by half. But it must be done soon. Every moment that passes, means the seal loses its effectiveness. If it fails completely I don't even want to think of the mess we have on our hands. The Nameless free again is one nightmare I don't intend to live again, because it would be much more dangerous the second time around." Time said stressing the seriousness of the situation to each of them.

"If it comes to that, remember were still speculating. We should wait a few weeks to see if things don't work out by themselves. Just incase they don't I have already initiate emergency plans and the protectors of the realities have some clue to what's going on. The most important thing we can do now is be patient and conserve our strength. It will take all our power to find the right champion who is destined to save us all. Let us only hope that the Killgonas don't find out what were doing." Nature forewarned them all

"Agreed. It is nearly dawn. I suggest we get some sleep. There's nothing more we can do now. Meeting adjourned." Wisdom said as he got out of his throne and picked up his symbol. The other three followed his lead and head for bed, hoping things would get better.

Back at the Temple Guardian was greeted by his wife at the steps of the Temple. She looked at him anxiously. "Where were you? I was so worried when I woke up and couldn't find you anywhere in the Temple. What was so important that you had to leave the Temple at this late hour?"

"Hush, Sapphire I'm alright. I took your advice to heart. I've just spoken with the Council. I told them everything that's been going on. They've decided to take action and do what they can to prevent a great tragedy from unfolding."

"I hope that they can. If not I fear our world and all others are doomed."

"Don't talk like that. Now we must get back inside before someone sees us," Guardian instructed taking her hands and leading her back inside.

They reentered their chambers talking quietly amongst themselves. They had no idea that Jasmine had seen the entire thing and now was wondering what was going on.

"What could possibly be so wrong that Dad would leave the Temple? I wish they would trust me enough to tell me the truth," she whispered to herself as she climbed back in bed.

Chapter Five

The Nameless wandered aimlessly around its prison angry at still being stuck here. True there was no life here, but there was no way to continue on its quest either. It needed to find a way to escape and soon. It needed to be back in real time and space so it could change that fabric into lifelessness. Only then could it truly die.

Trapped for so long in this miserable anti-universe by those wretched Entities, it had lived far longer than it wanted to. How dare those pesky interlopers interfere with its work? Its goal in life was very noble. The universe began as nothing so why shouldn't it return to that way?

The Nameless had fragmented memories of its own birth. It recalled being part of nothing, but then in a spark of light, it had been granted a cursed conscience. It now felt the awesome weight of life bombarding it. The pain was so intense it didn't know how to deal with it. It yearned for the peace and quite that had existed for so long.

It knew who had caused it this terrible pain. It was the race known as Entities. They were responsible for the Nameless's pain. They were the ones who continued to spread the gift of life across the cosmos along with their ideas. They were pure evil in its mind. That's why it had created its servants, the Killgonas, to aid it in its quest.

It had been doing fine on its own long before it created the Killgonas. Surviving by absorbing time and space fabric, it had felt no pleasure or joy in what it was doing. It only did it because that's what its instincts said to do. By destroying everything then it could finally rest forever.

It had been shocked to discover beings that were similar, but not alike to itself. Similar in the fact that both had been created by the Big Bang and that they needed energy to survive. But that's where the similarities ended between them.

The Entity race wanted to expand the universe, fill it with life. They tried to stop it from continuing its mission because they believed it was wrong. The Council of Four had even tried to alter it so it wouldn't do what it did anymore. When it refused their offer, they tried to kill it.

To protect itself and complete its mission it needed help. It used its power to convert fragments of a dead star to form a race of attack dogs for it. There where two hundred pieces that were transformed into two hundred helpers. Half of the dangerous beasts were female while the other half was male and the females were a lot deadly then the males.

The Killgonas served their master loyally. They didn't care that their sole purpose in life was to kill themselves in the end. The greatest honor for them was to help the Nameless complete its quest and be returned to their natural state. They would never betray their master because they were connected to it.

When the Nameless had been locked up and the Killgonas scattered they were lost for a long time. But soon they learned they could telepathically commune with the Nameless in its prison. After discovering this they decided to free their creator from its dreadful prison. Since that day nothing had slowed them down in their own quest.

The Killgonas had assembled in one of the newly extinct realities that they had made their home. They had been tremendously busy lately with their plan. They were attempting to break the seal that kept their Master locked away. If everything went according to plan all their hard work would be worth it.

The leader of the Killgonas was Killnala, a strong, powerful, prideful female Killgona. The Nameless had chosen her to be its spokesperson and to lead the Killgonas in its absence. She looked like all the other Killgonas except for a small scar on her right fore claw.

She smiled lavishly at her kinship ready to speak to them. "Silence my brethren! This meeting is called to order! All our efforts are about to come to fruition. Soon we will cause the seal to overload and give our glorious creator enough energy to break free from the shackles that keep it in the anti-universe. With its help we can finally destroy the entire Entity race once and for all. Because once they're gone, nothing will stand in our way of returning the multiverse back to single universe of lifelessness. No more noise, no more life, nothing! I urge you to make sure that nobody gets in our way," she preached. Her tail curled around her body in contentment.

"I don't want to interrupt you, Killnala, but I think your forgetting something. I'm almost certain that the Acolytes have notified the Council of what's been going on. If they have then they're certain to come up with a plan to stop us. Celestial Gods only knows they've been able to keep one step ahead of the last three and half eons," Killroary, Killnala consort and second in command, told her. He placed a clawed hand on her shoulder trying to restrain her euphuism. He gave her a look that told her to keep her emotions inline.

She shook his hand off and snarled at him. "Why do you doubt your own people? How can you even believe that our ostentatious plan will fail? You're the one who came up with it in the first place! We are immortal, powerful, and dangerous creatures. Nothing will get in our way of completing this plan and I like to see anyone try and stop us! I'll tear them to shreds!" Killnala shouted. Others soon joined in shouting their own threats.

Killroary didn't look impressed. Such theatrics were hardly worthy of beings such as themselves. He narrowed his eyes at his mate sending a message loud and clear. It was time to regain order. She nodded indicating she got the message. She turned to face the crowd.

"Silence! We are acting like animals. We are not some primitives wallowing in the mud blindly! Look around this beautiful dark, black, empty extinct reality we created. The Nameless made us its chosen ones. We alone have been entrusted with the sole duty of giving back the freedom it so rightfully deserves!" she roared.

The others cowered in fear as she smashed her tail around and smiled evilly showing off her impressive dental work. No one wished to upset her or otherwise they end up dead. With a flick of her claws she dismissed them. They quickly scurried away not willing to anger her anymore.

There was much work still to be done before the Nameless could be freed. Steps needed to be taken to ensure that nothing went wrong. The Killgonas wouldn't allow all their hard work to go to waste because of Entity interference. They had waited three and half eons to free their Master and they wouldn't wait a second more.

The minute they were alone Killnala exploded. She pounced on top of Killroary shoving him to the ground. Then she rolled around and flung him halfway across the reality. He limped backed over to her unsure what he had done to upset her so much. He even asked her.

"What is your problem? Have you forgotten that the Master named me as leader of our race and you as my second? I chose you to be my consort because of your skills and brilliant mind. Never in our entire lives have you questioned me. Today however you overstepped your boundaries as well as your authority! Your lucky I'm in a forgiving mood otherwise your punishment would have been worse. Let me make this clear to you. If you have a problem with me take it up with me before I speak to the others not during! Do I make myself clear?" she snapped at him literally.

Killroary refused to be frightened. He didn't back down instead he reared up to his full height and breathed on her. "Your overconfidence will be the end of us I just know it. What you're truly mad at is that I questioned your role as a leader and how effectively you can carry out a plan. If you think I want your position you're very much wrong. I'm only looking out for your best interests. I don't want you to end up hurt if something goes wrong. The Council of Four will do their best to thwart our plans. All I'm asking is that we take into consideration all the possibilities and then go ahead with the final phase of the plan."

"A delay could lead to our defeat! Look at all we had to overcome, the sacrifices we made, and the pain we endured to get this far. I know that we've had our fair share of setbacks. One more could ruin everything for us. If that happens we'll never free the Nameless from the anti-universe. None of us want that do we?" she argued tapping her claws together anxiously.

"Nevertheless, I don't believe we're ready to move onto the next phase yet. The creator would want to know if there was the slightest chance we fail. Why not ask the Nameless its own opinion on the subject?"

"I don't know. I suppose I could if only to satisfy you, but I don't like this. Leave me alone while I contact our creator. I don't want any disturbance understand? I'll let you know how it goes." He nodded his head and left.

Killnala took several deep breaths and tried to center her thoughts. It took a great deal of concentration to reach across the vast distance and merge minds with the Nameless. She was stressed out and angry, which blocked her attempts at first. Finally she felt familiar presences in her mind.

"Nameless, your humble servant Killnala wishes to speak with you. I have wonderful news for you. Everything is going according to plan; it won't be long now until you're free again we eagerly await your return. Without you to guide us we are lost."

"Excellent Killnala, I'm pleased. You and your brethren have done well. Your reward for all your efforts will be most grand. I sense that you are keeping something from me. What else do you have to say to me?" the Nameless thought to her. *"What is the problem that makes you tremble in fear?"*

"There is no problem per say. Killroary feels that there is reason for concern is all. He believes that the Entity race will find out about our plans and stop us. This past century we have been a little more active then usual. If there half as smart as I think they are they might have noticed something. Those pesky Acolytes would have noticed something and told their stupid Council. If that has occurred they are certainly making plans to stop us. Master, what am I to do?"

"You were right to contact me. Those beings are very dangerous indeed. You must find out for sure if they know anything and if they do what their plans are. Send one of your kinsmen out to see if they can learn anything. Now do you have anything for me to eat? I need to regain my full power."

"No, not today Nameless. I promise soon you will never be hungry again. I leave you now. Killnala out," she said awakening from her trancelike state. She reared up to her full height and bellowed "KILLANA!"

A slightly smaller female Killgona phased into existence in front of her. She bowed respectfully in front of her. "You summoned me, mistress? How may I be of service?"

"Yes I have a task for you to do. Discover what the Council of Four is planning. Report your findings to me immediately. Don't reveal your mission to anyone else, understood?" she threatened.

"Consider it done mistress. By this time tomorrow we will know if those tasty Entities have a clue about our plan. Be back soon," Killana assured her before vanishing again.

Later she was having dinner with Killroary. When he heard about what she did he was skeptical to say the least. "How exactly do you expect her to learn anything Killnala? It's impossible for our kind to reach Entara otherwise we would have brought the fight to them long ago. But we have no way to reach a place that's outside normal time and space. You have sent our best informant on a wild goose chase."

"That's where you're wrong. You males are all the same. You doubt my superior intellect. You're to busy thinking to act on your gut instincts. Trust me when I say that Killnala has her ways of finding the right information. Besides isn't this what you wanted? To find out for certain if there was a threat to us?"

"Perhaps or perhaps not. I wanted results without the risk of losing life. Don't give me that look. I'm as ruthless and bloodthirsty as you are; I'm just a little more thorough when it comes to the hunt and protecting our best interest," he replied

"Fair enough I suppose. I can't argue with logic like that. Maybe I'm just overworked causing the extinction of a reality is fun, but tiring. It's been ages since I had a chance to simply relax or hunt for sport. I would kill to have some non-recognized Crystal Carrier energy right now. My element is the hunt."

"You have killed more Entities and devoured more of their precious Crystal Carriers then any of our kind. Your efficiency is to be applauded. It's also what I love most about you," he told her linking their tongues together in a passionate kiss.

Their private moment was spoiled when Killana materialized in front of them. She was in her humanoid form signaling trouble. She was panting and one of her nails was chipped indicating she had been in a fight. "Sorry to interrupt this tender moment, but we've got trouble on the horizon."

Ten minutes later every single Killgona was assembled together in the dead space again. They talked quietly amongst themselves wondering what was going on. Many were curious and others surprised at being called back here so soon.

"Quiet down already! This is an emergency meeting. What we have to tell you will have a profound impact on our plans to free our magnificent creator. So I suggest you pay close attention to what I have to say!" Killnala roared.

Killnala gestured for Killana to step forward. She was still in her humanoid form, which shocked many. As she opened her mouth to speak a hush fell over the crowd and her voice was magnified tenfold so everyone could hear it.

"What I have discovered is the most significant find since we learned we could still talk to the Nameless. I went undercover to a reality where there are magical realms with fairies, witches, heroes, and all that disgusting stuff. There I took the liberty of finding a mystic and through my more aggressive methods of persuasion, learned the most disturbing news."

"It seems that the Acolytes are taking extreme measures to defend their precious realities, including contacting the Council of Four. My source had a lot to say about them. Since using their full powers could obliterate their beloved Entara and shatter the multiverse, they've decided for another plan of action."

Killroary slithered forward. "The Council seems to believe that the energy barrier that prevents the mixing of the realities and helps reinforce the seal can produce a backup seal that's more powerful then the first. This will be accomplished by resetting the energy barrier. Although the details are sketchy, we know that they plan on doing this by using a normal Crystal Carrier and an Entity working together in tandem. We mustn't let them succeed at any cost."

"How do you propose we stop them? I mean do you have a clue to which Entity their sending on this mission or who the Crystal Carrier is?" Killarthur, Killana mate, asked. The rest of the group voiced their own concerns and anger at learning their plan was threatened.

"Unfortunately no we don't. That information wasn't obtainable to us. But that is because the Council hasn't decided yet. They feel it's in everybody best interest to wait and see what develops. That gives us time. Believe me when I say I wouldn't come back without vital information if I could get it," Killana replied

"Then how do you propose we stop them? What are our best options? Destroy the barrier, search in vain for the Crystal Carrier, or how about a full out assault?" Killarthur demanded impatiently.

"Unfortunately we can't attack them directly without depleting our forces. Nor can we destroy the barrier it's to strong. Also the protectors of the realties have been warned about us and are working harder than ever to guard the barrier by keeping up the delicate balance. That leaves us with one course of action. We must discover the identities of the Entity and Crystal Carrier so that they can be eliminated," Killnala explained to the crowd.

The Entity Eaters conversed amongst themselves. It was their sole purpose in life to serve their Master, how would they going to discover the information they need to succeed? The only place it could be found was one of two places they couldn't go.

"Please, we must have order. I know our task is nearly impossible, but we will find a way. Already we are working on a way to breach the security of Entara to find the information we need. As soon as we discover the information we need a strike team will be sent out to eliminate the threat," Killnala reassured her people.

"I will personally see to the destruction of those who oppose us. We have waited to long for this moment to be stopped. I only ask that you be patient a little longer before we celebrate."

The assembly agreed full heartedly with her. Cheers rang throughout the group all praising her. Killnala never failed them before and she wouldn't start now. The Nameless would be freed on time. After a few more minutes of discussion, they left once more; this time for good, they hoped.

Killnala waited impatiently for them to leave. When the last Killgona had left she turned to her two trusted friends. "That should satisfy them for now. I don't have the time or energy to waste comforting them. Despite this minor setback, I still plan on releasing our creator as scheduled. Walk with me!"

She slithered forward with them right behind her. She didn't know what she was looking for in this empty space, but she needed something to keep her interest. "What do we know for certain about this plan to reset everything? Does it have the slightest chance of working?"

"Unfortunately it sounds like this plan to reset the barrier has merit. The science behind it is sound and they've seemed to have taken into account every possible factor. I don't know how we can sabotage their plans. It seems to me we have no way of preventing this," Killana said, evenly gesturing as she walked with them. She changed back into her normal form to continue the talk with more ease.

"I must point out that since we don't have all the details or know if they have a backup plan, we can't plan an effective counterstrike. The only advantage we have is that they haven't yet moved forward with their plans. But time is running out. It will take time just to figure out how to secure the knowledge we seek," Killroary claimed.

Killnala turned to face them both. Holding up a clawed hand, she silenced them. "Enough. I don't want to hear anymore bad news is that clear? While it may be difficult, it's not impossible to get what we want is that correct? Yes then? All right it's good to know we have a way. We don't have a whole lot of time to find out what we need to know. So I suggest that you start thinking up a way to breach Entara security. Also Killana start finding out what kind of reality is considered normal. I want to make sure we blend in properly."

"Don't worry my love. Soon we will have everything we need to ensure the success of our mission. Nothing will be able to stand in our way. Not the Crystal Carriers, not the Entities, and certainly no hand picked champion. Nothing can go wrong with this plan."

"I hope your right Killnala. Because if your wrong and we fail your punishment will be most severe."

Chapter Six

Five weeks had passed on Entara since that fateful day when Guardian had brought the disturbing news to the Council's ears. They had hoped if nothing was done things would work out on their own accord. But that was not the case at all. If anything, things were getting worse both for the multiverse and Entara.

The planet Entara was linked to the Council. They were a part of it and it was a part of them. They needed one another to survive. What they felt affected the overall condition of the planet. Right now their uneasiness and anxiety was causing strange things to ensue. Three weeks ago the blue green oceans had changed to fiery orange frightening many people. The moonset and sunset had switched one day causing a lot of confusion. Meanwhile, the contents of the library books had vanished and the wildlife was starting to go insane. The peaceful utopia was quickly disintegrating.

The Council was having another meeting. Reports were coming in from all over the world of new disasters every hour. It had to be stopped soon before people started rioting or ended up dead.

"We can't keep things under wraps much longer I fear. At the rate the seal is starting to dissolve at, we could be looking at a complete failure in a matter of days instead of weeks. We need more time. Do the Acolytes have anything new to report that could assist us?" Time asked tiredly. He hadn't slept in weeks and it was showing. He was in a perpetual loop of growing up, dying, being born and growing up.

"The Acolytes have managed to slow down some of the Killgonas progress, but they haven't been able to stop it. They have taken the liberty of issuing new rules about using the reality bubbles and tightened up security measures. Hopefully that will give us the time we need," Wisdom reported. He rubbed his forward in attempt to stay alert. His skin was starting to peel due to the amount of stress he was under. Already he had lost his ability concentrate for long periods.

"We have to take action soon. The people are getting suspicious of the things going on and are losing faith in us. Without the support of the people we lose much of our power. I also feel the need to point out that the Crystal Carriers are demanding answers to why there's an increase of trouble in their realities. When they start asking questions you know that's not a good sign. The Killgonas have gotten even bolder then usual in my opinion. I fear for the entire multiverse and our home if this plan fails," Emotion added, looking gravely at each of the members in turn. Wrinkles had appeared on her face from all the confusion she was receiving from everyone. She had nearly lost it completely days ago with the overwhelming emotional input she received.

"We can't wait any longer. It seems that doing nothing has caused a greater problem then we thought. We must move forward in our plan if we are to have any chance at saving all that we hold dear. Once our champion is chosen we must contact the twins and debrief them on the mission without giving away too much," Nature admitted. Her dress had dulled in color and she had lost much of her flair. Life was ceasing to exist for her.

"I'm still unsure about this. We are making a lot of assumptions and asking a lot of these two girls. The twins are even adults yet. Am I the only one who is concerned that we're putting to much pressure on the girls to succeed?" Emotion expressed, concern laced in her voice.

"Are we asking to much of these two? Perhaps we are, but they are the key to our salvation. They will have no insight as to the true reason they've been called forth. All that they will know for certain is that they need to teach a Crystal Carrier. By keeping the truth hidden the Killgonas won't learn about our attempts to reset the barrier or that we have two Entities on the job. Surely this will help us in the long run," Wisdom reasoned with his wife.

"What about the Chosen One? That person will have no protection whatsoever, and we can't force them to aid us even if it is their destiny. It's against our principles to force someone to go against his or her free will. By doing so we would be inviting trouble," Nature pointed out.

"Enough Nature enough already! We have heard it all before. The time for conversation and strategizing is over. The Nameless and its abominations must be stopped at all cost. We have found a solution to our problem so let's instigate our plan of attack at once," Time shouted, banging his scepter on the ground

"Calm down Time! You must control your temper. We're all our on the edge and we're all reluctant to give in to our darker tendencies, but like you pointed out we don't have a choice. If we are to save the multiverse we must cross some lines," Emotion avowed peacefully trying to keep the peace between everyone. Still it didn't change how she felt about them betraying their beliefs.

"She's right and once we use our powers there's no turning back. We must be absolutely certain that we understand the consequences of our actions and are prepared to deal with them when the time comes," Wisdom reminded them. He looked at each of them in the eye making sure they understood the importance of what they were about to do.

"I believe we are. My friends please try to understand that I understand your concerns, but the need to protect our home comes first. Surely you all feel the same way?" Time asked staring at each one in turn. They nodded their heads knowing he was right.

"Very well then, I see no other alternative We shall cast our powers to find our champion. But I pray to the Celestial Gods that this plan succeeds. Shall we begin?" Nature inquired placing her sphere in its slot.

The others each placed their symbols into the appropriate slots and placed their palms on the table. The table began to glow bright silver, then green, next blue, and finally magenta. The symbols began to hum an unearthly song as their powers connected. The Council clasped their hands together and they began to chant in an ancient language. The entire chamber grew dark, and then a single beam of light connected the four items as one and then shot up from the center of the table and connected with the miniature sun on the ceiling.

The chamber began to shake violently and preternatural sounds filled the room echoing all over the place. The quartet of elders rose from the ground and hovered in the air. A sphere of energy rose from the beam of light and hovered in the center of the group. Images flashed at superhuman speed. The symbols were judging billions of people from millions of worlds trying to find the champion. Several minutes passed as the Council's power looked for the right person. Finally it stopped. The sphere showed a single picture of a young human teenage girl with blond hair and blue eyes. A number identifying her reality appeared in the bottom corner of the bubble.

The Council landed back in their thrones and studied the image. "That is our Champion my friends. She is the one destined to save us all because she is unique. According to the information our symbols have gathered about her she is different then any other human in any reality. This girl is connected to us by a psychic link. She can see, hear, and even feel anything that happens to us. That alone makes her a thought after prize," Nature said still amazed by what she saw.

"We must guard this information with our very existence. The girl's identity must remain closely guarded secret. Even Star and Nova can't know who she truly is, at least not right away. It's the only way we can protect her," Time advised them.

"That's a sagacious precaution. If Star and Nova don't know who she really is then the Killgonas can't get find out she's the Champion and attack them. I also suggest we keep a near zero communication silence between the planet and us for a while. That will help assure that the chances of the information being intercepted drastically. I also think that Star and Nova should be unaware that the other one will be watching them," Wisdom said wisely.

"We should also see to it that there are no Killgonas in the reality before we send them. I've read the girls history and it seems that they don't have a lot of experience handling Killgonas one on one. They always have worked as a pair. I don't know if they can handle being separated," Emotion insisted.

"All of it will be taken care of before hand. Star will be debriefed separately from her twin on what she's supposed to do. After she leaves, then Nova will get her turn. Have their parents been informed yet?" Time asked.

"Not yet, they're unreachable at the moment. Sun is overseeing the formation of a new RG star and it will take a while before it's done. Moon is experiencing some difficulty with one of his moons. Apparently, it started to fall into a decaying orbit around a thankfully dead planet in reality 3456, the Diago reality. That one is a lot of fun and pretty tricky because everything is held up diagonally," Nature replied sadly.

"We can't use Star and Nova without their parents consent, can we? If we do they won't be able to receive the extra protection they need. Then again they are mature young ladies old enough to make this decision. Besides, their half birthday is soon making them seven and a half eons old. Certainly they can decide this for themselves how to handle this situation," Emotion pointed out.

"Not if we want to keep them in the dark or jeopardize our chances to succeed. Their parents can ensure that the girls are prepared for their mission and keep it secret from everyone. I don't like it much either, but we will need consent. We're already on thin ice giving the girls no warning about what's going on. We should take a break to clear our minds. The answer will come to us after we rest for a while. Also we need more information on the girl and prepare ourselves for the task ahead," Wisdom calmly stated.

The others nodded their heads in agreement and removed their symbols from their slots. Instantly the picture and all the information about the girl vanished inside the table. They marched over to the far right wall and Time tapped in order on the hieroglyphs.

A section of the wall slid up allowing them room to pass into their private chambers. As they entered the room none of them noticed small black hunter probe incased in an energy bubble. It detached itself from the wall to explore the room as the Council went inside to sleep.

The probe glided through the air down to the table. Hovering over the table it projected force field reinforced holograms into the slots. The slots glowed for a moment as they were tricked into believing the symbols were inside them. The sphere rose up from the table and displayed everything about the girl. The probe began to quickly download the information into its memory. The probe needed to quickly finish its mission before the protective bubble disappeared. Once that happen it would be unable to return to the Killgonas. Before it could obtain any vital statistic information on the girl the doorway slid up again. The hunter probe turned to deal with its unexpected guest. It produced an energy absorber to use against the threat.

"I thought I sensed something, just let me check to make sure everything's fine," Emotion told her friends as she reentered the sanctuary. She hurried over to her throne to run a security check. Suddenly her spatial awareness went nuts. She looked up to see what was causing her senses to go crazy. That's when she saw the hunter probe coming straight at her.

She ducked out of the way and rolled behind the table as the probe buzzed passed. Powering up her heart shaped Emotion Wand she sent a wave of anger at the probe in an attempt to destroy it.

The probe simply absorbed the energy sent at it. It used the energy to power itself and keep up the bubble. It then shot a beam of light nicking Emotion in the shoulder. She screamed in pain as rainbow colored blood trickled down her shoulder.

That shot had hurt her far more then she was willing to admit. She could feel her molecules starting to lose cohesion with one another and her energy levels were going down. Another well place shot, and she would die. Gritting her teeth she focused on staying alive by firing a burst of full-blown rage at the probe.

The probe flittered out of the way. It let loose another burst of energy, this one nearly wiping out half the room. Emotion barely managed to get out of the way. This fight had to end soon or her home would be gone.

The normally calm and serene Emotion aura was blazing with power. "How dare you defile this private sanctuary! I don't know why you are attacking me and frankly I don't care. I know whom you report to and I won't let you take back what you have learned to them," she shouted

The probe ignored her speech and started to buzz loudly. Emotion fell to her knees as her energy and thoughts were sucked from her body. Her entire body trembled and she began to feel extremely weak and dizzy. Her life force was quickly being drained out of her and sent back to feed the hungry Killgonas.

"No, I won't allow you to win this battle," she said weakly. Summoning all her strength, she erected an emotional barrier. The clear white wall protected her for the time being. She had to act fast before the barrier crumbled. "I am Emotion, member of the Council of Four. I won't be defeated so easily, especially not by a simple probe!"

Levitating to the top of the ceiling she linked herself with the mini sun to increase her powers tenfold. Pointing the wand straight at the probe she let loose a flood of unsuppressed, uncontrollable, pure emotion. No one, but her could handle that much emotion and survive, certainly not a simple hunter probe.

It exploded into a thousands pieces all over the ground. Emotion lowered herself to the floor and stepped cautiously forward to examine the remains her wand at the ready. The probes remains were smoking still and spark of electricity were shooting from the mess.

As she bent down to retrieve the probe's memory core, the only piece still surrounded by the protective bubble, she sensed what was powering the bubble. Her fingers were about to brush the core when it disappeared in a puff of smoke. "No," she whispered quietly.

That's when the other three members burst through the wall and into the room. They gasped in horror at the ruined sanctuary. Wisdom ran over to check on his wife while Time waved his scepter over his head. Instantly all the damage was repaired as time reversed itself. He looked at Emotion with a grim face. "What happened here?"

"What happened? A hunter probe, that's what happened, attacked me! To top that off an Entity energy bubble protected it! I barely managed to escape with my life! You know who had to have sent that thing don't you? By the way, where in the cosmos where you?!" she demand angrily brushing off her husband.

"Emotion, please calm down. Remember your energy levels. You mustn't tax yourself so much. Please try to think of peaceful thoughts. You'll heal faster that way," Nature urged her using her plants to fix her up.

"We sensed something was wrong, but we were unable to reach you in order be of any assistance. Someone had altered the space between the doorway and the room. It was causing us great pain. It dissipated when you destroyed that machine. Surely you know we never leave you to do battle alone," Wisdom filled her in astonished she would even think that.

"Well, it's nice to know you didn't abandon me. That does leave us with a bit of a problem though. The probe's memory core disappeared before I could retrieve it. The Killgonas will attempt to retrieve the information it stole from us once they get their claws on it."

In the extinct reality Killnala slithered back and forth impatiently. Killroary sat down at a table in his humanoid form so he could work more easily with the memory core. "How much longer until you have access to the data?"

"Patience, my love. Most of the probe's memory was damaged in the attack. What little remains intact will take some time and skill to retrieve. This can't be rushed," he informed her carefully studying the memory core.

"How much time? I don't like being kept waiting. It took you five weeks just to build the probe and figure out how to use the last of the Entity energy to send it to Entara. You better hope you got something we can use otherwise you'll be waxing my scales for a week!"

"Enough already, I get the picture. Give me two; maybe three hours and you'll have what you want. I don't know for sure if I got anything useful. We'll just have to hope. Why don't you do something else to pass the time? I know that you're dying for a chance to cut loose and change your shape," he suggested. He picked up a tool and started to work on his project.

Snapping her tail in annoyance Killnala slithered off to pout. When she reached the area that had been made into her private sanctum, she let out a breath. Being in charge of an operation to force an energy surge so they could power up the Nameless, was more then a little exhausting. Her stress levels were extremely high. This was giving her a terrible pain in her neck.

'Maybe Killroary is right. I do need to relax. All this stress is really causing me to lose it. Maybe a little shape shifting exercise wouldn't hurt a bit,' she thought to herself.

Closing her eyes she pictured herself as a cube. All of those right angles and flat surfaces made it quite a challenge. She felt herself shrinking and her body reshaping itself till it was a perfect cube. Content, but not satisfied yet, she went through a series of quick transformations to test her skills. She turned into all kinds of shapes and beings trying to find some kind of peace. No Killgona could ever match her speed and skill.

Finally she decided to change into her victims. It gave her a huge thrill being her victims. This way she knew exactly how hopeless and afraid they had been when she ended their miserable lives. Others might call it murder, but she called it life. She had just finished her exercises when Killroary appeared in front of her. He looked at her grim faced. "I have completed my task. I don't have much to tell, but what I do have is very valuable."

Excited by the prospect of good news the two raced to the lab. "You better have real good news. Our window of opportunity is closing. We only have seven weeks left! I need that information now."

"I understand that my dear. I wish I only had a lot of good news, but I don't. You get both good and bad news. So please try to remain calm," he told her, bracing himself incase she struck him out of anger.

"Don't just stand there. Tell me the good news already," she snapped impatiently. All of this secrecy was starting to annoy her.

"The good news is the probe was able to discover the name of the Entity the Council has selected, as well as a hazy description of the Crystal Carrier. The bad news is we don't have a name for the girl or any vital information that could help us in locating her. Nor do we know anything else about the Council's plans incase this attempt fails."

"It doesn't matter if they have a backup or whatever precautions they've taken. Soon it won't matter at all. I know how they work. They are so predictable. Not to mention I've had dealings with the Entity they've chosen for this task. It seems I'll finally have a chance to take my revenge on Star for what she did to me," she said laughing manically.

"How can you be laughing about such a serious matter? Star is the only Entity to have ever stood up to you and won."

"You think I have forgotten that? I deliberately cut myself so I would have a permanent reminder of my shame. I'm laughing because this is the perfect chance to exact my revenge. That goody goody has too much faith in her powers. That, along with her dependence on her twin Nova, makes her have an easy weakness to exploit. No doubt the Council will use both girls in some way on this mission."

"I plan to get rid of Star for good and with your help, we already know what reality the girl lives in, where she can be found and almost a detail sketch on her. This gives us an advantage. Those idiotic Council members will waste their precious time worrying about the probe. We will leave at once for our mission. I just need to give final instructions to our people, then we're off to conquer the entire multiverse."

The Council was in a heated debate. The probe's attack had greatly shaken them. It had been centuries since something like this had occurred. Also this changed their plans.

"That probe was sent by the Killgonas. There's no doubt about that in my mind. They wanted all the information we had on this mission and it seems to me they nearly got all of it. Thank the heavens that you damaged the probe Emotion. Hopefully we got rid of all the information it stole," Wisdom said.

"But how did they know about it in the first place? That's what concerns me the most. The only way they could have learned about our plans was from one of a Crystal Carrier or us. Since none of us told anyone it had to be the former," Emotion said tiredly.

"If that's true, then they're going after the girl. Our plans have to change. The twins must be sent now we can't wait. I know without parental consent we'll have to deal with legal ramifications as well as deny the protection to the girls, but there's no choice. But those girls fought in the war and understand that sacrifices must be made in order for the greater good," Nature stated evenly. Clearly she was agitated by the turn of events because she was chocking her ivy.

"Before this all over, I fear we will all do things we regret. Something seem more nobler then others, but we must always keep our goal in mind. Send word to Guardian to prepare the reality chamber and have a messenger bring Star and Nova here. We can't afford to waste anymore time," Time concluded.

Nature nodded her head and pressed some keys on her armrest. Speaking quickly and quietly she sent the orders out. With that done she looked her husband in the eye knowing there was nothing they could do now to stop the events they set in motion. "I hope you're planning to give a little help to the girls because I doubt they can handle this on their own."

"We will, my love I promise you that. They will receive gifts best suited for helping them in this quest. Each of us needs to think hard about what we want to give them. I'm more concerned about our Champion. We can offer her no protection. She must try to survive on her own. All we can do is pray that she can live up to her destiny," he said pointing at his wife's globe. All four members stared at the image of their champion that gave them hope.

Chapter Seven

Killnala tapped her clawed hands together impatiently. The information the probe had gotten was very disturbing. Something had to be done to ensure the freedom of her Master. "How much longer till we leave? We are on a timetable here may I remind you? Don't forget the Council might have already sent that annoying little good doer Star and her bratty twin sister, Nova."

"Don't be so impatient, Killnala. Be thankful the probe and our informant were able to get us the information we do have. You need to be a bit more patient everything will workout in the end."

"What we do know isn't much. You've managed to locate the girl's reality, narrow down her probable location by process of elimination, and discover that she has no protection from the Council, but none of that will matter if we don't have a name!"

"I assure you the girl will be much easier to locate and destroy then you think. Once we have her energy and the Entities we can give it to the Nameless tripling its power. You and I can track her by her aura so stop worrying so much."

"Whatever! When do we leave? I already packed the extra energy pods and the rest of our stuff. We should get going."

"As soon as you give final instructions and we eat something we can go. This journey will tax us greatly because we have to phase through so many realities to get to the proper one. Once there, we have to ration our food supply because those energy pods won't last forever. We'll need to hunt for more food later."

"Which won't be hard to secure since what we need is so abundant. Also with our shape shifting powers no one will be able to tell where aliens. Humans, why did it have to be humans? Star helped create those vile beings with the Celestial Gods ages ago. How it makes me sick to even pretend to be one," she spat.

"Easy, my love, easy. You mustn't let your anger cloud your mind right now. I know these last few weeks have been difficult for you, but you can't jeopardize our chances now. Remember we have one sole purpose in life and that's to serve our Master. You rule us, and in return we serve you," Killroary told her.

"I know that this plan of yours has been the product of nearly two and half eons of work. Your moment of glory and recognition is upon the horizon, and I know that the Nameless will reward you greatly, but you must remain calm no matter how hard that is. I know you can do this Killnala."

"Don't you think I know that? I can't afford to fail this mission. I am the oldest, strongest, and wisest of us. Everyone respects, obeys, even fears me because of that. I don't want think about failing because I can't! My very existence is on the line along with the release of the creator," she yelled at him. Tears were streaming down her face as she let out her pent up emotions. Never in her entire existence had she told anyone her darkest fears.

"Calm down and stop crying. Nothing will go wrong if you believe in yourself. You're the most confident person I know. You are the best there is and with my help, you will succeed, so stop worrying will you? I'll protect you from any harm," he said taking her claws in his.

"You better be right about this. Get our stuff from my sanctum. I'm going to go speak with Killana and Killarthur. I'm leaving them in charge of things so they better not mess up," she warned slithering off to talk with the two.

"Killana! Killarthur! Come here this instant! I need to speak with you two!" she shouted. The two obediently came over and waited for her to speak.

"As you are aware, you two are my most trusted lieutenants. I need you two to take care of things while we're away. Killarthur, I want you to take the males and harass the protectors of the realties. Keep them guessing about what's going on. Killana, you and the females cause as much chaos as possible. I want those Entities to exhaust themselves. The more they fight the more energy we can collect. Remember, we have seven weeks to go until the prime realities generate their maximum energy output. We need to be in position to steal that energy and transmit it to our Master. After that it can break free and destroy those Entities."

"Don't worry my Lady. Everything will be just fine trust me. You can count on us to get the job done," Killana assured her.

"Just take care of this little problem and we're good to go," Killarthur said.

Killroary appeared by her side. "Its time to be going. Here's your snack to tied you over until we arrive at our destination." He handed her pod of energy, which she gulped down.

"Right. Remember what I told you. I want to make sure that nothing goes wrong," she ordered. Grasping her consort's claws she phased away to another plane of existence.

Killnala and Killroary's journey took them a long time to complete. In order to reach the reality they wanted to they had to pass through all eleven planes again and again each time they entered a new reality. The journey was very taxing and it was about two hours later when they finally reached the right reality. Finally the two Killgonas materialized just outside of the town they wanted to be in. Cars passed by without noticing them because they had chosen to be invisible. They took a deep breath and let it out as they adjusted to the new reality.

Killnala staggered for a moment, worn out by the trip. She was feeling sick to her stomach. "Ugh. I hate when we have to multiphase and especially when we travel through the dream plane. It makes me sick seeing all that lovely stuff. Could you excuse me for a moment?" She disappeared behind a nearby tree and started puking her guts out.

"Feeling any better?" Killroary inquired a few minutes later. She straightened up and nodded. She began to rub her scales near her face in order to speed up healing.

"I'm fine really. It's just been a while since I traveled this much. So where and when are we exactly?"

"Peru, Illinois. The date is October 15th 2005. I'm almost positive the girl is in the immediate area. We should be able to track her down quite easily," he told her confidently.

"Careful, now you're the one who's getting cocky. First thing we need is to establish a base of operation. Then we get the layout of the area, next we make sure that there are no Entities in the area, and lastly we hunt down our prey. Any arguments?" she asked. He shook his head no. "Good lets get started."

They took to the air looking for a place to stay. Finally they found secluded area near a park, which they altered for their purposes. They made sure that the place was secured tightly before they took off again to see the town.

"I'm pleased. We haven't seen a single sign of an Entity yet. We must have gotten here first. When do we start the hunt?" Killnala asked her mate. She was eager to complete the mission and get back home so she could properly greet her Master once it was freed.

"We should start our hunt for the girl on Monday. She would be in school making it quite a challenge to find her, but we do have to rest and regain our strength. Speaking of strength we should stop staying invisible because its taxing us. I suggest its time we changed into our human form so we don't attract attention from any curious passerby who might see us," Killroary advised her having already begun to change.

Killnala growled angrily before willing the change to come. Her dragon like body reshaped itself until it was human. She had black hair with a blue ponytail. She had extremely long lashes and dark blue eyes that went well with her alabaster skin tone. She was tall and extremely muscular. Her nails were extremely long, extremely sharp, blue and loaded with a deadly poison. Her pointed teeth glistened in the sun. Her light blue tendrils ran from her forehead to her hairline. She wore a skintight blue body suit with black accents on the side and black boots.

"This body may be weak, but it will be a great deal of help in our search for the girl. Besides, it doesn't matter what body I'm in I still can take down Star or Nova," she told him who looked identical to her except for being more masculine.

"Remember, we have to be careful of how much activity we do. Our food supply is low and we can't contact the rest of our kind unless it's an emergency," he reminded her. "Not to mention that just because we got here first doesn't mean we should count out Star and Nova's resourcefulness. They're probably on their way here as we speak."

Back on Entara Star was in the park watching her little brother play and talking to her friends. "I was able to finish the Creative Writing class assignment last night. You know, the one expressing how we feel about our powers? I was very pleased with my ability to actually translate how I feel

65

onto paper. I mean the joys of justice, goodness, and life is so underrated if you ask me," she said laughing.

"Oh really? What about me huh? Face it, sister; your powers are pathetic compared to mine. People embrace the darkness and evils in life a lot more then their willing to admit. Its part of what makes them who they truly are. I'm not saying that injustice, evil, and death are the best things in the world, but they are needed. Face it, sis, we need one another," Nova surmised.

Before Star could reply to that a messenger appeared in front of her. "Miss Star? Miss Nova?"

"Yes, we're Star and Nova. How may we be of service to you?" Star asked puzzled by the messenger's appearance.

"I have a message for you both. The Council of Four has urgently requested your presence right away. I'm to escort you to them straight away," the messenger explained hurriedly.

Star looked at Nova confused. This didn't any sense to either of them. Why would the leaders of Entara want to see them? Shrugging her shoulders she turned to her friends and spoke, "Faith, will you and Sporty take Asteroid home for us and watch him till we return?"

Faith nodded her head and gathered up Asteroid up in her arms. "Don't worry. He's in good hands. Just go and see what they want. Relax I'm sure the Council doesn't mean you any harm. Come on Sporty let's go," she said flying off with Asteroid in her arms.

"Take care you two. Be sure to tell us what happens. Bye!" Sporty said jogging off.

Star and Nova followed the messenger quietly to the Grand Meeting Hall. Soon the two of them where outside the doors to the Inner Sanctuary waiting to be let inside so the Council could see them. The messenger faced them to deliver one final report. "The Council will speak to each of you in private. Please try to relax. I assure you that the Council means neither one of you harm." With that he was gone.

Star paced nervously. The last time she had met with the Council was during her last exams. That had been a nightmare. Being under their eyes was nerve wracking to say the least. She hoped whatever they wanted to talk about wasn't too important.

"Star, enter our sanctuary. Nova, please wait outside to be called," Nature called to her as the doors creaked open. Swallowing loudly she walked inside. The doors closed behind her with a bang.

Star walked forward nervously until she was standing right before the Council. She gazed up at each of them nervously. She bowed respectfully hoping to get in their good graces. "You wish to speak to me Council Members? If I've done anything wrong, I'd like to know what it is."

"You have done nothing wrong, Star. In fact it is because you've done so much right that you've been called here today. Star, what we're about to reveal to you must be kept secret from everyone else, including your own family. Do we have your word you won't tell anyone of what is discussed in this room?" Nature asked.

Star nodded her head. "You have my word. I won't betray your trust."

"Very well, take a seat. As you know three eons ago the Nameless was sealed away in the anti-universe and since then the Killgonas have been trying to free it. The Temple Acolytes have revealed to us that those monsters have been manipulating the energy barrier so that they can capture the prime realities maximum energy output. Once they have that energy they can give it to the Nameless and it will be able to break through the already weakened seal. In order to prevent this, we must reinforce the seal with a backup one," Time explained to her.

"In order for us to get the backup seal we need the assistance of an ordinary Crystal Carrier and an Entity working as one. That's where you come in. Your mission is to train the Crystal Carrier and assist her in creating a power surge that will reset the barrier causing a backup seal to form," Wisdom explained patiently to the frightened girl.

"This task isn't as easy as it sounds. The reality where the Carrier exist is a normal one, and she has no protection whatsoever against the Killgonas who are after her. She is unaware that what she thinks is nothing more then her imagination is very real. Also, in order for this to work you would have go alone and you have only seven weeks to teach her what she needs to know. Can we be assured you could accomplish this task?" Emotion asked

"Rest assured Council I won't let you down. There is too much at stake for me to fail. I swear to you on my life I will stop this terrible threat before it comes to be," Star replied.

"Very well then. Because of the high profile of this case certain information will have to be kept confidential even from you. You will only be given the barest of facts, a few gifts from us and that's it. Remember, the girl is unaware of her role in all this. You must earn her trust and not pressure her too much otherwise we will lose in the long run," Wisdom cautioned.

"I understand the seriousness of the situation. I admit that I'm slightly overwhelmed by all this. I have never been given an assignment of this magnitude before, but I'm certain I can handle it."

"That is good to hear. It is time for you to begin your quest. My globe will download the bare facts into your mind. Mostly it's just a brief description of what she looks like, the layout of the place she lives, and a few other tidbits of information. Now, husband, I believe you must start the ritual. Please proceed."

Time stood up from his throne pointing his time scepter at her. The silver clock on the end began to glow and the hands raced around and around. "I grant you the ability to create a time warp in the event you need a quick escape," He proclaimed as a silver glow enveloped her.

Nature stood up and squeezed her globe tightly. A ribbon of green light wrapped itself around Star. "My gift is the ability to hear the voice of nature. Let it guide you when you are in danger."

Wisdom was next. He unfurled his scroll and read an incantation from it. "My gift to you is the ancient wisdom of limitless understanding of people and books. I hope it helps you in your quest," he stated as a pale blue light beamed the gift into her mind.

Emotion drew her cloak tightly around her neck before waving her wand around. "My gift is the ability to use the powers of love, imagination, and creativity to their fullest ability. This is gift is very powerful so be careful when you use it," she warned as magenta colored droplets rained down on Star.

As soon as the last gift was given she looked up at them, her eyes sparkled with a new intensity. Her body shone with the most incredible brilliance. Her energy levels were at an all time high and a million thoughts raced through her mind. She was ready for action. "I thank you all for the gifts you have given me as well as the information I need in order to complete my quest. I shall depart at once for the Temple."

"Before you leave, please inform your sister that we are ready to see her about another important matter. Go now and journey forth and good luck. The fate of both Entara and the entire multiverse rest in your hands," Time told her as he sat back down.

Star bowed and swiftly left the room. She didn't notice the grim looks upon the Council's faces. Closing the doors behind her she turned to face her sister. "The Council will see you now. I have to go home and pack some things."

Nova entered the sanctum of the Council curious about what was going on. Curtsying formally in front of the Council she spoke up, "Honorable Council, I am very curious to why you wish to speak with me. If there's anything I can help you with, please tell me."

"Nova, you are the Entity who represents injustice, evil, and death. Many people would consider you the ultimate evil, yet you are not truly evil are you? You have set limits and rules of what you will tolerate. It is because of this we require your help," Wisdom began.

"Your twin was just given an important assignment. We would like it if you kept an eye on her and helped her out without her knowledge. Also you must protect the girl she is training from becoming prey to the Killgonas," Nature said.

"That might be hard for me to do. Star and I are very close despite our differences and work best together. Still I understand your reasons and will abide by them," Nova responded even though she didn't. She also received the same gifts as her sister and then left.

The Council looked at one another with grim looks in their eyes. "It has begun. Let us hope everything works out," Time said evenly.

Back at her house Star had finished packing a few personal items for her trip she thought might come in handy. A few photos of her family, a few personal curios, and lastly her diary items that held a great deal of value to her. Slinging her bag over her shoulder she left her room looking for her little brother. She found him in his room putting together his models of different realities.

"Asteroid, I want you to behave until Mom and Dad get back. Sporty and Faith will be downstairs if you need them. Do your homework and please don't destroy the house," she yelled at him as she ran down the steps.

She was in such a hurry she didn't watch where she was going and tripped falling down the stairs. She landed on top of Nova who had just returned home. "Sorry, Nova. I really should watch where I'm going. Listen, something urgent has come up in one of the realities that require my attention so I have to leave right away," she hurriedly explained as she detangled herself from her sister. "Take care of Asteroid. See you later, bye!"

Star rushed to the Temple as fast as she could. She would have teleported there, but it was impossible to teleport inside the Temple. Finally, she arrived totally out of breath. Jasmine and Sapphire were waiting for her on the steps.

We were worried that you wouldn't come. What took you so long to get here?" Jasmine asked as she escorted her inside hurriedly. Her parent's had finally clued her in on what was going on. What they had told her upset her greatly. She feared that the Council's plan wouldn't work and everything she loved would be destroyed.

"I had to pick up a few items. I've never done anything like this before, at least not on this kind of scale with such deadly consequences if I fail," Star replied. She was confident that she would succeed with her mission and prevent the destruction of her beloved home. It wasn't like she had any other option.

"It's understandable, Star. You've been thrust into a situation that you don't completely understand. I know that the task may seem impossible, but we have faith in you. My husband will give you last minute instructions once we get to our destination," Sapphire told her as they walked quickly through the Temple.

They passed hundreds of doors leading to more frequented realties and climbed three flights of stairs until they reached the right level. After walking through a maze of corridors, they arrived at the right door. The two Acolytes took their leave of her. Taking a deep breath, she went inside.

Guardian was meditating in front of a glass covered reality bubble. He looked up when he heard her enter. Rising to his feet he hurried over to her and shook her hand. "I've been expecting you for sometime. I was concerned a bit when the Council chose you for this mission. Seeing that you're so young I have my doubts about you succeeding. However, I'm not one to question their orders especially about this. Are you ready to proceed?"

70

"Yes, I am. Please don't worry so much Guardian you'll get wrinkles. I won't fail in this mission because I can't. The stakes are simply too high. I will save Entara and stop the Killgonas from succeeding with their plans. Just tell me what I need to do."

"Very well. It's really quite simple. All you have to do is enter the bubble, and you'll be instantly transported to the reality. Remember, time passes differently while you remain a part of the reality. Your seven weeks will be just that in their time, but it may pass quicker here. I'm not really certain. You run a very high risk of getting injured. For security reasons you won't be able to contact us at all once your there, but we will be keeping a mental watch on you."

"I comprehend the risks Guardian. This mission will be the hardest thing I've ever done. But that is why I must do it. I have to do it. There's really no other choice."

He nodded in agreement. He turned towards the incased bubble and with a wave of his hands the glass cover vanished. The bubble glowed softly now that it was exposed to the air. Star shook his hand firmly before plunging headfirst into the bubble.

A vortex of colors surrounded her as she crossed the barrier that separated her beloved Entara from all realities. She twisted, turned, and spun around helplessly until she emerged in the reality. She was hovering in the sky, looking down at the city of Peru invisible to the naked eye. She landed in a park near the local junior high. Smiling at herself she noted the date was October 16th. Plenty of time to rest before she started her quest to find the Chosen One, whoever she may be.

Chapter Eight

In Peru's neighboring town of La Salle a girl was sleeping restlessly in her new room. Boxes were scattered everywhere in the small area. She had just moved into the apartment over the weekend with her family and still hadn't unpacked.

It was dark outside and the girl wasn't use to the new place or sleeping on an air mattress. Suddenly her alarm went off waking her from her sleep. She rolled over and shut the thing off. Groaning a lot she got up and made her way to the bathroom that was next to her room muttering under her breath, "New day Kali, new day."

It was a very hectic morning for Kali Shevlin and her family, which consisted of her mom, younger sister Keelia, and a Great Pyrenees dog named Oso. The entire apartment was a mess because they were still in the process of moving things from their old house to the new apartment. It didn't help they had more stuff then could possibly fit inside the new home.

Boxes were scattered everywhere, nothing was hooked up, and there wasn't a lot to eat in the fridge for breakfast. A lot of changes had occurred, but some things like her school stayed the same. She did have a new bus route and lost her paper route, which is was her only source of income. All of this was very frustrating and made getting ready for school that much harder. Finally she left for school hoping that things would work out for her, but she severally doubted it.

Meanwhile Killnala and Killroary where checking out the old place searching for clues. It was a simple white house in need of some major repairs. A dumpster stood in the driveway filled with trash. "The girl's aura is very strong here. In fact I sense it all over the immediate vicinity. She lived here till recently. But she's not here any longer. She's gone and I don't have her scent," Killnala said to Killroary as they sniffed the air around the place.

"You're right. We must have just missed her. This was an unexpected turn of events. Obviously the girl has changed location. That just makes this hunt more interesting for us. What do you suggest we do? Are you sure you don't have a scent?" Killroary asked uncertainly. He had already tried to use his tracking skills to find the girl, but could find nothing.

"We are going to the local high school and hunting her down. We know what her scent is even though it's pretty weak here. That should help us find her even hidden in a crowded school. Let's go before we're noticed," Killnala ordered as she took to the air. Killroary smiled and followed right behind her.

Star was also heading for the school. From her briefing she knew it was called La Salle-Peru Township High School or LP for short. It was situated on the dividing line between the two towns so half was in La Salle and the other was in Peru. Gliding through the air as a white mist she so she wouldn't be notice she was amazed by what she saw. Stores, houses, parks, a mall, and so much more it was very different from her home. For one thing there weren't as many people walking around. She didn't see a lot of wildlife and there was more traffic then she was use to. The school itself took her breath away.

The layout reminded her more of a collage campus then a high school. There was a huge football stadium and track near a building marked Dolan where carrier classes were held. The main building looked like a giant E and there was another gym and vocational building just across the street. A huge tennis court stood near a practice field and there where at least four parking lots plus the auto shop down the road. The entire school was made out of red bricks with designs carved into them and there was even a clock tower attached to the main building. It wasn't the Institution, but it wasn't shabby either.

Star hovered over the school observing the student's arriving. It was Monday morning and most students seemed to wish it were still the weekend. Several were getting off buses, or cars, or even walking to the building. They seem to be extremely chatty and most of them seemed to be excited about upcoming school events. She needed a plan if she was going to complete her mission on time.

She then proceeded to spread her essence all across the main building. She literally allowed herself to become the school so she could understand it better. Star knew the girl attend this school, so it was important to learn as much as she could about this location so she could find the Chosen One faster. The school's soul merged with hers as they became one. Every part of the school had a story to tell. In her mind's eye she saw every major event that ever took place there. The history of this building was incredible. It was a bit overwhelming to say the least. *How am I going to find one girl in all of this? It will be like trying to find a needle in a haystack.*

Unknown to Star, Killnala and Killroary were also on the grounds looking for the girl, but for entirely different reasons. They were on the roof of the East Gym, which was connected to the Vocational Building trying to sense their prey. Killroary sat on the edge of the roof sniffing the air. "She's definitely here already. I can sense the aura of a non-recognized Crystal Carrier. I just can't pinpoint her location."

"Most likely it has to do with the interference caused by the other students auras. This is a very large high school. While none of them may be as pure hearted or bright as our target, they're still strong enough to confuse our senses thus hiding her. Ironic isn't it?" Killnala said stiffly.

"What? I don't see the irony of the situation," he replied.

"The girl is supposed to be very powerful and unprotected. Yet a simple thing like the natural congregation of too many auras has hidden her from us. Quite clever if you ask me," she commented. "Our search for her will go faster if we split up. Search every little inch of that school and all the other buildings. You search the auto building down the street while I check the vocation building. We will meet back here to search the East gym in fifteen minutes."

Killroary nodded and then jumped straight off the roof landing on the sidewalk. Luckily nobody saw him. Smirking he headed off for his target. With his tracking skills he was confident that the target would be found and eliminated in no time at all. If they came across an Entity in the meantime well that was an added bonus in killing them.

"Boys. Such showoffs. He could have just used the roof access or glided down. With any luck no one will notice him. Well I guess its time to start this hunt. The bloodlust won't be contained anymore," Killnala said to herself.

74

She then stepped off the roof and plummeted to the ground. She landed gracefully and started her search. It would be very difficult seeing as how she would have to remain solid yet at the same time avoid being noticed. Keeping her temper in check would be another problem, but she was certain that she could handle it.

Star had entered the school through the golden doors under the clock tower and into the main foyer. She drew in a sharp breath at what she saw. The school was just as beautiful inside as it was outside. The tile floor had writing on it and the chandelier was lit with old fashion lights. To her right the doors to the auditorium were open and what she saw reminded her of a professional theater. In front and to her left she saw a staircase leading to the other floors and she saw two amazing stain glass windows. This wasn't a school it was a museum.

"Hey you, the girl in purple, your not following the dress code," the greeter from the greeter's desk told her pointing at her midriff. She got up from behind her desk and headed over to her.

Time for a small show of power, Star thought. Walking over the greeter she looked her straight in the eye and said, "Yes I am Ms. You and anyone in this school sees me following the dress code. In fact you're not going to remember me at all. You're going to simply see and then ignore me."

The greeter's eyes lost focus for a second. A spark of purple light appeared in them. She was being mesmerized. What Star wanted her to see would be a normal girl that she could instantly dismiss. It was a simple masking spell she hoped it would hold for the time being. In most realities people accepted Star's corporeal body.

Star left the women and headed for the library, which was just down the hall. On the wall above her was a beautiful mural of medieval dressed people on horses. "This place is astonishing. How am I ever going to find one girl in all this?" she asked herself quietly as she entered the library. It would be a good place to start her search. Hopefully she would find her first.

Kali was up on the third floor in room 300. A sign next to the door read Mrs. Boyland, Foods & Adult Living. Foods was what Kali was currently in. The classroom was moderate size. There were six kitchens, a washing machine, six tables, and decorations of foods all over the walls. At the moment Kali was talking to her friends Tiffany and Chris before class started.

"Its awful the new place. I hate the stupid white walls. I'm sleeping on an air mattress and half my stuff is still at the old house. Moving was possibly the worst thing that could happen to me," she whined.

"Yeah I can understand that. My family is still unpacking from when we moved in during the summer," Tiffany said. Her blond hair didn't go well with her Goth lock. Even though she was a freshman, Kali felt comfortable talking to her despite the fact she was a senior.

Chris put down his book. He looked at her concerned as usual. "At least your birthday was okay. You got your new books and a nice plaque of some tigers. Not to mention a cake. Your party is still Friday right?"

"Not anymore. I really don't want a party at the new place and no one really can make it. So I'm canceling it. I just can't see me ever having a real party ever," Kali admitted sadly. Life always seemed to go wrong for her and it was becoming more frustrating by the day.

Tiffany looked slightly upset to hear this. "I'm sorry you can't have a party. I know how much you wanted one. Maybe we can all do something to celebrate later?"

"Yeah you deserve something nice Kali. It's not fair you get stuck with the short end of the stick all the time." Chris added. He had been her friend since freshman year helping her out with all sorts of problems, but he had no clue how to fix this one.

Kali just smiled at them, but inside she was hurting bad. Nothing in life seemed to go right for her. All she wanted was to have a normal birthday party to celebrate turning eighteen and she couldn't even have that. Sometimes it seemed she never could have a normal life.

The bell rang and class began. She sat down at her table and paid close attention to Mrs. Boyland explanation about different types of foods. For some reason she felt like something was suppose to happen, but it didn't. Instead class passed normally and soon she was heading for second period American Sign Language.

Star was walking down the halls invisible to the human eye. Her search in the library had proven unsuccessful and she had searched the offices and teacher's lounge with no luck. The girl wasn't anywhere she had looked so far. Where could she be?

Killnala was also significantly irritated. Her search had turned up nothing so far. She tapped her nails in annoyance. "I'm not pleased by our shortcomings so far Killroary. Our search so far hasn't turned up anything yet. We still have to search the entire main building and the Dolan one as well. At this rate we aren't going to find her. Classes change every fifty five minutes with a five minute window to get to the next one."

"I know that. Even when she's in class we can't pinpoint her. She might be in a place we already looked. How do we narrow our search pattern?" Killroary appealed to his mate. He was fearful if she lost her temper the mission would end up a complete flop.

"I have an idea, but we have to work fast. We go inside the security office, download pictures of all students who match our description, then print out their schedule and check them out one by one. It may be slower, but it will work out in the end. The target shall be found."

"Excellent plan my dear. I wouldn't have thought of it. With our abilities and my hacking skills this shouldn't take to long. If we hurry we can finish before third period starts. We can spend the rest of the day hunting."

Flashing each other a dazzling smile they phased inside the tiny security office. There wasn't much in there besides a desk, computer, and a couple of walkie-talkies. It was thankfully empty for the moment, but that could change in a heartbeat.

Killroary sat down at the computer cracked his knuckles and got to work. He programmed the computer to find white girls with blond hair and blue eyes. That was more than half the school so he asked for only juniors and seniors. "We have about five hundred girls to check out, but she is definitely on the list."

"Hurry up and print out the schedules before we're exposed! Third hour starts in five minutes and I don't want to still be here. When the kids go past here we need to mingle with them," she whispered to him. Just as the last schedule was printed out the door the office opened up and in stepped one of the casual dressed security guards.

For a moment everyone was frozen in place. The guard, because two strangely dressed students, where in his office, while the Killgonas were surprised that they had been caught. No one spoke for a moment they where to shocked.

The silence was broken when the guard started shouting. "What do you kids think your doing in here? This place is off limits! You're going to have to come explain this to Principle Nelson right now. Security I have intru….."the guard started to say, but he never finished his sentences. In a blink of an eye Killnala was all over him.

Killnala snatched the walkie-talkie from his hand and crushed it. Yanking him inside the room with one hand she slammed the door closed with the other. She hurled him into the wall leaving an impression it. He slid down to the floor where she picked him up and lifted him ten feet in the air. Her eyes burned with anger and her entire body was surging with adrenaline. "I really hate being interrupted, especially by weak fools such as yourself. You people think you're the boss of me. Well I got a message for you your not!" She drew back her hand and extended her nails to their full length of six inches. With one quick fluent movement she slashed his face, chest, and the rest of his body injecting the guard with her poison. Opening her mouth wide she bit down hard on his neck letting his blood pour into her mouth. He screamed in pain, but she continued driven by the smell of blood. Finally she released him and he crumbled to the floor. With a swift kick to the head he was knocked unconscious.

She began to rub her tendrils in order to calm down, lower her blood pressure, and rid her body of the extra adrenaline. Her bloodlust had been appeased, but at what cost? She turned to face her consort who was looking at her with an unreadable expression. "We better get going before someone comes to investigate the noise. If they catch us here we'll be seriously delayed. Would you stop giving me that look already? He's not dead merely knocked out. I didn't give him a full dose of poison only enough to paralyze him temporarily. You think I'm stupid enough to leave a body? We don't need that right now."

Killroary just shook his head and gave her half the schedules. Wordlessly they turned and left the office leaving the bloody guard to be found. They had more important matters to attend to then a dying man. It wasn't like if the man was discovered the humans would think to look for a pair of Killgonas now was it?

The rest of the morning passed without incident. It seemed that something or someone was preventing the two teams finding each other let alone one girl. The Killgonas had eliminated more than half the people on their list. They had gotten rid of all the juniors and were working on the seniors. They were both confident they would find the girl.

Star was getting very concerned. She spent all morning looking for her Crystal Carrier to no avail. It was lunchtime and she was exhausted not to mention starving. She had combed the entire main building up and down, room by room with no luck. Some Entity she turned out to be. So far she was failing miserably at her quest. She leaned against some lockers waiting for the C Lunch to begin.

That's when she sensed it for the first time. An aura of pure goodness and love filled her entire body. All around her she got the feeling of peace and serenity. She was close to her Carrier, really close. She looked at the locker she was leaning against number 2040. It was directly across from the library the place she started her journey. Was it possible that the locker belonged to her girl? Had her search finally come to an end?

The bell rang and her eyes scanned the crowd. What she saw next was the ultimate irony. A blond hair, blue eye girl wearing purple glasses stopped at the locker. She was wearing a long sleeve purple shirt and a pair of faded blue jeans. A minute later an almost identical girl joined her. The girl was a little larger, wore a green shirt, blue jeans, and a key dangled from her neck and black glasses. The two of them stopped to chat with each other for a few minutes. After she left the girl removed her glasses putting them away and grabbed her sack lunch before heading into the lunchroom.

"I don't believe it. She's the one. No wonder I didn't find her sooner. The Council showed me a picture of her without the glasses. They concealed her identity sense she only wears them here and not at home. Not to mention she's a twin so I'm sensing a double aura. I got to learn more just to be sure I found the right girl and I better be certain before the Killgonas find her," she whispered quietly to herself. She quickly followed the girl into the cafeteria to make sure she stayed safe.

Kali had no idea at all that she was being watched. All she knew for certain is she had her favorite lunch and was with her friends, Rebecca, Rebecca's twin sister Christine, and Jake and his girlfriend. Lately she was beginning to feel they only tolerated her presence and that they weren't really her friends anymore.

The entire day had been pretty normal so far, but Kali still couldn't shake the feeling that something wasn't right. The strange sensation that she was being watched wouldn't be dismissed from her mind. "Hey do you guys get the feeling we're being watched?" she asked. She hoped that if they did they would start taking her a bit more serious.

"You're just imagining things again Kali. Would you just eat your lunch already? Christine what do you think of this image?" Rebecca asked showing her latest design off. It was a picture of an anime character from the girls' online story site.

"Looks good. I really think the eyes should be bigger though," Christine critiqued. Both girls where big anime artist and charged money for their work. They had a successful business.

Jake didn't even seem to notice Kali. He just continued laughing and smiling with his girl. This was the typical scene lately at their table and Kali was getting fed up with being ignored. She wished she had some real friends who would talk with her and hang out with. So far that didn't look like it was going to happen.

Star was sitting at the table directly across from her listening in on the whole conversation. She was mentally checking off the list of requirements for the Crystal Carrier. The girl, Kali, was the right age, looked like the picture she had, obviously loved reading if her giant book was any indication so that meant she was imaginative, and lastly when she probed her thoughts she found startling images of her. No doubt in her mind, Kali Shevlin was her girl. The Chosen One, the girl, the Champion of the multiverse.

Now that she knew who she was supposed to train it was just a matter of protecting her until she could introduce herself properly. Earlier she had sensed someone in dire peril and come across a security guard near death. It had taken a lot of time and patience to heal him and mind wipe him of the attack. She couldn't afford another to do another one. "Her heart is heavy with pain yet her soul is full of love. Her mind is riddled with heartache, betrayal, and loneliness. My Crystal Carrier has been hurt often in the past. Yet, somehow she finds the strength to keep on going with her life no matter how terrible it may be. I find her to be most unusual," she mused.

Star tailed Kali to her last two classes of the day, Adult Living and Study Skills. All the time observing how different the Chosen One was compared to other Crystal Carriers she'd encountered in the past. If she didn't already know the truth she be very skeptical about the girl who sat reading the book. She was so engrossed by the tale she just shut the rest of the world out.

It wasn't easy to avoid Kali's mind. She broadcasted her past quite loudly. Her dissimilarities may make a difference in the long run, but right now it just made her an outcast in society. Something she never run up against with anyone else before so this would be a challenge Star mused to herself. She thought about all she had learned and what she could do with that information to help in her quest.

One major difference and obstacle for Star was that poor Kali had Bipolar/ADHD. Her parents were divorced and her older brother was away at collage. She was extremely intelligent, but lacked the ability to really socialize. She didn't go to school functions preferring to read, play outdoors, or write stories. Her favorite shows were cartoons and besides loving country and songs from movies plus didn't have a sense of humor. She also had a closely guarded secret that even she couldn't penetrate. All this added up to one complex person who might or might not be willing to accept her destiny and help save the multiverse from destruction.

Kali wasn't your typical teenager and was miserable because of it. Whenever she tried to change who she was it just made things worse. Kali didn't have the support she needed at home to be whom she truly wanted to be and was constantly picked on at school to the point where she had retreated to a small circle of friends and loved ones. But still her imagination burned brightly, she had a pure heart waiting to shine, and unlimited amount of love for the world. As she boarded the bus home, Star couldn't think of someone better for this task, but that didn't stop her from pitying her. She hoped that if Kali did embrace her destiny it would help her in the long run solve her problems and make it easier for her to accept herself as she was.

Killnala and Killroary also had the girl in their line of sight. She had been near the bottom of the list so it had taken some time to get to her. But it had been worth the wait because they knew they had finally found their prey. They weren't very impressed by what they saw.

"This is the best the Council could come up with? A freaking weird little eighteen-year-old senior is the Chosen One? Their standards sure have fallen far. Look at her; she doesn't seem very powerful at all. No way could someone like her take out anyone bigger then her let alone safe all reality. This is the biggest cosmic joke ever," Killroary said laughing his head off.

"Looks can be deceiving as we both know. Can't you see her aura or are you to blinded by your overconfidence? Even partially hidden it has the glow of a full-fledged Entity! No Crystal Carrier has that type of aura especially, not an unrecognized one. This girl, Kali, must be given further observation before we make our move. Only after we know her greatest weakness shall we strike," Killnala informed him coyly.

"What? *You're* not going to attack her now? Have you lost your mind? You've never been this cautious before. Usually I'm the one holding you back. We can't wait to attack. Star could make her move before we have a chance to slay her!" He barked

"This state of affairs must be handled adroitly. Too much rides on this for reckless actions. She isn't aware of it, but the girl has special powers that protect her even now. She doesn't even realize the great destiny that lies before her. It's our job to make sure she never finds of. If we attack her while she's with Star we get to kill two birds with one stone. We just have to be a little patient. Soon we shall feast and the Nameless will roam free once again," Killnala chortled happily.

Chapter Nine

Kali got off the bus and went inside her new apartment. Upon crossing the threshold of her new place she tripped over a box lying in the hallway. Rubbing her bruised hip she got up and looked around for her mom. She noticed a note tagged to the fridge saying she had gone back to the old place to finish clearing out the house and bringing their stuff here.

She went upstairs and collapsed on top of her air mattress. She screamed into her pillow and cried, "Why me? Why do I get stuck with the smallest bedroom with nothing to do? What did I do to deserve this?"

Putting in her new CD she cranked the volume up to drown out her sorrows. She let the music take her away from this place. "I hate this stupid place. The room's to small, my rug doesn't fit and is all bunched up, I'm lost without my books or any of my other personal belongings. The VCR/DVD player is down and we don't even have the computer up! Without the computer I can't talk to Agent-G or Slick! To top all of it off my baby, my cat, Hotaru, has to go live with Dad until I can get permission for her to come live here!"

"Kali will you shut the hell up and turn that wretched music off! I'm trying to get ready for work and I don't have time to listen to you complain. Get a life already!" Keelia, her younger sister snapped. She was in the bathroom getting ready for work. She was a photographer at a portrait studio in the mall and made more money in a month then she had every two month by delivering papers.

In Kali's mind Keelia was perfect in everyway. She had nice fake auburn hair and flawless skin that went well with her nice clothes, good grades, and lots of friends. She was involved with a lot of extracurricular activities and already had her license, which she rubbed in her face all the time. Her favorite things to do were boss Kali around and if possible humiliate Kali. She never had a kind word to say to her older sister. In her heart she knew this wasn't true, but she couldn't help but feel this way at times.

"Would you just please leave me alone Keelia? Is it too much to ask for that just once? Can't a girl get some privacy in this place or is that too much to ask for? I have a right to complain and sulk if I chose to. My life was just altered greatly and you're not being very sympathetic. So just leave me alone!" Kali replied angrily. Slamming the door close she counted to five trying to regain control of her temper. Why was it no one seemed to understand her? Sometimes it felt like no one really cared about her.

Star was downstairs in the living room listening to the sisters argue upstairs. It bothered her that the two of them where fighting. Nova, Asteroid, and her may have had their differences but they always worked out their problems and supported one another. She just didn't understand how sisters could hate each other so much. "I really wish I could take your entire troubles away child. But I can't just wave my hands and make things better, it's just not possible. But you must experience this change as well as others head on. It is the only way you will learn to deal with unexpected surprises. Handling things on your own is the first step in your training."

Turning into pure energy she phased through the ceiling and entered the correct bedroom. She wrapped herself around the crying girl soothing her, giving her some comfort. The room filled with a sense of peace, and Kali started to feel like living again. She picked up her baby doll Sauta; her most prized possession, and hugged her tightly letting her love flow through her body into the doll calming down.

A little while later Kali went downstairs to watch some TV. While she was watching her program her mom came home. Keelia came flying down the stairs ready to go to work. She didn't even glance at Kali as she ran out the door. "I have to go back to the house and finish cleaning with Sally. I'll be back later so will you please feed Oso and take him for a walk outside? Think you can handle all that?"

"Yeah, Mom, I think I can handle it all. I'm eighteen not eight. Come here, Oso; we're going to go outside. Go on I'll be fine," she reassured them clipping on the leash and going out the back door.

She took Oso out to the empty lot next to the apartments. She saw her Mom's van leave and let out a breath she been holding. "Yeah sure, Mom, leave me alone again! I hate being left alone all the time. I wish I was doing my route or riding my bike, but they took my route and my bike has a flat tire. Not to mention everything that matters to me is packed up still. Why can't I ever catch a break? Is it too much to ask God for some companionship? For once in my entire cursed life can something good happen? I think you owe me!" she shouted to the sky.

"You know something child, you can't go blaming the Celestial Gods for all your problems. They don't like it much, but then again who does like being screamed at?" a voice said from behind her. It was soft and melodious and definitely that of a young female.

Kali spun around scanning the empty lot searching for the source of the voice, but there wasn't anyone around. What was going on? "Whose there? Show yourself. I must warn you Oso is trained to defend me," she bluffed. Oso only protected her mom.

"Really Kali, you don't need to resort to bluffing. I would never harm you. It goes against everything I believe in. I doubt that I could even if I tried," the voice said again this time from right next to her. Suddenly Kali felt the weight of a hand on her shoulders and squeezing gently.

That was enough for her. Yanking hard on the leash she took off running as fast as her legs could carry her tearing through the bushes that divided the lot from the apartments. Forcing the back doors open, she jumped inside pulling in Oso and locking the doors behind her.

Panting hard it took her awhile to catch her breath. Oso nudged her with his nose trying to comfort her. "It's okay, boy, its okay. No reason at all to be scared. I probably was just hearing things. Man I'm thirsty; I'm getting a soda. Why don't you go lay down?" she instructed as she headed into the tiny kitchen.

Oso complied, but growled slightly as he sensed another presence enter the room. Kali was returning to see what was bothering him when something tapped her lightly on the shoulder. Screaming loudly, she dropped her soda. Whipping around she saw no one around. "Relax there's no reason to get jumpy. There's no one here, but me."

Grabbing a paper towel she bent down to clean up the mess she made when she noticed it was already taken care of. Now she was officially spooked. What was going on? "Something really strange is going on here.

Normally I like the supernatural, but this is getting a bit much for me."

"Believe me, there's nothing supernatural about any of this. Please don't run away I need to speak with you. I promise I mean no harm to you at all. Just trust me okay?" the disembodied voice said.

She didn't run instead she fell onto the couch and watched mesmerized as a shower of blue and purple sparks ran down from the ceiling until they took the corporal form of Star. Her jaw dropped slightly as the sight of a teenage girl hovering in midair.

Star held up her hands in a gesture of peace not wanting to alarm the poor girl. She spoke in soft, soothing voice, "Please don't be frightened of me. I mean you no harm whatsoever. I've been waiting for just the right moment to introduce myself to you. My name is...."

Kali interrupted her midsentence. "I know who you are all ready. Your name is Star and you're the Spirit of Justice, Entity of all Goodness, Creator of Life. I made you up sometime ago and had my online friend, Agent-G illustrate you and Nova. He really did good work because you look exactly like his image. I'm pleased to meet my best original character. So what are you doing here in my living room may I ask? Or how come I couldn't see you earlier if you've been around all day. Where's Nova isn't she with you and most importantly how is this even possible?"

"Whoa, whoa, whoa. One question at a time please, you're giving me a headache. I was aware of your psychic link with my people, especially to me, but I had no idea it was this strong," Star said in amazement. Kali's reaction to her was one she hadn't suspected at all. Most Crystal Carriers were scared when they first met her and not all that enthusiastic. This was rather welcomed surprise.

"What do mean by psychic link? Are you saying I'm connecting to you? The only reason I'm not freaking out by all this is I had this crazy theory that anything we made up was real in another reality or alternant dimension. So glad I'm right."

"You're very close in that deduction. Many people have a subconscious link with other realities. This link is established between people with powerful, creative, and caring aura's during a fluctuation between the reality bubbles," Star explained to her as she took a seat next to her.

"But doesn't Entara exist outside normal time and space? If I recall correctly it's situated between the anti-universe and the multiverse. So I don't see how I could have established a link between your people and me. Until you appeared I thought I made you up."

She shrugged her shoulders in defeat. Petting Oso on the head she continued. "Look I'm not even going to pretend I have all the answers. That's something the Council should handle not me. I will try to answer some of them, but I can't promise anything. What I do for certain is this. Every person ever born knows about the Entity race and the importance of Crystal Carriers. Our story is written in your blood. This is very important as you will soon learn."

"The reason I'm in your living room is because I wanted to introduce myself in a comfortable surrounding. I was invisible earlier; that's why you couldn't see me. Nova is back on Entara doing who knows what for the Council, and anything is possible if you believe hard enough. Does that answer your questions?"

Kali just snorted at that and the fact that she didn't believe Nova was back home. Those two sisters couldn't live without one another for more then a day. Something of great importance was up and she was determined to find out what. "I don't mean to be rude or anything, but I have to ask you something. Why are you here now specifically? I have a feeling it isn't to meet me just because I've been writing about you or that I've been dying to meet you."

"You are smarter then you look. I'll never underestimate you again. No, this isn't a social call, but believe me when I'm finished you wish it where. I was sent here on a mission more of a quest by the Council. This is of the highest importance and you should treat it as such."

"The Council? Forgive me Star, but you never have exactly seen eye to eye with the Council in the past. You hate taking orders from them or at least you did in the past. You think I got that wrong in my writing?"

"No, it's true we don't always share the same views, but that's natural. I'm a child remember not an adult. Its possible you're seeing future events that have yet to unfold because right now I do act accordingly and have never objected to anything they've done."

"Enough about that. Lets talk about you. You're the reason I'm here. Your life is going to change in a big way."

"I've been chosen to train you in the ways of a Crystal Carrier. Our time is limited. In approximately seven weeks the prime realities will produce their maximum energy output. The barrier will send the energy to the seal to reinforce it, but its never going to make it. The Killgonas are intent on capturing it and giving it to the Nameless. Once it has regained its full power, it will break free of the anti-universe and destroying everything. You are the only hope for Entara and the entire multiverse."

Kali looked at her as if she was crazy. "You're kidding right? How can I be a Crystal Carrier? I don't have any special powers or done anything grand! I'm just an ordinary girl in a normal reality. There's nothing special about me. Your wasting your time with me because I have no talents, I can't even drive, and I'm very different then you're run of the mill Carrier. What can I do to help you?"

"I'm not joking about this Kali. You know me better then that. You have a great talent for writing and your caring nature towards animals is obvious to anyone. If you believe in yourself there's no reason you can't succeed. Don't deny fate the chance to guide you on your path of destiny."

"If you say so, I don't really have a lot of confidence in myself these days. I don't think I'm that special, if you get my meaning. Look at my life and me. Compared to my sister and a whole lot of other people, I'm a failure, a freak, and an idiot. No on likes the real me and they never will. Even my mom hates me," Kali cried softly.

"I don't believe that for an instant and I don't think you do either. I've been watching you and I have to tell you I think you're the most amazing person I've ever met. You've had such a hard life and been hurt often. Yet you always seem to come out on top, which is pretty amazing. You are loving, imaginative, smart, and most importantly of all, you never give up. I say that qualifies you as a Crystal Carrier," Star told her putting an arm around the girl.

"Tell you what I'll do because you're a special case. I'll train you in the ways of a Carrier, protect you from any and all harm, and lastly tell you more about my life if in return, you show me your writing, be a friend to me, and lastly save the multiverse. Deal?"

Kali wiped away her tears and smiled. She took her hand and shook it firmly. "Deal."

"Well what would you like to do first? I mean its only six thirty, and I would rather start training later when your more refreshed. Maybe we could have dinner? I haven't eaten in ages," Star suggested.

"I'll get something fro us to eat then. Hope you like cereal because that's all we've got. You know, I don't understand you at all Star. I wrote you to be like a regular teen, but at the same time I wanted you to be serious, philosophical, and passionate about stuff. How is it you can be all that at the same time?"

"It depends on the person and the situation. People view me the way they want to view me. I have to make sure I always am in charge no matter what the situation. I try to do my best with my powers while relying on my own beliefs, school lessons, and the way I was brought up. Overall, I always seem to be calm, collective, and a little bit cryptic."

"Tell me a little more about Entara please. I've always imagined it to be a perfect blending of trillions of cultures with nature along side of it. Is that true?"

"Well, yes and no. It's hard to put into words to an outsider. Entara has wonderful seas with tons of life, billions of creatures on land and in the air. My favorite place next to the Temple and the park is the mall. It's not your typical mall. It takes up five blocks and is shaped like a giant star. Every store, display, and food court is designed for us," she described, creating an image in the air. The image was far grander then the Mall of America, which Kali had been to.

The two girls chatted for hour, happily basking in each other's company. Star gained a much needed insight about Kali and her personality. It was even clearer now why the symbols of the Council had chosen her. It would be a great honor to teach this girl how to use her powers.

Kali also felt like she had gotten something of equal importance. A real friend who would always be there for her no matter what the reason. She needed that right now. Also finding out that something she had imagined was real had a profound effect on her. She wondered what else she imagined was real.

Unknown to the two of them, the Killgonas where staked out across the street watching them. Despite the fact the apartment building was behind another one and their prey was inside they heard and saw everything. Killroary, who was usually the calm one, was swearing and panicking at what he was observing.

"Don't you see? We've lost our one chance to get rid of her. Your plan backfired right in front of our faces! Star has made contact with her!"

"And you where telling me not panic. Look at them, there's no connection between them yet. Besides, have you forgotten about the most basic rules about the Crystal Carriers? They are only given full protection from us when their crystal has emerged. Meeting Star may help speed things along, but not by much. We still have a window of opportunity and I won't waste it. Trust me, Star will not be able to save herself, let alone that girl when we strike!"

"Might I suggest then that we go hunt for some energy? I still can't figure out what destroyed our reserves back at base, but right now were low on supplies. We need to find someone easy to feast on and fast," he stated. He was still trying to figure out what happened.

Earlier they had returned from staking out the school to discuss their next move only to find their base totally trashed and all their energy pods gone. The only thing not destroyed was their communication device so they could still talk to the rest of their people. The faint scent of darkness and evil had lingered in the air, but they couldn't match it to any known Entity or anything else that would attack a Killgona. No animal could have done it and the intruder hadn't left anything they could track him or her down and kill him or her with. It was very mysterious.

The two dragon-like beings in human form raced down the deserted streets at speeds of one hundred and seventy five miles an hour. It was barely past nine, yet the town seemed shut down for the night. There was no one in sight, which was good for them. No witnesses to observe them as they attacked people.

"Slow down! We can't keep up these speeds! At this rate will burn out by morning. Have you located a suitable target yet?" Killnala demanded a little while later. She was panting hard and continuously rubbing her tendrils in an effort to stay awake.

"As you know we don't need a complete energy feed just enough to keep us going for the next few days, right? Come on, I've got the greatest idea. We're heading to the hospital to feed. These patients won't be believed seeing as how they're all restricted to the mental ward!" Killroary barked with laughter.

They went to IVCH, the local hospital, and crept up the side of the building. They then melted right into the brick wall and reappeared unharmed on the other side. From then on in it were easy pickings as they feed off the energy of the patients. After an hour of gorging themselves they headed back to base. They spent the rest of the night cleaning up their camp and preparing for tomorrow.

The next day Star went to school with Kali while staying invisible. Both of them were extremely tired. Star had spent the night answering a never ending stream of questions. It was past midnight by the time Kali had nodded off.

"You must be very cautious of where you go and who your with. I know that the Killgonas are nearby and they are very sly and cunning. They will try to separate us in order to kill you more easily and they won't hesitate to get rid of anyone who stands in their way," Star whispered to her urgently before classes began.

Kali glared at her angrily before quickly looking around. First period was due to start in five minutes and students where shuffling inside. "Will you please refrain from talking to me verbally while other people are watching? I already have a reputation that's bad. I don't need to add to it," she hissed to her before sitting up straight.

It was very difficult to concentrate on what the teacher was saying. Her eyes would wander following Star around the room. It was distracting to say the least. She had often seen on TV people who could see things that others weren't able to. Having it happen to her was annoying.

The two of them finally found a free moment alone in the girl's bathroom as she was heading to third period gym. Kali dragged Star into a stall and locked the door. She glared angrily at the Entity and let out a deep breath. "What is with you Star? Are you trying to get me into trouble with the few teachers who like me? Mrs. Boyle and Mrs. Ruggerie didn't like me squirming around in my chair like that! I have enough trouble remembering all the signs in Sign Language class without being sidetracked."

"I'm sorry if this isn't working out to you're convince, but I hope you haven't forgotten why I'm here. We have seven weeks to prepare you for your most difficult task in your entire life. Saving the multiverse comes before school."

"You're not an hindrance to me, Star, really. I love having you around me, and I'm psyched by the fact you need my help and all. But try to remember that I'm eighteen and I have school to do among other things. This is my senior year and I need to make it count."

"Perhaps you're right. As a student myself, I should try to empathize with you. I know from probing your mind that your high school years haven't been that great. You want your senior year to stand out as the best. With my help, child, it will be one to remember forever. Now come on, we're going to be late for gym."

"Thanks and could you stop calling me child please? I'm a year older then you. Have you ever played the game badminton? I'm really good at it in my opinion. I can smash that birdie halfway across the gym!" Kali informed her proudly as they entered the main gym together.

Star watched Kali from the sidelines making sure no trouble came her way. So far nothing seemed to be wrong. However she couldn't help, but feel as if they were being toyed with. She wished Nova were here to help her, but she was back at home.

It wasn't until fifth period art class that Star decided to step in to help out a bit more. She had been looking at the extra credit drawings in Kali's sketchbook admiring her hard work. They weren't great, but they were still good. There was defiantly some talent. The images that drew most of her attention were of her, Killnala, and Nova. They were very detailed and there were sidebar notes about each person.

She turned to ask Kali what had prompted these designs when she saw a boy harassing her. The teacher, Mrs. Sarver, was at the back of the room, too far way to do anything. It was up to her to do something about it.

"Would you stop it already? I'm trying to get this project done and your bothering me. Go away," Kali told the boy angrily.

"Ooh, the psychopath is getting mad. What are you going to do? Freak out like you always do or maybe cry!" the boy taunted.

Star walked up behind him and sprinkled little strips of purple energy onto him. He went rigid for a minute, and then he spoke, "I'm sorry for that. I was being incredibly rude and nasty. Excuse me."

Star smiled triumphantly and winked at her. "Don't worry about him. I just gave him some strips of concentrated positive energy to get him to change his attitude. It was up to him to decide what he was going to do. Go back to working on your project. I'm going to go do a little sketching on my own."

Meanwhile Killnala and Killroary where in the library, which was directly across from the art room in the middle part of the E. They were pretending to be looking up information for a school project, but in reality were keeping an eye on their prey. So far they hadn't found a weakness they could exploit and it was aggravating them to no end.

"How much longer do we have to do this? I hate acting like you. Ever since we got here I've been acting more like you and you have been acting like me. Why?" Killroary asked in a low voice.

"I'm not sure. I was proceeding cautiously because this is my only chance to rid us of the threat posed by her being alive. Hitherto I sense someone else's hand guiding our actions," Killnala whispered to him.

"Perhaps the Nameless is assisting us in some manner. If I'm the one worrying about everything, then your mind is clear so you can focus on the mission. Now that we've got that figured out, what have we learned?"

"Not much. If I didn't have solid evidence proving her true identity, I wouldn't be tailing her. She's not really remarkable in anyway. All I know for certain is what her teachers' grade books, and her records from the office have on her. We also know that she doesn't get along with most of her family, she's emotionally unstable at times, and doesn't really have friends. We're going to need more if we are going to discover her weakness. We need to interrogate her teachers, acquaintances, and family to discover the truth."

"Not to mention we need to get her routine down pat so when we make our move, it occurs when she's the most vulnerable. We don't need any blasted witnesses blathering their big mouths about what they saw to any of the authorities. Not that it will matter soon because once we have given the Chosen One's energy as well as the Entity's to our Master it will break free and destroy this pathetic place," Killroary prophesized with a glint in his eyes.

"Come on, let's blow this place. Those nosy librarians are coming closer. I don't need them pestering me about my outfit again," Killnala informed him as she stood up and calmly headed for the door. As she passed the check out desk she casually spilled all the returned books on the floor leaving a mess for the librarians to clean up. Her consort just shook his head and followed her lead.

Once outside she crossed the hall to Kali's locker and started examine it. "This is her locker. Shall we see what's inside?" Raising her hand, she got ready to snap the lock off with her nails when Killroary restrained her.

"We can't keep destroying property and causing a racket. We need to be a bit subtler. I have an idea that I like to attempt," he hissed. Focusing his thoughts he phased his hand through the lock forcing it open. Removing the lock he flung the door open and bowed mockingly. "We're in, but we have to be quick. Lunch periods change in ten minutes, and we're going to lose our ignoring factor in five."

"Then let's not delay. Start searching through her things. Hmm, I thought her locker would be more decorative. This is very plain."

"There's nothing in here worth our time. Just her coat, book bag, and books for class. That and her lunch. Hey didn't she bring her own lunch yesterday?"

"Yes. I guess she finds the cafeteria food inedible and I would have to agree with her. Look at the colors she prefers; blues and purples. If those are her favorite colors we could use this fact later on."

The airs around them begin to shimmer and a shiver ran down their spine. It was time to go. Locking up they hurried away just as Kali and Star came walking around the corner. That had been to close for comfort.

Kali was busy asking Star questions about what she had done in Art. "I don't understand what you did back there. I mean I know most of your powers if not all of them. What I can't figure out is how they work. That's my problem with creating characters. I can't always figure out how everything is suppose to work so you're just going to have to tell me. I want to know everything. I want to know it all. About the Council, the people of Entara and how they live, what's it like to have such awesome powers and how do you use them? What is the best part about being able to enter any reality of your choosing? Have you ever faced a Killgona before? What was the war like? Come on I want to know everything!"

Star raised a hand to silence her. All these questions were starting to give her a headache. "Kali I'd be glad to answer your questions, but later. Right now you have to eat something. Besides, what about our deal we made? I agreed to train, protect, and tell you everything if you would save the multiverse along with showing me everything there is about you. So far you haven't held up your end of the bargain," she pointed out.

"Well, we can't practice in school there are to many people. We'll have to wait until after school. Then my training can begin. Don't worry, I'm confident things will work out," Kali told her reassuringly. "Hmm strange I thought I locked this properly. Oh well let's go."

After school they went upstairs to her bedroom to start practicing. They locked the door and shut the blinds to avoid any disturbances. With a wave of her hand, Star, turned on the CD player and began, "You are different then most people around you. You have a pure heart crystal inside you just waiting to emerge. It is my job to help it emerge and teach you to control its incredible powers."

"What's our first lesson? Philosophy issues, power usage, or perhaps history? Whatever it is, I can handle it," Kali said rubbing her hands together eager for a challenge.

"Your first lesson is to find a way to magnify the power you already have inside you. Your writings, your love for reading, your interests and passions are your powers outlet. All you have to do is find the power behind them and let their light shine through you."

"You are already psychically linked to the people of Entara and have a special bond with me that can never be broken. That bond will grow stronger as your other talents develop. To unleash the full power of the crystal you must find a way to guide the light of your crystal heart. Only then will your Crystal Carrier necklace emerge," Star preached demonstrating with Kali's stuffed animal collection what she meant.

"That doesn't seem hard at all. All I have to do is an act of great good and this is in the bag right?"

"Sometimes yes and other times no. Be careful and try to relax. Trust your heart and let your instincts guide you. Remember that your thoughts and feelings must in tuned with your heart and soul for this to work. Now take a deep breath and try to use the power inside you."

Clearing her mind of her fears, anger, and bothersome thoughts she focused on the positive emotions. Listening to her heart and trusting her mind, soul, and heart to work as one she attempted to form a ball of power. Her right hand started tingling and the air seemed to crackle. Just as it seemed something was going to happen, everything returned to normal. Opening her eyes she looked at her hand with disappointment and confusion. "I don't get it. I did everything you said and nothing happened. For a split second I felt like I had it, but then it slipped away from me. What went wrong?"

"Patience, this takes a great deal of time. Each Carrier has a different trigger. What will trigger a response in one person doesn't mean it will do the same in another. You have to keep cool. When the time is right everything will click together. Want to try again?"

"Yeah, we have only seven weeks to find the secret to my powers. That is if I have any to begin with. Are you sure I'm not dreaming because this sounds like something Kelsey and I would make up."

"Trust me, Kali you are wide awake. This isn't make believe at all. This is very real and you do have special powers. I would as wager a guess that your twin has powers too because your twins and close. Now lets practice more."

They continued to practice all night, but were unable to active her inner powers. The same thing occurred the next day. Kali was getting greatly discouraged by all this. All her life she had dreamed of doing something like this and right now all she was doing was failing.

When Thursday rolled around the two of them took a break. Kali went home with Kelsey to visit Hotaru. It was a heartfelt moment between pet and owner. Star was touched to be able to see Kali so happy. Kali was petting, playing, and holding her cat with a look of contentment on her face. Kelsey also seemed to be acting nice towards her sister for a change.

Watching the twin sisters interact reminded Star of her own twin. Growing up they had their own differences mainly about moral issues, but they always worked them out. She really wanted to show herself to Kelsey, but was forbidden to do so. The only way she could do that was if there was an emergency.

Later when Kali was walking to her old house to finish packing it up Star sensed she had something on her mind, but was afraid to voice it.

"If there's something on your mind don't hesitate in asking me about it."

"It's just that Kelsey and I seem to have lost the closeness we use to have. It's been almost two years since we've actually been able to get along. She's always angry and won't live in reality. Is that the same relationship you have with your twin?" Kali asked hesitantly.

"All siblings, especially twins, go through a rough patch in their relationship. It's generally the teen years when you're experiencing the most difficulty. Right now you're both searching for an identity and it can be very frustrating. Kelsey loves you and one day I promise she'll mature. Till then you have be patient and let Kelsey find her own place in the world. Anything else on your mind?" Star questioned.

"Well there is one thing. Remember that site I send my fanfics stories to? You're in some of those stories and there are others that are top of the line professional good. Good enough to even be made into real episodes in my opinion. Are they also real in another universe?"

Star threw back her head and laughed merrily. "Oh Kali, why do you ask the question when you already know the answer to it? That website is another reality. The power emanated from their powers half of Entara and keeps the energy barrier running strong. I assure you that your friends Agent-G's and Slickboy's stories are one of the best I've ever read or had the pleasure of visiting."

Smiling at that tidbit of information they continued on their way still clueless that danger was nearby in the form of two Killgonas. Both of them sensed that Kali was still attempting to learn how to use her powers with no success.

"We were right. She came back to her old stomping grounds, but we're still not ready yet. Let us hope that we find out her weakness soon," Killroary commented. He was getting tired of stalking their prey and wished to commence with the hunt as soon as possible.

"Yes, but we've also gained more in depth information on her from this little stakeout. By Sunday we'll have our answer. I already have a vague idea of what her weakness is. I want to make sure though. Nothing can go wrong nothing," Killnala hissed.

"Let's leave then. These bushes are starting to give me a rash," Killroary told her scratching his arm furiously. Nodding they slipped out of their hiding place and continued to stalk her always making sure they were out of sight. By the time Saturday rolled around they had an answer to their question. Kali's greatest weakness was one that most humans shared. When Monday afternoon rolled around both Star and her would be dead.

Chapter Ten

The reality bubble pulsated intensely in its chamber. Guardian glanced around nervously as the room began to shake. The lights flickered on and off. Finally things began to settle down once more. Guardian let loose a breath he been holding. The chamber had been acting up for days and he was worried that the reality bubble would break. If that happened there would be no way for Star to return home.

He turned to face Sapphire with exhaustion on his face, "I am greatly concerned my dear. A week has passed since Star left us and look at what's happened! The reality is being threatened by evil and her Crystal Carrier hasn't used her powers yet. I fear that Star will fail and we will all perish as a result of it."

"Don't talk like that Guardian. You have to have faith that it will all work out. Trust in Star and the Council and things will work out. Giving up on hope only means you have already accepted defeat. Star will come through for us as she has in the past as will the Chosen One. The Nameless will be contained once more, the multiverse will be saved and Entara will once again be at peace. It will all work out you just have to believe that."

"You are right as always my dear. We knew the dangers that we would have to face and the consequences of Star's actions should she fail. It's just so hard to hold onto faith and hope when the end of our world and everything we hold dear is on the horizon," he replied sadly.

Sapphire lifted his chin up and looked him straight in the eye. "Not everything is lost yet. Even if the chamber is acting up it doesn't signify a lack of progress on Star's part. It's quite the reverse if you think about it Guardian. The Killgonas wouldn't be trying so hard to destroy her if she wasn't making any headway. We should take this as a sign of progress."

The chamber doors opened and Jasmine rushed in nearly tripping over her robes. "Mother, Father! What is the latest news on the mission? Has Star succeed yet?" she asked anxiously. She was very concerned for her friends well being.

Her mother shook her head sadly. "Nothing yet my daughter. We've lost contact with Star days ago. Besides the link we all share with members of our race, which tells us she's alive, we have no real way to know what's going on in the reality. All we can do is observe the reality bubble and hope for the best."

"I wish you stop saying that Mother. Its hard to keep up appearance with the outside world when you know the truth," Jasmine replied. For the past week Jasmine had been charged with running interference between the Temple and the rest of Entara.

"What news did you bring from outside? You normally don't go running around the Temple looking for us. It's so unbecoming of you. Is something wrong?" Guardian asked concern layered in his voice.

Jasmine nodded her head and began to wring her hands nervously. It was a bad habit of hers that she unconsciously did before delivering bad news. "You have no idea the amount of fear that the others in the Congregation are feeling. You two haven't told them anything at all about what's happening. The fear and tension in the Temple is enough to fill a black hole."

"Don't just stand their babbling Jazz. If you have something to say speak now. This is not the time to be hesitant," Sapphire said walking over to her and placing her arms on her shoulders.

"Tell us Jasmine has any word of what's going on in here gotten out?" Guardian demanded. The look in his eyes was dangerous and frightened Jazz terribly.

"NO! Father please don't raise your voice it scares me. Things are proceeding, as they should be. The prime realities are nearing their maximum energy output. The lesser realities are getting ready to receive the energy boost as well as the seal. But that isn't everything. The seal is starting to slowly disintegrate and the reality bubbles have become very fragile. They could break if someone attempted to use them right now. In plainest terms, the Temple is losing its power and its connection to the multiverse."

"That's not the worst of it is it? What about the rest of Entara? Have the changes stopped at all?" Sapphire asked.

"I haven't left the Temple at all, but those who have come in have told me things aren't the way they should be. It seems that the Council is losing control of their thoughts and emotions. Entara is undergoing drastic transformations that are having a very adverse effect on the planet. The entire populace is starting to get very afraid. I've done everything in my power to assure both the people and the Congregation that everything will be fine, but I don't think they believe me anymore."

Sapphire was hugging her daughter tightly stroking her head. She looked up at her husband sharply. "You have to speak with the Council now before something really bad happens. After all Sun and Moon are completely unaware of what their daughter is doing. I don't believe lying to a parent, especially a mother, is helping anyone anymore."

Guardian looked at his family and knew they were right. He'd been the one who had lied to Moon and Sun about their daughter. At the time it had been the right thing to do. But now they needed to know the truth. He turned and left the chamber. The time to reveal the truth had come.

Moon and Sun where at home in the gardens wondering where their precious twin daughters were. They had come home from work a week ago to find Sporty and Faith watching Asteroid. The girls had been unable to tell them anything except the girls had spoken to the Council before leaving their brother in their care.

Sun watched her son intensely. She was afraid that if he left her sights for a second he disappear to. "Asteroid! Gather up your toys and come over closer to your Dad and I," she called out to him.

Asteroid made a face. His mom was always protective of him because he was the baby of the family. Now she was the overprotective parent. "Mom! I'm not going anywhere you can relax! Jesus the twins disappear and I get handed the short stick."

"Darling, let him play. It's not like he'll vanish into thin air. Asteroid why don't you go get your toys and play by yourself. I need to talk to your Mom," Moon suggested to him. Asteroid grabbed his toys and ran over to play on the patio.

Sun looked at her husband sharply. How could he joke about something like this? It was unthinkable. "Moon I am not in the mood for jokes! In case you haven't noticed our daughters are missing!"

"Sun, please calm down. I'm sure there is a perfectly logical explanation for what's going on. After all Guardian told us that the girls hadn't been at the Temple so we know they must be here on Entara somewhere," Moon tried to reassure her to no avail.

"I will not calm down! Frankly I don't see how you can be so calm. Our daughters have vanished and I'm sure Guardian knows more then he's telling! If the girls were on the planet somewhere we would have found them by now. No one knows a thing and their friends can't even tell us what the Council wanted to talk to them about. I have been shut out every time I try to get answers! That doesn't even begin explaining half the crazy things that are happening lately!" Sun exclaimed near hysterics.

"What are you talking about? Look, I admit not knowing where the twins are worries me as well as being denied the truth, but I have no idea what's causing you to freak out so badly," Moon said trying to figure this out. What crazy things was his wife refereeing to?

Sun snorted in disbelief. Her dress was flying everywhere and she was starting to burn with the intensity of a newborn sun. "Are you blind or have you lost your mind? You cannot have noticed the strange things that have been having lately. The Temple is closed for the first time ever, the exams for the children were moved up, the planet itself is acting strangely, and finally the Council lied to us about knowing where Star and Nova are! You don't find any of that strange?"

Before he could reply the doorbell rang startling them. The three of them hurried to the front door. When they opened it they got the surprise of their life. Standing on their doorstep was the Council of Four and Guardian! To say the least they were surprised and a bit shocked.

"Mistress Sun, Master Moon, may we come inside?" Guardian asked urgently.

"Yes, of course you may. Asteroid go to your room and stay there until I come get you. Don't argue with me just go!" Sun ordered. Asteroid sulked for a minute, but did as he was instructed. He knew that having the members of the Council and the Head of the Temple Congregation in his home meant that things were serious.

"Please come sit in the parlor. I'll fetch some refreshments," Moon offered, but a look from Time halted him. Meekly he followed everyone into the parlor before taking a seat next to his wife.

Their parlor was beautifully furnished. It was modeled after an English one with walnut furniture and glass statues on shelves. Crystals provided a comfortable lighting and the wallpaper was of creeping vines.

Once seated Sun spoke up, "Let's dispense with the pleasantries and get straight to the point shall we? What is going on and where are my daughters?!"

"Sun please! You must forgive her. She's been very upset these last few days," Moon explained apologizing for her. He shot a look at his wife warning her to keep her temper in check. They had very important guest over and it wasn't a good idea to be rude to them.

"It's alright Moon. Your wife has every right to be angry and upset with us. When we finish revealing the truth about what is really happening to our beloved Entara to you, you'll probably be as well if not angrier. Just be patient with us. This isn't easy for any of us to explain," Emotion told him. Already she could sense the turmoil he and Sun were broadcasting.

"I guess it would be best to start at the beginning. Mind you both we don't have time to give you the full, detailed, story so this will have to do. As you know the seal that keeps the Nameless locked up is reinforced by the energy produced from the energy barrier that keeps the realities separated. Recently that is no longer the case, as the daily renewals are losing their effectiveness," Guardian began heavily.

"What do you mean the renewals are failing? If that happens the seal will lose its power and the Nameless will be able to break free destroying everything in its path. That includes the multiverse and Entara!" Sun exclaimed startled by this revelation.

"How is this even possible? Why haven't the Acolytes taken care of the problem already? Why is this the first time we've heard about it and what does this have do with Star and Nova?" Moon demanded.

"It's possible because of the Nameless servants. The Killgonas have been busy manipulating the energy barrier getting ready to free their master. Soon they'll be in position to do this by capturing the last of the energy they require. The Congregation tried to deal with the problem, but we were unsuccessful.

I had to secretly contact the Council and bring them up to date on what was going on," Guardian replied tiredly.

"When Guardian contacted us we discussed our options. It was risky for us to engage the Killgonas directly. The casualty rate would have been too high. Another way had to be found to deal with this problem," Wisdom told them.

"We had to begin to make some hard choices. None of our early attempts to ward off this catastrophe worked. We tried limiting power use, moving up the exams, and even warning the Crystal Carriers. None of these measures seem to help much. The Killgonas kept out witting us every turn. It seemed inevitable that the Nameless would be released again even after we tried everything to prevent it," Emotion stated as calmly she could.

"I guess not informing the general public of the possibility of the Nameless breaking free from the anti-universe was out of the question. Just because we've lived in a peaceful utopia for so long doesn't mean lying to us will keep up the illusion of safety," Moon remarked sharply. He was in total disbelief about what was happening.

"We didn't want to create a panic that's why we lied initially. Don't you understand? It was difficult enough imprisoning the Nameless and making sure the Killgonas couldn't reach Entara in the first place. Their natures are so unpredictable it was a shock to learn centuries ago they could talk to their master even while its trapped. Learning about their plot we acted on it by using our symbols to search for a chosen Crystal Carrier who could help us by creating a backup seal to insure the Nameless staying put," Nature said.

"My wife speaks the truth. A plan was devised to create a backup seal by having a non-recognized Crystal Carrier and young Entity working as one. To make sure this was accomplished we needed someone ready to step in if things got desperate. Your daughters were chosen for the quest," Time told the parents, his word hitting them hard.

"We had no choice about using your daughters and we had to lie to you about their whereabouts. It was the only way to protect them and the mission. After five weeks things were beginning to deteriorate. We did a ceremony to find our Chosen One and were about to ask you for your permission to use the girls when a probe attacked us. After that we had no choice, but to summon the girls and give them their assignment while minimizing the information they received. To protect everyone's best interest we had to do some unethical things. Lying to you was the only way they would be safe," Wisdom intoned gently knowing that his words didn't change the facts.

"For the good of all Entara and the entire multiverse the twins are completely unaware of the other one being in the same reality. Star left through the Temple and Nova left through a portal we created. Hopefully this measure will prevent the Killgonas from finding both of them," Nature explained trying to reassure them everything was okay.

"Please tell us, have you kept in contact with my babies? Do you know if they're safe and sound? Please I must know the truth for once," Sun begged the Council.

Everyone looked up at Guardian who wasn't meeting their eyes. He was the only one who knew the truth. "I'm sorry to say that shortly after Star left we lost our ability to speak with her. I was unaware of Nova's involvement, so I'm not surprised I haven't heard a thing from her. Since the reality bubble is acting strangely I have no way of seeing what's happening. All I can tell you is that I sense she's alive. Please accept my humble apologize."

"Your apologize won't do us a lot of good if my children are dead! I can't believe any of this. You four are supposed to be our leaders and look at what's happened. Our world is in chaos, our greatest enemies are on the verge of freeing the most dangerous creature to ever live and to top it all off you sent my babies into known danger without our permission thus leaving them without vital protection! Have I left anything out?" Sun exclaimed uncontrollably. Everyone shrank back as she lit up with the energy of a newborn star.

"Do you have any sort of backup plan incase this all blows up in our faces? I have faith in my daughters' ability to handle any situation they encounter. Still I feel better knowing there's a Plan B. How do you plan to protect the multiverse and more importantly our home world of Entara from total annihilation?" Moon inquired.

"There is a backup plan, but unfortunately its pretty desperate. The protectors of the realities are on stand by, ready to fight for their worlds. Many are eager to avoid a confrontation at all cost if possible and protect the delicate balance of good and evil. Still they will hardly be able to stand on their own against a full fury attack by a Killgona," Time said to the two of them. Taking a deep breath he continued.

"Entara is in the most dangerous position. Guardian and the rest of the Congregation will be the first line of defense should an attack occur. After them there will be all the adults followed by the children. The Council will be a last resort. It's all we have. You two and your son will be a very valuable to us in the coming battle. If you decide to help us out it could mean the difference between victory and defeat. We need you to help rally the Entities together. Please help us," Wisdom asked.

"How can you even think that we would want anything to do with this? After everything that has passed between us recently you want me to risk my youngest in some crazy plan of yours? The only way that's going happen is over my dead body. I can't even trust you enough to tell me the truth about my twins. Why should I allow you to endanger the safety of my son?" Sun said angrily as hot tears streamed down her face. The air around her began crackling with the intensity of her power increasing.

Suddenly the ceiling shook and Asteroid fell straight through and onto the floor. He grinned at his parents sheepishly. He'd been eavesdropping in the music room, which was above the parlor when he heard what was going on. He decided he had to act before his mom ruined everything.

"I'm sorry about the eavesdropping, but I was concerned. Its not often we have such important guest over. If half of what I just heard was true then we have to act now. Mom, Dad, please don't ignore this. Don't let your anger cloud your common sense. It is our duty as Entities to protect life in all forms, including our own," he pleaded with his mom.

"Son, I don't think you fully grasp the whole situation here. You're to young to have an opinion in this matter," Moon stated.

"Don't say that Dad it won't work on me. I know enough about this to say that my sisters wouldn't want us to not help out because we're being selfish. I can rally the kids together and help lead them in battle. I know I could be a great leader. You two are one of the most respectful adults on this planet. You could lead the adults in the fight for Entara if it comes to that, which it most likely will. Please Mom let us help them," Asteroid insisted.

"Asteroid I can't do it I just can't. The danger is too great. Don't you understand honey? I'm not strong enough. I would die if I lost you in this fight," Sun told him picking him up and placing him on her lap. She looked at her youngest child afraid he would break right in front of her.

"Mom how is this fight any different or less dangerous than when the Nameless was loose the first time? I know I was pretty young and didn't see as much fighting as everyone else, but I still was a part of it. I'm older now, more powerful, and a whole lot smarter. I want to help and I know deep down inside you do to. Being selfish won't bring Star and Nova home safely, but being prepared might help them out in the long run," Asteroid pointed out.

"You have to admit he does have a point my dear. Despite what the Council did to us it was in the best interest of the greater good. Now it's our turn to help the greater good. Please Sun, let go of your anger and listen to what they have to say," Moon pleaded with her. He took her hands in his and held them tightly.

"Very well then, for the good of our people I will assist in this plan. What do you want us to do?" Sun asked calmly.

"We need you and your husband to help prepare the populace in case your daughters fail. Make sure they understand the situation fully because we can't lie anymore. Everyone must be in perfect health and the top of their game if we are to avoid a great amount of causalities. Do you think you're up to the task?" Wisdom inquired.

"You can count on us. We'll make sure that everyone's prepared and that no one panics," Moon assured the Council.

"Just keep Entara as normal as possible will you please? Whatever you feel is reflected upon the planet and its scaring people. Our job will go much smoother if we had some stability," Sun advised.

"Don't worry about a thing. We'll take care of the planet. You just concentrate on your job. Asteroid I sense much bravery in you. Be careful you don't become overconfident," Emotion warned the boy getting up.

"Don't worry Councilwoman Emotion. I will keep my emotions in check. The children of Entara will soon be at your disposable, ready and wearing to do the task you've asked of them," he assured them.

"Excellent we must start at once then if we are to be prepared. You three will begin immediately on your task. Meanwhile Guardian, you should return to the Temple and try to buy us some more time if you can. We will attempt to reestablish contact with the twins. We'll stay in touch with each other updating one another the moment things change. We must be ready for anything as the events unfold around us," Nature informed them getting up.

"We must return now to our sanctuary and see what we can do. Hopefully this will all work out for the best and we won't have to use our powers," Time said heavily as he rose to his feet.

Wisdom and Guardian both rose to their feet followed by the family. Everyone shook each other's hands. After final goodbyes the guest departed leaving the family alone. They had much to do and a lot to think about.

"This is so much to do and we have only a short amount of time. Oh Moon I'm so afraid," Sun cried.

"So am I my dear, but we must have faith and trust that everything will work out. Now come you two we have work to do and only six weeks to prepare for it. Let's go do what we do best," Moon said guiding his family back inside.

Back in the extinct reality Killarthur and Killana were going over the days work. Trying to keep everything on time and make sure nothing went wrong was an even harder task then they thought it would be.

Killana scanned the view screen intensely as she monitored the energy output levels of the barrier. Soon it would reach maximum output and the rest of her kind would aid her in securing it for the Nameless.

"Energy levels are approaching maximum output. The sentries reported to me earlier that the more the protectors try to preserve the energy barrier the weaker they become. All of that extra energy should make a delicious treat wouldn't you say?" she asked purring contently.

Killarthur reared up to his full height and looked at her with a glint in his eyes. "Wonderful my dear, simply wonderful. Those idiot Council of Four members forgot to warn them of that side effect when they asked them to step up their duties. Once we've eliminated the entire Entity race, obliterating Entara and destroying the realities will be a piece of cake. Nothing can ruin this glorious chain of events. Tell me any word from Killnala or Killroary?"

"I received a transmission a short while ago from them. They've found the target and after careful observation are ready to eliminate her," Killana informed him.

"Good. The Master will be very pleased to learn that. The Crystal Carrier precious energy along with Star's energy will increase its power by tenfold. Speaking of some primitive creature, do we have anything to eat?"

"I caught a fairy for us. From that reality I went too a while ago when I was searching for information. She's near death so she won't be that hard to digest. Come on," she said slithering off to her private areas.

They soon came to Killana's private area. Lying on a bed of pillows was a fairy. Her pale blue hair and white wings hung limply against her body. Her pink dress was shredded to pieces and she was bleeding from open wounds. She was so weak and near death she didn't even acknowledge them as they slithered up next to her.

The two predators eyes burned with an intense hunger. They circled around the doomed girl wrapping her up in the tails holding her in place with their back claws. Using their front claws they pried open her mouth. Taking a deep breath they sucked the remaining life giving energy right out of her. Once she was dead they proceeded to dismember her and ravished in the kill.

Once done, they cleaned up their mess and went back to work. They only paused long enough to kiss each other savoring the sweet taste of blood and energy lingering in their mouths. But the time for romance was over. They needed to contact their Master and give it an update. Soon the two where kneeling on the ground in intense meditation. The Nameless was growing more impatient each day. It wanted the day when it would be free to roam again to come already.

Report my minions. How soon until I'm free again? The multiverse grows more alive with each passing day because of my absence. This can't continue for much longer. Not if I'm to return things to the way they were, the Nameless thought to them. Its voice echoed like a drum in their heads.

Only six more weeks my lord, then you will be free once more. Sooner once Killnala and Killroary eliminate the only threat standing in your way, Killana reported trying to sound more confident then she was.

We also have some food for you tonight. Its not much, but I hope that this energy will satisfy you for now, Killarthur said his voice quivering. He transferred part of his meal to his Master and waited anxiously for a response.

The Nameless devoured the energy meal without giving it a second thought. It wasn't a lot nor did it satisfy the desire to personally eliminate life. For now it would have to do until it could grow stronger. *Thank you for the snack. It was satisfying and helped me greatly. Please continue with your plan. Make sure everything is ready for my release. Soon I will roam free once again and the multiverse will become nothing again. That will be the day to end all days. The day I finally succeed in my mission and those horrible Entities pay for what they did.*

Chapter Eleven

Killnala sat down at a table in a local coffee house and ordered two cups of coffee; heavy on the cream and sugar. The waiter quickly wrote down the orders and hurried off to get the drinks. He shuddered as he made his way to the kitchen. Those two gave him the creeps. A few minutes later he returned with the drinks and quickly departed. Killnala picked up her cup and took a big sip savoring the flavor. She let out a sigh of contentment, "Heavenly. I'll say this for humans, for all their weaknesses and primitive life styles, they do brew a good cup of coffee."

Killroary, who was slouching in the seat across from her, put down his cup frowning. "I have to agree with you there. This beverage tastes almost as good as freshly squeezed energy. It's such a shame it will disappear forever when the Nameless is freed. But that's life isn't it? Now why are we here when we should be at Kali's house?"

"As you have been telling me for centuries patience is a virtue. Soon all the pieces will be in place and the multiverse will fall. I just wanted to savor the moment before our eventual victory now instead of later."

"Victory? As I recall we haven't won anything yet. You are getting cocky again. We need to stick to our plan if we are to eliminate Kali and destroy Star."

"Oh enough worrying already. The plan will work, its absolutely foolproof. For something so remarkably simple it's quite evil. All we need to do is wait until she's alone with that dumb dog, then when the moments right we strike hard and fast. We're holding all the cards Killroary and Star don't have a clue how to beat us. Neither of them will be able to escape our trap so for the last time will you relax?"

"I know that we agreed on the plan, but I'm getting impatient. Your change in hunting tactics is scaring me. Usually you like to scare the prey so badly that it panics, then you toy with it, and when they're nearly insane you end their pathetic lives. None of this watching and waiting for the right moment to strike."

"This is a different sort of prey. Our prey has no powers or special abilities to protect herself at all from our attacks. She's going to use her brains and wits in order to evade us. When I end her life, I want to make sure that I had a worthy opponent so I guess I'm not acting as impulsive as I usually do. In the end it's all the same. We win and the Nameless is free," Killnala said simply as she finished her coffee.

"Don't you want revenge on Star for what she did to you during the war? After all she's the reason you have that scar," Killroary pointed out.

"Of course I do," she said snapping at him. "I'm entrusting you with the duty of softening her up for me. Once we've made her weak it will be a lot easier to take care of her. I can't wait to kill her and present her body to our Master. Now on to more important matters have you got word from home yet about the situation?"

"Everything is just fine. Killarthur reported to me that the multiverse should be relatively unprotected when it comes to the final assault. Killana wanted to add that everyone is at peak condition ready to do his or her duty. The Nameless grows stronger with each passing day, but also more restless. It wants to be free now," he reported calmly.

"Good. I had my doubts about leaving those two lowlifes managing things, but they proved me wrong. If they haven't screwed up things up by now their not going to. Now we should be going. There's a lot left to do before the main kill," Killnala barked at him. The two of them headed for the door without paying.

That's when their waiter stopped them in their tracks, "Where do you two think you're going? You still haven't paid for your drinks yet. So please pay right now and you can go," he told them bravely.

Both of them gave him amused looks and scoffed at him. Pay for their drinks? Why would they do that? "We don't have any money to pay for the drinks. Now if you excuse us, we have a previous engagement. Get out of our way," Killroary told him politely as he tried to get around the guy.

The waiter stood firm. He wasn't about to be pushed around by some punks, "I'm afraid I can't let you leave then. Either you pay up this instant or

I'm going to have to call the manager over here. Believe me you don't want that."

Killnala rolled her eyes and grabbed the guy's wrist tightly nearly breaking it. "You don't want to make a scene in front of all these nice customers, do you? Besides you really don't want to mess with us. I'm giving you one chance to keep your pathetic excuse of a life, so I suggest that you back off if you know what's good for you."

"That's it, lady. I put up with your punk look and bad attitude, but I won't stand for you assaulting me. I'm going to have to call the police," the waiter snapped wrenching free and heading off to call the police.

"You just made a grave mistake, your last one. Killroary, shift us into another plane will you please, while I deal with this minor annoyance," Killnala ordered.

Just as the waiter reached the phone everything around him vanished. It was instantly replaced by a nightmarish landscape filled with weird sights and sounds. "What in God's name?" He heard a low growl from behind him. Slowly he turned around and what he saw made him nearly wet his pants.

While Killroary had reverted to his true form, Killnala had chosen to morph into something truly hideous. A twenty foot tall, white furred monster that had a long pointed teeth and horns. But the worst part of it was its six huge, glowing eyeballs. Both creatures let out a primal roar and charged.

"AHHHHHHHHHHH! Someone help me!" the waiter screamed as he tore across the landscape as fast as he could. He didn't get far before Killroary tripped him with his tail. He went sprawling across the ground and was pinned down by the weight of a full-grown Killgona. "Help me!"

But no one came to his rescue. Killnala came over and picked him up with one of her paws. Growling angrily she started to squeeze the life out of her prey. The man struggled to get free, but the lack of oxygen was getting to him. Soon it became too much and he blacked out.

Killnala was in her element. The thrill of the hunt, the scent of blood, and at the moment of the kill was coursing through her body. The lusting desire to feast upon a fresh kill was overwhelming. She couldn't keep her impulses under control anymore. She had to devour this rude little whelp and now.

She opened her jaws wide letting saliva drip from her teeth. She positioned herself so she could bite him in two and then scoop up his corpse into her mouth. Moments before she made the kill Killroary snatched the waiter from her clutches. She turned to her mate and roared at him. "GIVE ME BACK MY KILL!"

"We don't have the time or energy for this. Don't waste your efforts on this idiot. He learned his lesson about respecting people who are his superior so lets go. We have to prepare for the hunt," he hissed at her. He glared at her, watching her carefully to see if she would challenge him.

Killnala's instincts screamed at her to attack, but her rational mind prevailed in the end. "Fine, but next time we do it my way. I'm sick to death of this cautiousness and waiting. It may have been vital for our hunt, but right now all I want to do is dismember someone! My blood is screaming for a kill and I don't know how much longer I can wait," she told him angrily as she reverted back to her human form.

Working together they left the dream plane and returned to the living plane depositing the poor waiter in the middle of the busy coffee shop. Patrons began yelling and waiters dropped their trays as they raced over to check on the man. He was bleeding badly and his right arm was broken. He was curled up on the floor in a fetal position muttering incoherently. No one noticed as the two Killgonas slipped away unnoticed.

"What's the situation on Nova? We've been here a little more than a week without sighting her. That makes me very uneasy," Killnala informed her partner as they strolled down the street. She kept glancing around looking to see if anyone was following them. For days she thought she saw something out of the corner of her eye, but nothing was ever there. That feeling was stronger then ever.

"It's true that we haven't seen or heard Nova at all the while we stalked Star and Kali. That is very strange. Twins usually stick close together, but maybe Nova was kept out of the loop this time," Killroary suggested. He also glanced around trying to find their mysterious stalker.

"It's a possibly that we have to consider. The Council of Four might just pull a stunt like that to put us off guard. But I'm unwilling to take that chance. We've put to much time and effort into this only to be blindsided later on. We are six weeks away from unleashing the most deadly force ever known to the multiverse and I won't risk a bad tempered teenager to mess it up. If Nova is here, like I suspect she is, then we must find and deal with her," Killnala said in an icy tone.

"Then I suppose we should redouble our efforts in locating her. Nothing must get in our way. Besides this will give us a few hours to fine tune our attack plan for later on." The two of them laughed manically as they melted away from sight. They had work to do.

Star was getting very frustrated with her quest to train Kali in the ways of Crystal Carrier. Time was running out. If she didn't do something soon the Nameless would be free, and all of Entara and the entire multiverse would cease to exist. She had no idea at all where the Killgonas were and she was unable to contact home to ask for advice. She was also unable to use any of the gifts the Council had given her to help Kali out. To top it all off, Kali still couldn't use her powers and should no sign of receiving her crystal necklace. Things were starting to look pretty hopeless.

"What am I suppose to do? I can't just stand here doing nothing! There is too much at stake for me to fail. Why did the Council select me for this job? I can't do this I just can't do this," she moaned sadly. She sighed loudly as she picked up a folder that contained Kali's novel. With a quick glance to make sure nothing was wrong in class she decided to read the novel. The story was one that perked her interest.

Last night Star had been trying once again to activate the powers locked with in Kali with no results. Deciding they both needed a break Star had sent Kali downstairs to watch TV while she explored the bedroom. That's when she came across the story about her, Nova, and the Nameless. Star had started reading it hoping to find something useful, but nothing turned up. She was now reading the chapter on her and Nova meeting with the Council. It was disturbing how much was fact and what little was make believe. It proved that Kali was unconsciously linked to her people.

"If this story is an accurate representation of what has happened, the it also tells me what will be. I hope Kali knows what she's doing. Ten chapters had been written so far with at least five more to write. Still I hope that it has a happy ending." Closing the folder she looked at the entire class smiling. It was uncanny how much the kids reminded her of her own classmates. She opened her mind and let their thoughts enter her mind. The more she learned about them the easier it was to understand them. Still it was rude of the class not to listen to the teacher talking about the different types of fruit. *Mrs.*

Philosophy would kill us if we acted up like these kids, she thought.

Suddenly the temperature severally dropped in the room. It felt like the room had been plunged into the ice age. Several students started shivering and shouting. People were huddling close together for body warmth and the teacher was calling down to the office. None of this made any sense. There were no open windows and the heater was on full blast. It was a warm day out. Something was up.

"I've got to check this out. But I can't just leave Kali unprotected. Until her crystal emerges, she's still considered prey. But if I don't check this out someone could get seriously hurt. What do I do?" She had to remember everything she had ever been taught in dealing with a crisis situation. Holding her palms slightly apart, she focused her energies. Soon a small ball of light began to form. It grew bigger and brighter till it was the size of a beach ball.

Holding the ball of light over her head she tossed it over Kali's head. It hovered for a few seconds sparkling. With a small pop, it exploded encasing her in white force field. It would move with her and keep others out of her personal space. The field itself was ingenious. The field itself was comprised of good energy and time and space fabric making it nearly impossible to penetrate. The field itself ran on self-perpetuating energy so it wouldn't run out of power. It would take a Killgona at least an hour to get through.

Satisfied her Crystal Carrier to be would be safe for the time being, Star decided to go look for the source of the disturbance. Teleporting to the custodian's office, she found that no one was there. Frowning she rummaged around until she found a spare walkie-talkie. Flicking it on she caught the end of a message.

"Julie I repeat something is stuck in the heater causing the temperature to drop."

"Can you guys fix it, or should I call someone for you?"

"No, I think we got it. It will take at least fifteen minutest to repair, but no major damage done. Ten-four."

"Ten-four" The line went dead. Placing the walkie-talkie back she let out a breath she'd been holding. So it wasn't an attack. Everything was all right.

"A blocked heater. What a relief. I'm so glad it's nothing serious. The custodians can handle it. I need to get back," Star said heading for the door.

As she walked to the door she began to shiver uncontrollably. Rubbing her hands together she attempted to warm herself up to no avail. It didn't make sense. Entities normally didn't suffer from the elements. They could control their body temperature and other internal body functions with a fraction of their minds. While she was stuck in her corporal form and integrated into a reality she lost some control over her body functions, but nothing to this degree.

She sank to the floor withering in pain. Her energy levels were dropping fast and she couldn't keep her thoughts in order. "I don't understand. It should be getting warmer in here not colder. I can feel myself getting weaker. Only a creature designed for this temperature would be happy," she stuttered.

Suddenly a stray thought from a Killgona Survival Training class entered her mind. Born in the vacuum of space Killgonas thrived in extreme cold. It gave them a distinct advantage over other life forms, including Entities. "This is an attack! I got to get down to the boiler room now!" she thought frantically. Summoning up what power she could, she teleported into the boiler room crashing to the floor. She was so weak from the cold she couldn't stay invisible.

All the custodians spun around, "Hey, what are you doing in here?" one of the custodians demanded while the other two surrounded her.

"I'm not in a talkative mood right now. Just get out of my way if you want to live," Star said staggering to her feet. Pointing at each one in turn she immobilized them and strolled past them towards the boiler.

Using her telekinesis she cautiously removed a small black cube. It had glowing numbers on it ticking down. It was a bomb! Quickly she encased it in a bubble just as it exploded releasing a deadly poisonous gas. Thinking fast she used her powers to dilute the gas before it harmed anyone else.

She sank to one of her knees exhausted by what she had just done. Rapid power use after being weakened by the cold had drained a lot out of her. But that's what this was all about, weakening her and warning her to be ready for the real attack.

After modifying the custodians' memories she went to the nurses office in hopes of finding something to ease the pain. Making sure she wasn't seen, she found the medicine cabinet and willed it open. She scanned the contents for something, but was disgusted that there wasn't any pain medication. Willing it closed she left.

She was in so much pain she could barely move. She crawled into the girl's bathroom and locked herself in a stall hoping all she needed was time to heal. But the Killgonas must have done something else besides making it extremely cold, because she felt weak as a kitten. She waited a while before going after Kali. It was forth period by this time and she stumbled into the classroom and saw Kali was perfectly safe.

Before she could join her she crashed into an empty desk causing it to fall over. Everyone looked up startled by the noise and for a mere moment Star flickered into existence in front of everyone.

Kali gasped in surprise hoping no one noticed. None of them knew what had caused the desk to fall over. She needed to get out of there right now and help out Star.

"Mrs. Rexius, may I please go to the bathroom?"

"Fill out your planner and you can go," Mrs. Rexius said. Quickly she filled it out, go it signed, and left.

A few minutes later Kali and Star were alone on the landing just outside the classroom. "Where in the world have you been? You just vanished from sight, leaving me completely unprotected. The only thing I had to keep me safe was this fancy shield of yours. I was really worried about you and right now you don't look so good."

"Believe me, it's not as bad as it looks. Entities can take a lot of damage without getting seriously hurt. I'm starting to feel much better already trust me."

"Don't you dare lie to me. I'm linked to you remember? I know that you've lost some of your power and at least one energy reserve trying to heal yourself up. If this gets worse your thoughts and energy won't mix together. Will you at least tell me what happened?"

"All you need to know right is that the sooner you connect with your inner power, the sooner we'll both be safe," Star huffed at her. "Now you best return to study hall. I'm going to make sure there aren't any more surprises hidden in the school. Don't worry I'll be careful."

"Alright, but please be careful. I would hate to lose you," Kali said hugging her before she returned to the classroom.

Star spent the rest of the day looking for more traps and seeing if she could find her elusive counterparts. She had no idea that one was closer then she liked to think.

Killnala smirked as she watched Star from the roof of the Dolan Building. Being able to see all planes at once had certain advantages. It was like having X-ray vision only better. "Foolish Star. You have no idea that you are setting yourself up to fall by going on like this. By the end of today I will have my sweet revenge upon you and I will pave the way to my glorious future on your dead body. The Nameless will happily reward me once your dead," she laughed insidiously.

Oh, I just love being pure evil. Killroary come in! Do you have anything new to report to me? Is the trap set? she asked telepathically.

Nothing new to report I'm afraid. All is quiet over here. My search for Nova has turned up nothing. She is either not here or I simply can't detect her. It doesn't matter anyways. Our trap is ready for use. I've tested it myself to make sure nothing goes wrong, he answered.

Excellent, my love. The school day is nearing an end. I shall join you shortly. The minute our business is concluded we are going home and setting our Master free. Killnala out," she said, severing the connection.

She bore her eyes into Kali's back watching her like a hawk as she read a book in Study Skills. "Soon, very soon you will be mine. So enjoy your last hour of life while you can." With that said she went to meet Killroary.

Kali was unaware of the danger that awaited her. All she wanted to do was go home and unpacked her room. Maybe even watch a little TV while she was at it. However, Star was insisting that they practice again.

Arriving home she went inside and settled into her new after school routine completely ignoring Star. It wasn't that she didn't believe her; it was that she was afraid of letting her down. What if she could never unlock her powers and stop the end of the multiverse? What would happen then?

Finally after watching cartoons on the cartoon channel, she grabbed her coat. This time she was going to get her powers to emerge. "Come on. I'll get Oso and we can go practice in the lot. You coming or what?"

It was fairly dark and there wasn't another soul in sight as the trio entered the lot. Star shivered in the cold air still weak from her efforts earlier. "Brr. It's freezing here. Why do we have to practice here?"

"Why not? It's the perfect place to practice with no one watching. It's not that cold out Star. Besides, you're the one wearing a halter-top so you have only yourself to blame. Now come on, lets get started. I really want to see if I can use my powers," she said excitedly as she let the dog run.

"Okay then let's try something simple. I want you to talk to Oso."

"Talk to the dog? I already do that. I thought you were going to challenge me. How is talking to Oso going to help me out?" Kali demanded as she tugged on the leash. The enormous dog stopped pulling her and started sniffing some plants.

"That's not what I meant girlfriend. You love animals and you have a special connection with them, especially your cat Hotaroo. Maybe if you focus on your bond with animals you can awaken your powers. Its worth a try at least."

"I'll try it. Just don't expect much to occur. OSO! Come here boy, come here," Kali called to the dog. Instantly he came running at her.

Right before he reached her something happened. From the four corners of the lot a beam of light appeared trapping them inside. The lot soon vanished from sight as a gray mist surrounded them. Ghostly images flirted among the mist scaring Kali and Oso, who began to bark furiously.

"What is going on? What is this place? More importantly, how do we get home? Star answer me!"

Star silenced her with a look. Her eyes narrowed as she took in her surroundings. "Be on your guard. I have a feeling I know who is responsible for this little trap. We've simply been moved from one plane to another. I speculate that were in the astral plane. This is the plane where spirits travel from place to place, which explains the ghostly images. In reality we're still in the lot so in order to return home, we need to get back to our proper plane."

Suddenly they both heard the disembodied laughter that sent shivers down their spines. Oso growled and barked angrily as Killnala and Killroary both materialized a few feet in front of them. The two creatures looked at the trio hungrily.

"Your not going anywhere, trust me on that. We control this place so neither of you can escape so don't bother trying! I'm personally going to ensure that by slaughtering you," Killnala informed them as she sized them up. "Oh where are my manners? I forget to introduce myself. I like my victims to know who their killer is."

"Don't bother I'll save you two the trouble. I created you in my story to be the ultimate killers. You are Killnala, the leader of the Killgonas. You're smart, cold, and have one nasty temper and tend to get ahead of yourself. He's Killroary, your consort. He's a bit more level headed and likes to think before he acts. Yet when he hunts, he's more brutal then you are. I don't like either one of you one little bit," Kali informed them, glaring hatefully at them. She had hoped these two wouldn't come to life like Star had.

Killnala looked at her amusingly. "So your not as dumb as you look. Good this will make the hunt more interesting. Rest assured, your little link won't save you from me. Now about that mutt, I think we can do without him don't you?" With a snap of her fingers Oso was gone.

"What did you do to him?!" Kali demanded angrily. She wanted to throttle the Killgona, but Star held her back. This wasn't the time or the place to lose their cool, not if they hoped to survive.

"My mate just sent him back to your home. Don't worry about him. Worry for yourself or to be more precise, worry about Star," Killroary said cordially. His muscular form was itching with anticipaticion for the kill.

"What's that supposed to mean? If you're trying to confuse me, it's not going to work."

"He's not trying to confuse you at all my dear. He's pointing out your greatest weakness. Your weakness is that you care too much. Books, animals, TV, you care a lot about those. But like most of your primitive race your love for family and friends hinders you in life. Why do you think I had Killroary help me with weakening Star over there? She's not running at full strength so she won't be able to protect you from him. That leaves me to take my sweet revenge. Enough talk. ATTACK!" she ordered.

"Run! Don't let them harm you. Your shield will protect you from most attacks, but not all of them," Star yelled shoving her away before firing a starburst, a purple star shape blast, at Killnala.

Killnala dodged the attack and leapt high into the air. Doing three front flips she extend her nails to full length uncurled and took a big swipe at her. Star tried to get out of the way, but didn't quite manage it. The poisoned tips grazed her in the shoulder, causing her great pain.

"That's only a sample of what I plan to do to you. You're the only one who ever truly humiliated me, defeated me in front of my Master! I bear this mark on my hand as a reminder of what you did to me all those eons ago or have you forgotten?" Killnala demanded as they continued to battle. She fought with her claws while Star fought with her diminished powers. Neither one gaining or losing an advantage.

"Foolish Star, why do you delay the inevitable? You know that you will die by my hands no matter what you do! Finally after all this time I will have my revenge or did you forget about why I have a scar?" Killnala demanded as she tried to bite Star's head off.

Star created a barrier of justice, which resembled a purple scale, to separate the two of them so she could catch her breath. This battle was taking a lot out of her and she needed to conserve energy. It was her only hope to winning.

"No, I haven't forgotten. How could I? It was the most terrifying moment in the entire war for me. I was only three eons old at the time, a mere child. I had been sent to stop you from causing the extinction of the planet whose people would one day become the most adaptable in the multiverse."

"Your precious jewel of a planet, Earth! Your entire family had worked together along with those supposed Celestial Gods to create it. The Nameless wanted them silenced because of all the diversity was killing it. I volunteered for that mission thinking a child wouldn't be my greatest problem."

"But I was a problem wasn't I? The day you came I poured my whole heart and soul into protecting the planet. I was able to tap into my full powers for the first time. I sent you and your master packing. That was my crowning achievement in the war," Star reminded her. She kept glancing around hoping to see a way out of the astral plane. So far she had spied nothing and she was really worried about Kali.

"And for the longest time that defeat has haunted me. I've never been able to live down the shame. No more, today you die!" she snarled charging straight through the barrier like it wasn't there.

Star waved her hand freezing her in time. Star started to turn away when Killnala broke free and kicked her cruelly in the back sending her flying.

"Your stupid parlor tricks won't work on my. You Entities may have minimal control over everyone else's thing, but you're not the Master of Time! Let's take this up to another level!"

Meanwhile Kali was running for her life as fast as she could. But the gray landscape seemed endless. Everywhere she turned there was more mist. There seemed to be no escape. Suddenly she tripped and fell to the ground. She struggled to get up, but was kicked in the back and fell forward.

Killroary stood over her licking his pointed teeth in anticipation. "You know originally Killnala was going to get you, but I convinced her to let me have you instead. I want to make sure things go right. Say goodbye!"

Kali closed her eyes figuring it was the end. She desperately wished that the shield would extend itself. After a few minutes of waiting for the end to come and it didn't she cracked her eyes open. What she saw stunned her. The shield had grown both in size and intensity. Killroary was pounding on it trying to get through, but to no avail. "Ha, ha, you can't get me."

"That shield of yours will eventually break and I will be able to get you. Just because you managed to extend the shied around yourself doesn't get us off your back. You have to have a crystal around your neck for that to happen and that's never going to come to pass."

"And you're going to stop me from getting mine? Fat chance. I'm going to get rid of you first."

"How? You can't fight at all or even defend yourself from an assault. You're just a weak, defenseless, little girl,' he said amused.

Kali literally saw red as she heard that comment. No one called her weak and defenseless. She jerked her knee up hard causing the shield to strike him in the groin. Before he could recover she lashed her foot out forcing him off her. Somersaulting backwards she came up and got into a fighting stance. "Want more you filthy creature?"

He didn't respond instead he charged straight at her, ready to slice her in half when she punched him hard in the stomach. He doubled over in pain just as she struck him in the jaw with her elbow. He attempted to grab her only have her throw him over her shoulder. "I don't need to know how to fight in order to survive. Instincts alone will keep me alive!"

The two battles raged on each side giving it all they had. Some supernatural force guided Kali as she fought like a ninja master in order to survive while at the same time Star struck hard and fast with diminished strength. The Killgonas also fought with tooth and claw in this life or death struggle. Neither side gained an advantage or lost any momentum during the struggle. Both sides were determined to be victorious. It seemed like the battle would never stop.

But soon the tide turned for the worst. Star was losing. The poison was eating its way through her system slowing her down greatly. Her own powers were greatly weakened and her corporal body was severally damaged. She was desperately searching for a way to unlock the gifts given to her, but she couldn't.

A vicious kick to her side sent her sprawling to the ground. She tried to get up, but she couldn't. Killnala stood over her grinning madly. "Your finished Star. After so long I will finally have my revenge. Say good night."

"NO! STAR!" Kali screamed as she raced towards the fallen Entity when all of a sudden she found herself wrapped up in Killroary's tail. She struggled in vain to get free, but he just squeezed tighter causing her to turn blue.

"You're not going anywhere Carrier! Prepare to witness the demise of your friend Star. Don't bother screaming for help; no one can here your cries."

Suddenly he screamed in pain and released her. He rolled around on the ground twitching in pain and smoking. A large red novaburst soared past him hitting Killnala squarely in the chest sending her airborne. Kali looked up in the sky grinning knowing only one person could have done that.

Hovering in midair, surrounded by a glowing red aura, was Nova. Her hands where charged up for another attack and she looked pissed off. "Leave my sister and the Chosen One alone! Go back to where you came from, you demonic lizards!"

"Nova! How did you get in here?" Killnala demanded angrily. She rose to her feet, struggling to figure out how this pest got inside her foolproof trap.

Nova landed next to her twin and helped her up. Kali stood behind the two of them for protection. Nova glared hatefully at Killnala and Killroary. "You let me in. I'm the Entity of Evil remember? Your evil actions allowed me to create a small portal to enter the astral plane and come to the rescue. Enough talk; time to fight."

"Thanks for coming, sis I really needed your help right now," Star whispered.

"You're welcome. We'll talk later right now let's hope we can alive in this fight long enough to escape. I'm not feeling to good," Nova replied. It was only then that they noticed that Nova also looked like she had been through the ringer and back. Nova had several burn marks all over her body and was bleeding profoundly from her right shoulder. Her hair was scorched and she had a few bruises on her face. Her clothes hung limply on her body. There was no question in their mind she had been in a fight recently.

Both Killgonas reverted to their true forms and linked together. Once they were holding clawed hands they began to glow a bright blue. The landscape around them started to ripple. An intense pressure built up around the trio. Soon the three of them where quivering on the ground trying to breath.

"We have to get out of here before we run out of air. You two have any ideas?" Kali gasped.

"One. If Star and I combine our powers together we might be able to escape from this plane. But I'm low on power and severely injured," Nova panted.

"We have no choice. Together we have a chance of unleashing Time's gift. A combined time warp will not only get us back to the living plane, but will also regulate how much time has actually passed since we got here. We can recover in your room once we trap those two here. Still I'm unsure of the consequences of such drastic action," Star warned them struggling for air.

"No time like the present to find out. We had better hurry before they finish sucking the air out of here. Kali, hold tightly on to us this will be a bumpy ride," Nova instructed crawling over to her sister.

The two of them took each other's hands and cleared their minds of everything. Both of them concentrated hard on the power inside of them and the brilliant gift they had received. Soon a bright silver glow surrounded them. The air crackled and the wind whipped around them. Suddenly a huge silvery hole opened up behind them. Without hesitation they all jumped in it just as the Killgonas came at them on a final run. The hole sealed up behind them and blew up effectively trapping the two creatures in the astral plane for the time being.

The girls reappeared in Kali's room; both the twins were on the new bed that had just arrived in pain. Kali ran over to check on them, fear plain in her eyes. "You two look awful! Is there anything I can do? Hey, why do you both look so worried? We barely survived that encounter, but we did. We should be celebrating."

"Child, our energy reserves are almost depleted. Our powers are nearly gone and the Killgonas won't rest until we're all dead," Nova gasped. Red blood dripped on the sheets staining them. It was mark to how serious the situation was because Entity blood was rainbow color not crimson.

"We might die before our quest is complete. Then all we worked for will be lost. The Nameless will be freed and the entire multiverse will be destroyed because of us," Star coughed as she winced in pain.

"Don't you two worry about it. I'll think of something you can count on it. I won't fail you. Nor will you die, I promise," Kali said. She was frightened beyond belief after what she experienced, but she wasn't going to show it. She couldn't afford to be scared right now when Star and Nova needed her help.

"There's more, Kali. You have less time now then before. When we combined our time warps together we caused a surge of time energy in the multiverse. While time is still flowing normally here, its sped up everywhere else," Star explained.

"The maximum energy output draws nearer. If you don't gain your powers and reset the barrier soon, the seal will lose its effectiveness," Nova added.

"How much time do I have?" Kali pressed the twins urgently.

"The rest of the week plus an additional three have passed in our time. You only have two weeks left," Star said.

Kali looked at her stunned. Two weeks to save the whole multiverse? They were doomed.

Chapter Twelve

Kali looked at the two Entities dumbfounded by the news she had just received. How in the world was she supposed to save the whole multiverse in a mere two weeks? She hadn't even been able to summon a single power yet and now this. "Are you absolutely positive that we have less time then before to save the world? I don't mean to doubt you, but in your present condition, can I trust your judgment?."

Star started hacking up a storm coughing up mucus, saliva and blood. She shivered intensely and weakly wrapped the blanket around herself. Trembling she replied shakily, "W-w-were positive, Kali. There ii-s-is no m-m-mistake. Nova and I can feel the change in the flow of the time stream. It is subtle, but it's there. We're in trouble if the Killgonas become aware of the change."

"I fear that they may already know, dear sister. From what my observations of them revealed, they were planning for any contingency and this is one of them. Oh it hurts so much," Nova moaned holding her side in pain. Never in either twins life had they been in this much pain.

"Move your hand and let me see. This doesn't look good. You're both bleeding and losing energy at an alarming rate. I have no idea how badly your real bodies are damaged since I can't see them. Since I'm not a doctor, I can't give a diagnostic on your entire condition, I can tell you're both in seriously bad shape. I'm going to get some bandages and the first aid kit. Hopefully there will be something to help you two. Just rest, I'll be right back," Kali promised, hurrying into the bathroom.

With some help from the twins, Kali was able to bandage them up and temporarily stop the bleeding. Both girls still looked pretty bad and they where losing their glow. In an attempt to lighten the mood, she decided to ask Nova how she had gotten here.

"I got here through a portal the Council created. I was sent to make sure that Star succeed in her mission and protect you from harm. If something went wrong I was to step in and take over. It wasn't easy hiding my presence from you two or those pests. Several times I was nearly detected by both parties. I followed Star in the hope of finding you. Instead I was drawn to your twin sister, Kelsey. Her anger, rage, and temper drew me directly towards her. By sticking close to her I went unnoticed by the Killgonas," Nova managed to say before she started gagging on her own saliva.

Kali watched helplessly knowing there was nothing she could do to stop it. After a few minutes Nova was able to continue. "I'm fine really. Don't look at me with horror in your eyes it doesn't suit you. Your twin isn't evil, if that's what concerning you. We just have a lot more in common. So much in fact that I forged a link with her incase I needed to use her later on."

"Use her? In what way do you mean by that, Nova? How could Kelsey aid you?"

"Several ways. I could use her as a decoy to protect you or I could pick her brain for information. Mostly I used her as my extra eyes and ears. She was perfect because the Killgonas ignored her."

"Still it must have been hard for you not to contact me. What did you do after Kali was discovered? If you were supposed to be helping her develop her powers and keep the Killgonas at bay, why didn't you?" Star inquired.

"I [cough] did do what [cough] I [cough] was told. I found their base of operations and destroyed their energy pods weakening them. I messed up several other plans of theirs and made sure that both of you returned here safely everyday. I had to use Nature's gift, the voice of Nature, to protect you from their earlier traps," Nova said weakly.

"What traps are you referring to, Nova? I'm sure Star would have dealt with them. There was no need for intervention," Kali tried to assure her as she took their temperature. While waiting she cleaned their wounds out and sterilized them to prevent infection.

"No choice. When they where searching for your weakness I combined my powers of death, evil, and injustice with Nature's so I could delay them and discourage their lust for slaughter. That was not easy. I saved plenty of innocents this way. I may be the Entity of Death, but I don't welcome it," she explained.

"How did you know they where going to attack us in the lot?" Star asked. She winced as blood started to soak her bandages. She ran a trembling hand through her hair and gasped as several strands came loose.

"I overheard them discussing their plans over coffee earlier today and knew I had to break cover to save your hides. But I was weak from using my powers so much, trying to contact home, and I had been injured at the Killgonas base. That's why I'm in such poor shape," she said concluded her tale.

"I commend your bravery and your loyalty, Nova. But your actions have put everything we've worked for in danger. Both of you are in dire need of medical assistance, but we have no way to contact your people. I can't take you to the hospital because there's no way to explain your condition to them," Kali told them as she rewrapped the bandages over the wounds. She looked the thermometer and it read ninety degrees and dropping fast. This wasn't a good sign.

"I agree with you about the medical facilities not being able to fix us up. We are simply losing too much energy too fast and our corporeal bodies are losing too much blood as well. I can feel my thoughts slowing down, losing their valuable connections that keep my real body in one piece. I would gather that we are near death," Star said weakly.

"Then you've got to return home. There's nothing more you can do for me here. Please, I don't want you two to die because of some stupid loyalty to me. Go back to Entara and get healed," Kali begged them both.

"That isn't an option. Our duty is to you, and nothing not even our own safety and health, will stop us from completing this quest. We must make sure you are safe from harm. Killnala and Killroary won't hesitate to kill you. You are no longer safe anywhere. We must figure out a way to protect you from harm while you are at school or at home," Nova insisted.

"We could use Wisdom's gift. We can alter it slightly so that she would be safe at home and school at all times. That would also include anything that reminded her of either place. She'd be virtually impossible to touch," Star suggested.

"Wait a minute you two. You can't do that I won't let you. Using the Council's gifts takes a lot of power and life force out of you. You're not strong enough to use those gifts at the moment. Even if you were, I wouldn't allow it. I can't let you guys place yourselves in greater danger because of me. I order you not to do this," Kali ordered them.

"We have no choice in the matter. We can't let them get you. You are the key to stopping the Nameless. Nothing else matters, Kali don't you understand that? Please try to understand that we are doing this not only to save you, but everyone everywhere. Don't worry everything will be okay I promise you," Star assured her. She brought her hand up and stroked the girl's cheek.

"Star, I don't want you to do this. There must be another way that doesn't result in your death. How can I save the multiverse if you die?"

"Have faith and trust in my sister and me. We know what were doing. Now stand back and give us some room," she ordered gently.

Both twins sat up and clutched each other's hands tightly. Closing their eyes they began to chant in their native tongue. Their auras changed from their usual colors to a blazing blue. The faint outline of books and scrolls could be seen as they wind picked up. Suddenly a blue stream of energy shot out the window heading for the school. A second beam enveloped the apartment. The twins held on to each other as long as they could before they broke the connection. Both girls slumped to the ground unconscious.

"STAR! NOVA! NO!" Kali screamed as she attempted to awaken her friends. But nothing she did woke them up.

Both Entities had started to fade from existence and were breathing in short shallow breaths. They had used too much energy trying to protect her from harm. Now they were going to die because of it and she couldn't do anything to stop it. "Come on wake up please wake up. There has to be something I can do to save you two. I'm not just going to sit here and watch you die. There is a way to save your lives I know there is so tell me what I have do!"

Star's eyelids fluttered open, and she tried to speak, but her voice was gone. There was one way to save their lives and she had to tell her what it was. Desperate to get her message across she summoned all her strength and began to fingerspell a word.

Kali stopped crying and cleared her eyes so she could see better. "What is it Star? What are you trying to tell me? B. O. N. D. Bond? What do you mean bond? Are you talking about a bond shared by sisters, friends, or family what? I don't understand. I need more."

.

Star pointed to herself, then Kali. Pointing to Nova she formed the letter for t in sign language, and then rotated around her mouth. That was the sign for twin. She finger spelled bond again. Suddenly it clicked in her mind. She knew what she was trying to say to her. After all she was linked to Star.

"You want to bond with me. Transfer your entire essence inside me and live off my life force until you're strong enough to reemerge. I don't know about this, Star. A lot can go wrong and the bonding process has to be perfect; otherwise both of us could end up dead. Also we have no idea what would happen to me if I had to carry you inside me. Are you sure there isn't another way to save your life? No? Then I guess we have no choice. Star you have my permission to join with me."

Star did the sign for the thank you before closing her eyes once more. She began to vibrate at high speeds until she dissolved into a hundred tiny purple bubbles. Floating over Kali, the bubbles attached themselves to her body. For a few seconds she looked like a sequenced statue. Then the bubbles were absorbed into her skin.

At first Kali felt completely normal like nothing had happened. She couldn't feel Star's presence at all in her mind nor did she seem to have any of Star's powers. She feared that the bonding had failed and she had just lost her friend. She started to stand up when she clutched her head in agony. She let out a moan and sank to her knees. Something was happening inside her body.

Her brain felt like it was going to explode. There was too much going on at once. Her mind was simply not designed to process the thoughts, feelings, and the world as Star did. Also she felt Star's memories forcing their way into her mind adding to the confusion.

Her senses had vastly improved. Her body felt electrified and her mind understood a thousand different complexities now. She had some kind of supernatural force around her and in the back of her mind she felt her link magnify. This was like being an Amazon!

"Star! If you can hear me at all give me a sign. I can't function like this on my own for very long. I need you to help interpret what I'm receiving. Please Star show me that you're still alive."

I am here, Kali very much alive if not a little weak. I won't be able to help you out directly in my current condition, at least not for a while.

I need to regain my health. I'll try to tone down my influence on your body and mind, but you're going have to be careful for a while, Star whispered gently to her. *First thing you need to do is take some deep breaths. Focus your mind on one thing at time. Next, I'll reduce the amount of interfacing for you. There, is that better?*

Kali slowly and cautiously rose to her feet wobbling a bit. She was sick to her stomach and she had a massive headache. After a few seconds passed the pain was gone. She was back to normal physically, but mentally was another story. She felt more confident, positive about life, and was very optimistic. She couldn't stop the rush of emotions going through her body. It was like wrapping up in a warm blanket of love. She had no idea where all of this emotion was coming from.

It's from me. Now that we're joined together we have become an entirely new person, two minds one body. You have to get use to me inside your mind. Also I have to resist the urge to use my more active powers if I'm to heal. Now we must hurry, Nova is running out of time. She needs to bond with someone soon if she is to survive, Star urged.

"But I can't possibly support both of you in my mind! It would kill me. Besides Nova needs to join with someone similar to her if she's to have any hope to recover from her injuries."

It's not you she's going to bond with; it's your twin sister Kelsey. Remember, Nova has linked with her already, so part of her resides inside of Kelsey's mind. It's a good thing you two are twins, we'll heal faster because we are twins also and we share the sister bond. Take us to her now please.

"I can't drive and Keelia has the van currently. It would take too long to have Kelsey brought here. So what do you suggest I do?"

Star sighed loudly inside her head, *We teleport there, of course. You must hurry there isn't much time. Touch Nova and think of your dad's house. You have my low level powers so use them.*

"Won't that make you weaker? What about my own powers? More to the point, what about Killnala and Killroary? They eat Entities and now you're inside of me putting us in more harm then before," Kali questioned skeptically as she locked her bedroom door.

I don't think it matters to the Killgonas where I am as long as they kill me. They want you dead as much as me. At least inside of you I can protect you better. As for me I appreciate the concern; you needn't worry. My low level powers such as teleportation and invisibility are like what breathing is to you. It won't prevent me from healing at all. I'm hoping that by using my powers, you can tap into your own special powers, Star explained gently.

"Well, let's get this over with. The sooner we leave, the sooner we can get back before mom notices my absence," she said. She nervously placed a hand on Nova, who by this time had nearly vanished from sight, and concentrated hard picture her dad's house clearly in her mind. There was a slight ping, and soon Kali found herself in her dad's living room. Kali placed Nova on the couch and stood up looking around for help.

Tess, Kelsey's cat and Hotaroo's cousin, hissed at the intruder's sudden appearances. Hotaroo on the other hand, jumped up into her mistress's arms pleased to see her. "I'm glad to see you too. But right now I have more pressing matter to attend to. Kelsey! Kelsey get in here now!"

Kelsey, who had been typing in the computer room, came racing out surprised to hear her twin's voice. "Kali? What are you doing here? Oh my God! Is that whom I think it is?" she asked gawking at the sight of Nova lying on the couch inches from death's door. Not in a million years had she expected this.

"Yes it is, and I'll explain in detail later what's going on. Right now I we need your help in order to save her life. We want you to bond with Nova. It's the only thing that will save her life," Kali insisted.

"You better have a good explanation for all this. I'm about to become the host body for the Entity of Evil. Show me what I need to do," Kelsey replied as she kneeled down next to Nova.

"Just stand still and don't move. Nova, relax and flow into Kelsey. It's your only chance," Kali ordered her. Her voice echoed with the wisdom and urgency of her sister.

Nova didn't say anything. It was doubtful she could. Instead she turned into swirls of black energy and surrounded Kelsey. The girl yelped in fright, as she and the Entity became one being. Kelsey glowed a deep scarlet with a black outline for several moments. Her dark blond hair changed to black and her eyes both turned crystal blue instead of their normal one blue one green look. Finally she returned to normal and swayed slightly, falling into Kali's outstretched arms. "I'm okay, really. She's fine. Just a little worn out and confused by all that's happened to her."

"Nova can you hear me? It's Star your sister. Answer me please!" Star said speaking through Kali.

"Hey, ask before you use my vocal cords will you? Besides, what about Kelsey is she okay? Is she okay?" Kali replied hotly.

"We're both fine. It's just a little strange at first. Kelsey may have your curiosity, but none of the tact. I've explained the situation to her and she is most eager to help out," Nova reported using Kelsey to speak for her. You could tell it was her by the edge to her voice. There was something edgy and tough.

"It's not fair to me. Why do I get stuck with Miss Injustice here, while you got Miss Justice inside of you? Also why do you get all the cool powers, the glory of saving the world, and everything else why I don't get anything? I mean why does all the cool stuff happen to you," Kelsey complained.

"You think I wanted this? You think it's cool to have two monsters on your tail intent on killing you or how about having the fate of the whole multiverse and the planet Entara resting on your frail shoulders? Maybe you want to be constantly reminded what a failure you are because you can't do a single thing with your supposed powers. Add that to the pressures of my normal life right now and maybe you'll have some idea of the situation I am in!" Kali snapped at her.

"No need to be rude about it. I was simply stating an opinion," Kelsey sniffed.

"Enouck, Hes, Lep," came out of Kali's mouth as both Star and Kali tried to access her speech centers at the same time. What came out was utter nonsense.

"What did I tell you about using my voice?" Kali barked.

Sorry, but I think we have more important things to discuss then having to hear you two argue about old issues. Your sisters, twins for Entara's sake! I think it's time you two put aside your differences and try to get along at least for a while, Star asked, her voice echoing across her mind.

"Fine, well do it your way. But if she starts acting crazy I'm leaving no questions asked," Kali told her defiantly.

Fine, now may I speak? Star asked. Receiving permission she cleared Kali's throat and spoke, "Alright it's obvious that there is some tension between you two. That's natural between sisters and it's no different between twins. Sometimes you need help to solve your problems. However, now is not the time to discuss these issues."

"My sister is right. They know about Kelsey, but have greatly ignored her because her aura brightness wasn't as great. They may change their minds now that I'm inside her or they might want to use her against Kali. Nothing is for certain," Nova pointed out.

"How do I defend myself then? Do I have special powers or am I a Crystal Carrier too? What can I do to help out? I want to be part of this," Kelsey demanded angrily. All her life she wanted to do something adventures and this was it. Here was a chance to get out of her mundane boring existence and have real fun even if it meant being in constant danger.

"I don't know if you can help to be honest. The only reason at all that Kali has powers inside of her and is a Crystal Carrier is due to her link with Star and our people. You are her twin so it stands to reason you have a crystal and powers buried deep inside of you as well," Nova commented.

"If that's the case then, we have to prevent the Killgonas from snacking on you too. After that we have to come up with some kind of plan to activate my powers while keeping Star and Nova alive inside of us. Suggestion, please?" Kali asked as she paced the room.

I hesitate to suggest it, but we are desperate and it might come in handy for both of you two. Besides we don't want to waste it on anything else, Star thought hesitantly.

Good idea, sis. It would buy us a little extra time in training Kali. Time that we desperately need in order to train Kali and recuperate from our injuries. If all goes well we can train Kelsey too," Nova said catching her twin's drift.

Neither Kali nor Kelsey had any idea what they were discussing. So they decided to ask them.

"Will you two please spill it already? I'm getting mad hearing you two think to one another in my mind. You're as bad as me. Never giving a straight answer to any questions." Kelsey whined.

"Sorry it's just that we got caught up in the moment. You understand that don't you? What I was hinting at was Nature's gift to me. I still have it. Why not use the voice of Nature to watch the two of you and make sure we can get together quickly incase of trouble," Star suggested vocalizing this time.

"Forget it! That's a high level power and you can't access it right now. Besides, in your condition you can't use it without harming me. I would have to be the one using it and I don't think I could handle that much raw power coursing through me," Kali responded wrenching back control of her voice.

"Then I'll do it. I'm not scared to try something. How dangerous can it be?" Kelsey challenged her. If Kali were too afraid to fight she would step in.

"You can't, I'm afraid. I've used that power already. However if the two of you can work as one you might be able to use the gift safely. That is what it is for isn't it? To be used to help us."

"Okay Miss High and Mighty, and idea how where going to pull this one off? I mean do you have an instruction manual?"

"Would you cool it already Kelsey? Honestly you're worse then ever with Nova inside of you. Maybe this wasn't such a good idea after all," Kali, said exasperated. No one was listening to a word she said. She hated when no one listen to her.

"Enough! No more fighting, that's an order. Kali, I know you're mad at Kelsey, but you need her help right now. Kelsey, please try to take this a little more seriously. Now take Kali's hands and form an arch. Both of you close your eyes and form an image of Nature in your head. Feel her presence; listen to her voice inside you guiding your actions. Embrace the image and let the power flow from one to the other before circling back. Accept the gift and its tremendous power. You will find the peace you seek," Star instructed.

Doing as she was told, Kali opened her mind up so she could connect to Star's in order to feel Nature's gift. She felt a slight tingling in the back of her head and soon felt both hers and Star's mind merge as one. The sensation was incredible. For a brief instant the entire universe was hers to play with.

She felt an overwhelming presence remind her she had a job to do. Resigning to the fact she'd have to come back to this later, she left that particular area of her new mind. Once back to more familiar surroundings she began to tackle the task at hand.

In her mind's eye she formed a remarkable life like picture of Councilwomen Nature. She wrapped her conscience around the image feeling the gentleness and peaceful presence of the women. Faintly she could make out her voice. "I present thy child with the gift to hear the voice of Nature. Use it wisely in your journey."

The picture turned forest green and sprang forward startling Kali, who hadn't even realized she created the arch with Kelsey. The green light passed through Kali's right arm down Kelsey's and back to her through Kelsey left arm. With a tremendous boom, the girls fell apart gasping.

"That was incredible. Did you feel that raw power surging through us just seconds ago? I wonder what the voice of Nature does for us exactly," Kelsey exclaimed excitedly. She stood up gazing around the room itching to do something else with her new abilities.

"When is my head going to stop swirling? What happened to me? Why do I feel so dizzy and lightheaded?" Kali asked still woozy from the experience. She felt like she going to be sick.

Sorry about that dear. I should have warned you that you might get a little sick from the experience. Our powers aren't something most people can handle. That's why bondings are such rarity. I assumed because you were able to link together with Kelsey you be able to channel the power through her so there wouldn't be any problems. I was wrong, and I apologize for that. What's done is done. We have to move on, Star stated simply.

My sister is right. We must start thinking about the future if we are to have one. Any danger that we present to you while inside you is nothing compared to what the Nameless and its minions have in store for us. We must act fast if we are too avid the awful tragedy they have planned. Now let's go outside and practice, shall we? Nova said urgently already marching Kelsey's feet towards the door.

"Nova, would you please calm down and be a bit patient? For the Spirit of Injustice you sure are in a hurry. I thought that your actions would be a more subtle and drawn out. Besides how you know the voice of Nature has work and its safe outside?" Kali questioned.

"Most of the injustice in the entire multiverse is caused by people who are in to much of a hurry to find the truth. So that's why I rush things sometimes.

Besides, can't you sense Councilwomen Nature's gift working? We can," Nova and Kelsey said together.

"Sense what? Nova, while it may be apparent to you what has happened it isn't to me. Call me a coward if you think being overly cautious qualifies me as one, but I like tangible evidence before I risk my life."

"Come on, Kali, don't be such a sour puss. This is a once and a lifetime chance to do all the things we've ever dreamed about. To actually be involved with something bigger than us is something we always desired. Now you may think that this the time to be cautious, but I'm not wasting a single second of this. I'm going outside," Kelsey informed her opening the backdoor and racing outside.

"KELSEY! Wait a dang minute. God, she never listens to me. Why do I even bother?" she asked out loud as she stepped outside.

It was nearly sunset and the evening breeze fluttered around her sending shivers down her spine. Buttoning up her leather jacket she walked up the incline to where Kelsey sat peacefully by a tree. "What are you doing? You could have been attacked by Killnala and her consort with your carelessness!"

"If you haven't noticed, nothing bad happened. Take a look around you. The voice of nature has taken root in the trees, bushes, everything around us in order to protect us. If you listen closely you can hear the plants talking to one another."

"Since when did you become a philosopher? Kelsey, try to understand I'm not mad at you really. But this entire situation has me confused and a little freaked ever since day one. I'm glad that you're part of this, I am. I wouldn't want to share this with anyone, but you. I just wish that the circumstances where different so we could enjoy this more," she said sitting down next to her.

"I know and I'm sorry for the way I've been acting towards you lately. I have been really mean and controlling lately haven't I? Just because I'm miserable, is no excuse to be nasty and annoying. I guess that's why Nova was attracted to me originally. I sort of remind her of herself. Not that I condone injustice, evil, and death, but I do understand it pretty well. Let me help you with whatever your meant to do. Together there's nothing we can't accomplish," she said hugging her.

It seems that the situation is under control now. I don't think we have anything to worry about now. Let's both rest and discuss this tomorrow with a clear head. There's nothing more to be gained today, Star thought to Nova privately.

I agree with you whole heartily. We should be thankful just to be alive. The girls are content for now and we do really need to rest in order to recover. Take Kali home and rest. But tomorrow they're both getting a crash course in power use. The fate of the entire multiverse and Entara rest upon them, Nova intoned gravely.

Chapter Thirteen

The next day Kali awoke surprised to find herself levitating a foot above her bed. She screamed and fell on the floor narrowly avoiding the sharp edges of a box that had yet to be unpacked. "What is this, Star, what happened just now? Star? Star wake up!" she whispered loudly. She had to be careful not to wake her mom.

Five more minutes mother, mumbled Star sleepily. It sounded like she was sleeping in her brain! She didn't even know she could sleep while she was bonded to her. What else didn't she know? She was going to get her answers right now.

"Star, get up right now!" Kali shouted. She felt a jolt in her head as Star woke up. For a few seconds her heart raced and her eyes darted around the room before the Entity remembered her current condition.

Why did you have to wake me up so early? It's only 5:30 in the morning. The bus doesn't come until 7:25! She complained.

"This is the only time I have to myself. My mom and sister are still in bed. Meanwhile I check out my email and the latest updates on my favorite fanfics site. Just let me get dressed and we can get going."

A short time later Kali was sitting down in front of the computer typing in her password. A moment later she had access to her email. She smiled at all the reviews and updates that had appeared overnight. There was even an email from her online pals. "Ahh my own private paradise."

How long will this take exactly? We really should be sleeping or you could listen to me explain how my low level powers work, Star insisted

"Star, I love you a lot, sometimes I dreamed about being you. But right now I want to do my thing. After I'm done and ready for school, I'll listen to what you have to say. Until then, leave me be got it?" Kali snapped impatiently.

Don't take that tone of voice with me. I may be a disembodied Entity, but I still deserve your respect. I am only trying to keep us on task. Have you forgotten about Killnala or Killroary? Since we escaped their wraith, they'll be after us with a vengeance. You have to have some idea of what my abilities are and how you can tap into them in order to stay alive, Star rebuked.

"Don't you think I already know that? You keep reminding me about it every chance you get. I'm scared that the measures you've taken won't be enough to protect my twin or me. I'm afraid of a lot of things. Why do you think I'm reading fanfics? It's to calm my nerves down before I have a panic attack!" she slammed her hands down on the keyboard in frustration.

When she tried to remove her hand she found she couldn't. Confused she looked at them and yelped in shock. Her hands were disappearing inside the computer system! "What in the world? Star help! I can't stop this!"

Stop screaming your head off. You'll wake your mom and sister and that's one scene we both want to avoid. Calm down and take some deep breaths. What is happening to you is something that's very natural to me. You're merely spreading your essences into another reality. The fanfiction reality if you want to be accurate. That is the one reality, which the Killgonas can't get into. If you're ever in trouble go there," Star instructed her in soothing voice.

Taking control for a minute, she moved away from the keyboard and the computer. Slowly Kali's hands reformed and her stress level went down. With a snap of her fingers the computer shut off and everything that Kali had to get done for school was done. *"Now will you listen to me?"*

"Talk fast and make it understandable. I'm not as smart as you are."

Very well the, I'll try to make this understandable to you. When an Entity bonds with a host to survive the host gains the ability to access low level powers. My low level powers include; teleportation, invisibility, flight/levitation, spatial awareness, minor control over elements, aura reading, energy manipulation, and you can do some minor tricks with my special powers. Also my personality at times will overwhelm yours and come out. My powers are controlled by emotion so you must keep tight control over them. Be careful or you could end up harming someone. Also try to not use my powers if you can help it.

Killgonas can smell power use and will lock onto it. Once you're in an unprotected place they will kill you.

"Thanks for telling me about that. I'll try not to use your powers, but it's going to be hard. When do you think you'll be strong enough to leave my body?"

By the end of the week, hopefully. But it mostly depends on how much I rest. If I try to use my powers at all I risk hurting myself further. But if I try to use any of my higher level powers we could both end up dead. Nova would have explained this to Kelsey so you shouldn't worry about her.

"Somehow that doesn't comfort me much. I'm sorry to say this Star, but your sister seems to wild to take anything serious. How do I know she won't make things worse?"

Don't be so harsh and judgmental girl. Nova is one of the best students at school and has an excellent record of success with troubled Crystal Carriers. She'll handle Kelsey just fine.

"Hopefully Kelsey is in a listening mood. Kelsey has a tough time listening to anyone but herself. Also she rarely hears what there really saying. All the information goes through one ear and out the other."

Have some faith, will you? Your opinion of your sister is low. I wonder what caused it to become like that. Kelsey isn't as dumb and immature as she acts. Nova proved that by installing a link between the two of them proves Kelsey is responsible enough for this. Give her a chance will you. Keep an open mind will you? Come on we have to get some breakfast and wake the others. So lets get going.

Things where heating up at the Killgonas camp. They had finally gotten out of the astral plane and return homed where Killnala proceeded to throw a huge temper tantrum. She had reverted to her true form in order to rip and shred the place apart. Killroary was trying to avoid being hit by any flying objects.

"HOW? How could the three of them defeat us so easily? Our plan was perfect absolutely foolproof and they ruined it! We had that girl wrapped up like a present, Star on her knees ready to be slice in two and we got broadside by her stinking evil twin sister! How could we not know that Nova was here? How could she escape our detection for so long?"

"Its strange that Nova was able to avoid us for so long. At least now we know who destroyed our energy reserve pods. But we need to focus on the mission right now. If we are to complete our duty we must think about this clearly."

"How can I focus on the future when my lifetime nemesis is still alive? We should have been on our way home hours ago to celebrate and present the Nameless with the energy not playing musical chairs! Star and her blasted twin will have certainly doubled the protection surrounding the girl. We've lost our one chance to strike! The element of surprise is gone there is no way we can salvage this!"

Killroary slapped her hard across the face. "Get a hold of yourself Killnala. You're losing your cool. You can do this all you need to do is get a grip. Listen to me. Star and Nova were seriously injured in the battle. It's likely that their dead. Also their little time warp has made a mess of things giving us a chance to strike. We just need to pull it all together."

Killnala took a few deep breaths and blew it out. "Your right as always Killroary. Losing my temper isn't helping either of us with this dilemma. If we are to claim victory we need to stay sharp. It's just that we are so close to our goal, Killroary. After so many of eons we're about to triumph over our foes forever. I can hear our Master in my head more frequently these days. It wishes to know why we haven't completed the mission and returned with our promised feast by now."

"Tell the Nameless it shall have the feast of many lifetimes shortly. Right now we must feed ourselves and strategize our plan of attack. We don't know for certain if the twins are dead, they could have found a way to survive. Here I saved some energy from those mental patients for you. Try some you'll feel better," he said offering her some energy, which she eagerly consumed.

"Hmm, delicious. I knew you were the best person for the job of being my consort and second in command. Now let's analyze the situation. It's plain to me now that Nova was the Council's trump card to their plan. They must have been pretty distressed to send her without Star's knowledge."

"Smart enough to entrust them with special gifts. How else do you explain their ability to create the time warp to escape us? I wonder what else those meddlesome fools gave them," he mused.

"Whatever they received, they're bound to use them against us. Even in their weakened state an Entity would rather die then leave a Crystal Carrier unguarded. Their still here I know it. The girl may have new safeguards protecting her, but she still hasn't tapped into her own potential powers. If we can prevent that from happening we win this fight."

"But how can you be certain that they're still alive? I doubt Kali knows how to heal them. If she managed to save their lives then we have to find ways to get around the Council's gifts if we are to end their lives permanently this time."

"And we will find a way around them. No gift is absolutely perfect. There is a way to get around it and we will discover it no matter what. The time for patience and subtleness is over. Now we use brute force and directness in order to accomplish our goal. No one gets in our way and if they do we destroy them no questions asked. I want to get out of this miserable, wretched excuse for a reality by tonight!" Killnala informed him adamantly.

"Then let the real hunt begin! I swear to you by everything we hold sacred that we won't stop until the girl is dead, Nova is begging for her life, and Star is gasping on her dying breath. Together we shall triumph over our ancient foes and bring about the eternal silence upon the multiverse," Killroary promised as they took the air and headed straight for the school.

Meanwhile, Kali had arrived at the school and was struggling to deal with Star's powers. No matter how hard she tried to control her emotions she couldn't keep the tight grip required to keep the powers in line.

At the moment she was trying to keep her eyes shut because she could see peoples auras glowing brilliantly around them. She fell against one of the display cases by the auditorium doors trying to regain control as she watched the busy crowd walk by. Each person had a special glow around them indicating their status as a person. Many were a brilliant bluish purple color, a few of them were crimson red, and she saw at least two people who were ebony black color. Forcing herself down the hall she managed to get to her locker, which she yanked open and stuck her head inside in an attempt to clear her head. Taking a few deep breaths she calmed down.

"What do all those colors mean exactly? I thought auras where either the mystical life force that surrounds each of us showing off our individual health or the personal electro magnetic field that surrounds us."

It's both actually. However, there is a third one that you need to know about. The one that you're seeing now reflects the pureness of one's heart and soul. The color blue represents a person who is full of goodness and purity in their soul. Red means that people likes to stay neutral helping out both sides of the playing field while avoiding trouble for themselves. Black symbolizes a person who has nothing but darkness inside of them and indicates a high level of evil inside them. Entities use these colors to monitor people and help find potential Crystal Carriers.

"Your saying all these people has the potential to become Crystal Carriers? But if most people have a blue aura why don't they earn their crystal necklace? Why aren't there more Crystal Carriers?"

Because in order to earn your crystal a person must demonstrate that they can handle the raw power. Not everyone can handle the intensity of a crystal. You are one of the lucky few whom are able to.

"The people who where surrounded by black auras, can they change? Become good people or are they doomed to stay evil forever?"

It rarely happens, but they have the option of becoming good. Its difficult though to overcome the darkness in one's heart. The same goes for a person who is good. They can become evil and it would be next to impossible to regain their former glow. That's why neither Nova nor I like losing one of our Carriers to the other. It throws off the balance. That's why we treat the game of life like a chess game.

"Its true that Crystal Carriers who switch sides throws off the balance, but that doesn't necessarily make it a bad thing. Sometimes it just means that person wasn't comfortable with their color the first time. Hello Kali how is my twin treating you? Don't let her lectures bore you too much. You'll get wrinkles from them," Nova joked as Kelsey slid next the locker smiling happily about something.

"Nova, you're not supposed to use a host's body without their permission! You know that is incredibly rude and inconsiderate of you," Star exclaimed loudly using Kali's mouth without permission. People turned and gave her strange looks before continuing on their way.

"Hush, both of you. You're causing a scene and that's the last thing we need right now. Will you two go rest or something. Kali and I have something to discuss privately," Kelsey demanded hotly. The Entities complied, retreating to the far corners of their host's mind so the girls could talk in private.

"Finally I thought they never leave. I spent all last night talking to Nova about my life and hers. We have so much in common it's unbelievable. I no longer harbor any ill feelings about hosting her inside my body. She's a great person to be with twenty four seven."

"I'm pleased to hear you say that. It's a little different for me, but that's just because I've already spent a lot of time with Star. Having her inside me is making me a little unnerved. So is there anything else you wanted to say to me?"

"Yeah there is. You wouldn't believe the morning I've been having. I woke up levitating! And if that wasn't cool enough later I turned invisible; can you believe it? These powers totally rock! Everything we've ever wished we could do we can do. What else do you think we can do besides these basic powers?"

"I hate to be the one to burst your bubble, but it's not you or I really doing this stuff. Not if you wanted to be technical. It's the beings we're harboring inside of us this moment whose powers we're using. Our own powers, if we have any at all, are buried deep inside and haven't emerged yet. And keep your voice down a bit please; we don't want to attract the wrong kind of attention. Do you want the teachers to think you're crazy?"

"They're all immature idiots anyways so why should I care what a bunch of jerks thing about me? Come on, Kali loosen up. You're being way to serious again. Relax and have fun for a change. Do you realize that we have the power to get back at all the kids who ever tormented us? To make people actually act grown up for once?"

"I'm tempted I really am. But just because we have the power to do it doesn't mean we should. You and I have seen enough TV programs to illustrate that point. I have to say no to this. Kelsey, try to remember what we're trying to do here."

"You're letting Star tell you what to do. She's not in charge of you Kali. You can make your own decisions about what you want to do. Don't let her control you so much. I know your dying to try out some of these powers. Why not test them out here in the school? It's not like the Killgonas can get us in here."

"True, but what about the consequences of our actions? I don't think the school would survive if we used the powers. Didn't Nova bother to explain any of this to you? Both of us need to be careful with what we say, think, and feel. If we react poorly to a situation we could accidentally harm someone. I don't think you want that on your conscience. After school at your house maybe we practice with these powers, but until then will you promise me you won't use them?"

"Fine, I promise to try and control my powers. I better get going; see you later," Kelsey yelled heading for her first period. Kali caught a glimpse of what was going through her mind and frowned. She knew today wasn't going to be a good day.

"She's going to get us into trouble, I just know it. Kelsey's bad qualities are being augmented by Nova's persona. I don't want to get her into any trouble. Can't you do something about this?"

Star laughed gaily. *Just because we're twin sisters doesn't mean I control her actions. The same can be said about you trying to control Kelsey's. She's her own person with her own mind. She is going to do what she wants to do and you can't make her do anything she really doesn't want to do. Nova is a good person even if she is a little dark. She'll make sure nothing real serious happens. Lighten up, Kali. You're way to tense right now. How do you ever expect to find your powers if you're so tightly wrapped up?*

"Sorry, Star. I don't know why I can't relax these days. I guess I'm afraid that if I do let my guard down for even a second something bad will happen. I really don't want to be surprised again by a Killgona. Sometimes I wish I never met you and my life was back to normal. Are you sure that Killnala can't get to me in here?"

"Positive. Now you'd better make tracks to class. Remember, stay alert at all times just incase there's danger and above all else; don't use my powers if you can help it."

With that in mind Kali entered Foods Class determined to keep things in check. Things went smoothly for a while, but then it all went sour. Everybody was paying close attention to Mrs. Boyle explain about the upcoming test. Everyone that is, except two girls named Vanessa and Jen. Both of them where talking loudly while others strained to pay attention. It was getting annoying.

"Will you two be quite please? Others are trying to pay attention," Kali whispered to them. "I can't hear Mrs. Boyle speaking."

"Shut up, Kali, and mind your own business. We don't have to listen to you," Vanessa hissed at her.

"Yeah, we're not bothering anyone. So leave us alone," Jen replied. Then the two of them began talking again louder then before.

Kali turned back around trying to calm down, but couldn't. It was the same thing every day and it never stopped. It had been bad enough when they were sitting at her table now they were even louder at their new one. She never could get a moment of piece. It irritated her greatly. "I wish those girls would be quiet for once," she whispered angrily.

A tingling sensation rushed through Kali across the floor and snaked its way up Vanessa and Jen's body until it touched their lips. Instantly they lost the ability to speak at all. Both girls started to gesture frantically causing Mrs. Boyle to rush over to them to make sure they where okay. Everyone was laughing at the expense.

Kali looked at them in horror. She couldn't believe what just happened. How did that just happen?

I told you not to use my powers! What were you thinking? You could have harmed those girls permanently!

"I didn't or at least I didn't mean to harm them. What low level power was that anyways? I thought you told me all of them and that doesn't look like any of them you mentioned," she whispered. She watched the two girls helplessly. They were still mute with no signs of regaining speech.

I did tell you all of them. That was my special ability power. This is low-level justice working to correct a situation. You wanted those girls to be quite because they caused a disturbance and you got just that. You have to watch what you think and say otherwise it could happen. Your lucky this will wear off in a few minutes. You might accidentally activate them again and this time you could be linked to the cause. We can't afford that.

Kelsey was also struggling too. Nova had given her the same speech earlier about her low level powers and how to control them, but Kelsey was having a difficult time controlling her temper. The slightest thing would set her off, such as people who were acting immature. She couldn't stand it and was losing her temper.

As a result a rash of arguments were going on all over the study hall room and the teacher was loosing control of the class. Kelsey watched in disbelief as the injustice took grip everywhere and wondered how this had occurred.

"What is going on Nova? I thought that you told me your powers wouldn't be that strong if I accidentally used them. This seems to be a pretty strong reaction to me," Kelsey whined quietly.

This is nothing compared to the results of my stronger powers. Your own anger effected how long and how powerful the injustice would last. That's why you need to try and control your emotions or something worse could happen. This isn't all fun and games Kelsey. I hope you realize that now. Still, it is a surprise to me how much power you did tap into just by losing your temper for a moment. Even with the link between you and me it shouldn't be like this, Nova mused.

"Maybe it's not just the link. Maybe it's also because we're both twins and because we have similar personalities. Also you seem close to your sister and I was once very close to Kelsey. A natural bond plus a link to an Entity could be enhancing my ability to use your powers," Kelsey suggested.

I think you may be right, Kelsey. This bond you once had with Kali might be the key to unlocking her powers. If it is it could mean we finally have a chance to save everything we've been fighting for. I like to run this theory by Star, but I think you might have solved all our problems right now.

"Can you wait until after class before contacting Star? I don't want to cause anymore trouble so I need you to help me keep my temper in check."

Alright, but the sooner we tell Star about this the better chance we have of keeping the Nameless locked up in the anti-universe and putting an end to those idiot Killgonas once and for all. Time is running out for everyone, including for you and your sister.

Through out the morning there was more then one instance when the girls lost control for a second and accidentally used the Entities powers. Kali was nearly caught teleporting from outside the girl's locker room to the bathroom and was more alert to signs of danger in the hallway causing people to stare at her. Kelsey was no better. Through out her morning she had several close calls when she nearly went invisible due to embarrassment in second hour, caused a light to burn out in third, and lastly in forth she nearly destroyed her classroom by letting loose a mini tornado.

And that was nothing compared to other messes that happened when they passed by people. Fights were started quickly and then ended with ease, people had their personalities altered slightly, and the worst was when they glimpsed at a person timeline seeing them be born and die. Both Entities assured their girl's that this happened the first day of a bonding and things would get better soon. They just had to hold out for a couple more hours.

By the time lunch rolled around the two of them were worn out. Neither one of them had suspected that the bonding process would have this many side effects. It was worth it though if it kept Star and Nova alive. They sat down at their own private table and began talking in hushed voices.

"I don't know how much longer I can deal with this. I know I was excited this morning about all this, but after what I've been through I can see why you cautioned me. My fragile mind is near panic," Kelsey exclaimed.

"Well, you're going to have to get use to it. Star and Nova need more time to recuperate and they are. I can feel Star getting stronger inside of me. But they are still to weak to support themselves on their own. We'll have to make some sacrifices if we want to survive this," Kali informed her.

"You don't have to tell me twice. Nova and I were discussing something earlier that may be of some interest to you. If my idea works I can also access my own unique powers and assist you in your quest to take out the Nameless," Kelsey replied.

"Great I could do with some good news. Why don't you tell me what it is so we can get our own powers?"

"It's simple really. In every book, TV show, or game we've ever seen or played, powers are connected to a person's thoughts and emotions. It's similar to a bond or a link shared between close friends and family members. You're a Crystal Carrier because you have a link with Star. What if the source of your powers lies in your bond with me? After all when you created Star you based her off yourself and Nova me," Kelsey pointed out.

"You're right for once. As twin sisters we share a unique bond, a bond that is helping Star and Nova heal. Your argument is most logical. In order for me, I mean us, to tap into our powers we need to heal the broken bond between us. Only then can we stop the ultimate threat," Kali admitted.

How long will it take for the two of you to resolve your differences? It's already Tuesday afternoon. We have only eleven more days to save the world; Nova said adding her two cents into the conversation.

Oh hush Nova. They have almost two years of personal conflict to resolve in just a few short days. Give them a break will you? This isn't easy for them, Star said.

I don't know if this going to help out at all. We fight all the and never lost our powers.

There's a difference between them and us. We're Entities born with our powers and the knowledge of how to control them. A Crystal Carrier has to work to earn their powers and train to keep them in check.

True, but what if they can't resolve their differences in time? What if Kali can't activate her powers and if she can't what's going to stop the Nameless from destroying everything? I'm not trying to be pessimistic, but I have a sinking sensation even with her powers it won't be enough.

Don't you dare talk like that! Everything will work out in the end it always does. The multiverse will survive this crisis as it has withstood others. The Killgonas will be stopped once and for all and we'll have two new Crystal Carriers defending their reality from harm.

So you believe. But just because you hope for that to happen doesn't mean it's going to occur. Good doesn't triumph over evil all the time. I've proved that enough times to you.

I know that, but we can't give up hope. Any chance we have we have to take no matter how small it is. It's the only way we can guarantee a chance for everyone to survive.

Before the discussion could go any farther, the lunch bell ran. Reluctantly the two sets of twins separated sadly. They had really wished to discuss this a bit further, but now they would have to wait until after school before they could do anything else.

"I'll take the bus home with you for the rest of the week. Hopefully will be able to make some headway on solving our problems. If we don't then I hate to imagine how much worse off were going to be. I'll catch you later, Kelsey. Bye!" Kali called over her shoulder as she hurried outside. Her next class was down the street in the Dolan Building and she had to hurry if she didn't want to be late.

She was halfway across the parking lot when she stopped and stood still for a moment. Something didn't seem right. Something was causing her hair to stand on its ends and slight tingling sensation passed through her body. "I've got a really really bad feeling," she whispered before she broke out in a run.

That's when Killnala appeared in the sky right behind her. She was in her natural form and she had a murderous glare in her eyes. "There's no where to run little girl! This time you are mine!" she roared as she rocketed towards Kali her claws ready to slit her throat.

Don't stop running! Don't look back! Just keeping moving and get inside the building as fast as you can. The Councils gifts will protect you from her wraith. Trust me! Star urged her.

True to Star's word the gifts were already working their magic to protect her from harm. A green ribbon of light touched the branches of a nearby tree. The branches glowed and began to move with a will of their own. As Kali blew past the tree and into the building, the branches stretched out and wrapped themselves tightly around the pursing Killgona. Once they had a hold of her they refused to let go.

"Let me go you vile plant! You won't contain me! I will destroy you and everything else in this wretched excuse for a reality!" Killnala bellowed as she struggled to break free from the tree's grasp. But the more she struggled the tighter their hold became. Soon it was next to impossible for her to breath.

"Arg! I am Killnala, leader of the Killgonas, destroyer of realities, and the Nameless personal representative! You won't stop me from killing that miserable excuse for a life form!" she howled enraged as she busted apart the tree branches sending pieces of the tree all over the place.

Killnala was seeing red by this time as she caught sight of Kali sitting safely in her classroom. Lost in a fit of rage she charged the building intent on ramming straight through the glass to catch her prize. But before she could even get close enough to make contact a blue force field formed a protective barrier around the building sealing Kali safely inside and trapping Killnala out.

"NOOOOOOOOOO! I will not be deterred! Nothing shall get in my way of feasting upon Kali's freshly spilt blood! You will let me through this instant!" Killnala commanded as she repeatedly rammed the force field. But no matter how many times she hit it, it wouldn't break. Finally the combined effort of the force field plus exhaustion caused her to collapse on the ground just outside the main door. Her entire body shut itself down and it wasn't until much later that she felt someone trying to arouse her. Her eyes fluttered open and she winced at the sudden intensity of the fading sunlight. She managed to make out the form of Killroary who was propping her up.

"What happened to me? How long have I been out? Is that vile girl dead yet? Did you find out where the Entities are hiding? And where the Hell were you when I needed you? You better start talking or I swear I'm going to slit your throat Killroary!"

"Shush, my love. You're still recovering from exhaustion. All your questions shall be answered shortly, but I suggest we get out of sight. We attracting to much attention from passerby's," he told her as he gave her a hand up. Dusting her off they quickly started walking down the streets heading for home.

"To answer your questions in order you overexerted yourself trying to get through that force field created no doubt from Wisdom's powers. It's also safe to assume that tree that attack you was empowered by Nature. You've been out since Tuesday. It's now Friday afternoon and yes the girl still lives. Before you get mad at me for waiting so long to find you I think you be interested in some information I picked up about the Entities and the girl."

Killnala growled at him in annoyance. She didn't agree with his goals all the time, but if he had something they could use she would let it slide this one time. "Well whatever you learned better be worth it. I'm sick to death of these little surprises the Council gave the girls. They're nothing, but a major roadblock for us. How are we suppose to get anything accomplished if they keep employing them?"

"We're not, which is the exact reason for their use. We've seen three out of four gifts, which gives us a chance to prepare for the last one. What gift do you think that weakling Emotion handed out?"

"Something that's very powerful and no doubt dangerous to us. But I really don't care at the moment. So far we have nothing to show for our efforts and our Master's release is in less then a week now. We have to be ready for that at any cost. Now tell me about Star and Nova now!" she snapped at him.

So Killroary told her everything that he had learned in the last couple of days. He told her about how the Entities had bonded to the twins in a last ditch attempt to stay alive, how the gifts were set up exactly so the girls were next to impossible to get to, and their plans to fix the girls relationship to activate Kali's powers. When he was done he was frowning, "What are we going to do?"

"Why do you ask questions that you already know the answers to? We need to find a loophole and get rid of both sets of twins. With that much energy there will be more then enough for both the Nameless and us. Now come we have to plan the final destruction of the Entities."

In the meantime things weren't going so well for Kali and Kelsey. Each day after school they had gotten together and tried to work out their conflicts. So far neither one of them had been able to solve their problems and both of their tempers were near the boiling point. Finally it became too much and they started to have an all out screaming match.

"I'm sick and tired of trying to talk to you! You never take anything seriously! All you want to do is live in your little fantasy world. Why did I even bother trying to solve my problems with you its just a huge waste of time, because talking to you is like talking to a brick wall!" Kali yelled at Kelsey.

"How dare you! You're nothing but an arrogant, rude, self-centered bitch! You think you're so smart and that you know everything in the world and that I'm an idiot. And on an added note you love that stupid cat of yours more then me!" Kelsey shot back.

Back and forth the insults went each getting worse then the one before. The girls had asked Star and Nova to mediate between them, but it hadn't worked well. Both of them were to hurt and stubborn to back down.

Tell me again why you thought they would be able to resolve their conflicts by themselves? They hate each other! Face it sis we're too long lived a race and highly evolved to help mediate a dispute this huge. Instead of solving their problems they've just made them worse. Nova thought to Star.

While its true we may be long lived and highly evolved it doesn't mean we are above sibling rivalry, betrayal, and hurt. These past two years have been hard on both of them causing a huge rift to form between them. We have to help them find some middle ground in all this so they can at least attempt to work this out.

Well, I suggest we better hurry then. They're starting to use our powers against one another. I seriously doubt the house can withstand that much damage.

It was true; Kelsey's living room had become a living battlefield. The cats had taken refuge in the closet as the sisters used the Entities abilities to wage war on one another. There was no calming down or resolving their issues peacefully.

"I can't believe I've got you for a twin sister! You're an uncaring, nasty, and worship dad like a God! He's not and he's the worse parent you could ever ask for. He doesn't care about you or anyone else!" Kali shouted hurling a ball of energy at Kelsey's face.

Kelsey rolled out of the way and the energy ball hit the wall behind her leaving a huge scorch mark. She looked at the wall in horror before turning to face Kali with her eyes blazing full of anger and rage.

"What about you huh? You defend Mom, are way to critical, and always tell me what to do! I'm sick of it and I hate you!" Waving her arm around she sent a stream of water straight at her.

Levitating straight into the air Kali launched herself into a flying kick and hitting Kelsey in the side sending her crashing into the couch. Kelsey responded by hurling a cloud of darkness trapping Kali successfully inside. She tackled her sending them both head first into the TV. Both girls continued to wrestle around the floor for several minutes using more and more power on one another. Finally the powers simply shut off and both girls looked at each other in disbelief.

"What happened? I was winning!" Kelsey whined.

"You were not I was. I have no clue what is going on. Star? Nova? You two have an idea what is going on?" Kali asked.

So now you two want to listen to us? That's enough fighting from the both of you. You're making it harder for us to recover by draining us of our low level powers with all this fighting. I know you two have issues that go far back and that right now your not the best of friends, but you need to put it aside and work together. We have more important things to worry about then your petty bickering. So I suggest to you come up with someway to coexist right now or else Nova and I will have to get physical on you do you understand me? Star told both of them sharply.

The fate of the entire multiverse and Entara rests upon you two repairing the broken bond of sisterhood. I suggest you clean up your act because this isn't some game where you can press the reset button when things get bad. This is a life and death matter for the right to exist! Nova reminded them both.

You both believe in the greater good and putting others before yourself. Right now you need to act on those instincts and stop being so stubborn and hardheaded. With such little time left we need to pull together and try our hardest to succeed. So no more fighting, no more arguing about old conflicts, no getting sidetracked. Just the two of you acting rationally and responsibly, Star instructed gently.

"Alright, I promise to try harder in the near future not to be so stubborn and listen to what others have to say. But this isn't easy for me, Star. Letting go of more than two years of pent up frustration and angers isn't easy. I don't think I'll ever be able to get over them even with you inside me," Kali stated out loud. She was still holding her hands up in threatening position so she put them down by her side.

"Well, it's not any easier for me, and I have the one person in the entire galaxy who thrives on this kind of stuff inside me currently. While we're on that delightful subject when will you two be able to leave our bodies? I mean it's been almost six days."

"If nothing comes up probably tomorrow night, Sunday morning at the latest. It's hard to say each bonding is unique. There are a lot of different factors we have to consider. And because of all the power you two used you might have delayed our reemergence by a few days," Nova explained out loud as she took control of Kelsey voice for a minute.

"That's excellent new for my ears. With you two back to full health will have a better chance to finally accomplish our goal. Not to mention Kelsey will also be able to activate her powers and help me out."

"Now that's settled its time to go. Your mom was expecting you back an hour ago. Will stop by tomorrow night and the same time. Be ready for us and no more power use. Bye!" In a blink of the eye they were both gone.

Back at the Killgona headquarters both Killnala and Killroary were pouring over every bit of information they had gained in the last days. After careful examination of the last plan of attack and figuring out were they went wrong the carefully strategize a new plan of attack.

"I believe I've discovered the loophole we were looking for. The Council may be powerful, but they're not perfect. Their gifts only work as well as the girls employs them to. By carefully dissecting how each gift was employed, I have extrapolated a weak point in them. I know how to breach the security," Killroary stated.

"And when we catch them off guard with our sneak attack they'll never be able to escape or use Emotions gift no matter what it is. This time we got them good. I have a good feeling about this Killroary. By this time tomorrow night we'll be back home celebrating our hard earned victory. There is absolutely no place in the world the brats can hide from our wraith," Killnala crowed.

"Our mission will finally be complete and nothing will be able to stand in the way of the Nameless's glorious return. Not the Council, not the Crystal Carriers, and certainly not some Chosen One," Killroary added. The glint in his eyes barely masked his bloodlust. They headed to bed to rest up for the big night. They needed to be at full strength for tomorrow assaults.

A typical Saturday night at Kali's home was simple. While Keelia was at work and mom was in her room watching TV with Oso, Kali was downstairs at the computer with a soda happily chatting with Agent-G and Slickboy, her Internet best friends. These days they were her only friends she could really confide in.

Kali was reading the boys latest coauthored chapter for their latest fanfics. The story was called Hellfire and Brimstone. The story revolved around the boys' favorite comic book turned animated characters being kidnapped and tortured by an evil club and in their latest chapter they had written the superhero team had been planning a rescue mission. To say this was good was an understatement.

Kalitt*: This is a great chapter you two came up with. I've never would have imagined you could portray this much passion and detail in one story. Its almost like I'm there. That one chapter where you had that girl change sides was intense:*

AgentGV: *That was an impressive moment when we wrote that particular part of this story. It was very difficult because I didn't know exactly how to present it without getting someone annoyed. I had to stay true to my own character design and her character profile. It can be a hassle:*

Slickboy: *But when you have two people working together it can be even harder. We have to make sure each part of the chapter matches up with what the other one wrote. That's why I prefer working with OC because you have more freedom:*

Kalitt: *I have to agree with you there. Both of you have created such great OC characters. I mean Slick you have Jack "Slayer" Robinson and G you have Vincent "Mayhem" Freeman. I think you both did well introducing them into this story. They're the best:*

Slickboy *and* **AgentGV**: *LOL:*

Kali did just that. It felt good to be with her best friends in the entire world, even if they could only be here for her in spirit. In fact, she felt safest when she was talking to her best friends without a care in the world. Kali was about to respond to G's latest question about her novel when she heard a strange noise coming from upstairs. It sounded like a cross between a car backfiring and a door slamming closed. She got up suspicious of the noise. "Mom? Mom are you okay? Mom!"

Kali raced upstairs, her heart pounding something didn't seem right. She pounded on her mom's door screaming for her to answer her. She tried to open the door, but it was locked. "Mom open up! Mom can you hear me? MOM!"

Uh Kali?

"Not now, Star. Can't you see my mom is in danger? I have to get in there and make sure she's okay."

This is important. Look at the floor now! she ordered her.

Kali did and took a step back nearly losing her balance at the top of the stairs. A pale, blue, forked, tail was wiggling its way out of her mom's room trying to grab her. This time she did lose her balance and tumbled down both flights of stairs. She landed in front of her mom's old secretary cabinet bleeding from several open cuts.

Kali managed to crawl over to the couch just as a clawed foot from the entryway took a swipe at her. She headed for the kitchen only to be forced back by another claw foot. She was soon forced up against the porch doors panting.

"I don't understand this at all. I thought I was safe at home from attacks. How is Killnala getting around the protection of the Council?" she asked gasping for air.

Before Star could reply the front door flung open followed by a huge gust of wind. As she shielded her eyes they both heard a familiar laughter. There standing calmly in the doorway examining her nails, was Killnala.

"You screwed up big time, Star. Your precious gifts don't work in the in between places such as shadows, doorways, and time periods. Because of your little hindsight, I was able to play my attack accordingly. This time I will be the one walking away from this encounter."

"According to what your own murderous instincts? I know you better than you know yourself. You can't attack us if we stay away from the in between places."

Killnala chuckled lowly and smiled wickedly. "However will you be able to accomplish that my dear? There are to many of them, you can't possibly avoid them all. You can't avoid them forever and neither can Nova."

Kali's face paled dramatically upon hearing that. Her entire body went numb. She could sense inner turmoil upon learning the truth. "Your little friend is attack Kelsey right now, isn't he?"

Killnala nodded yes. "There shall be no escape this time for any of you. You will die and I will show no mercy. Say goodbye!" Extending her nails to their full length she pounced at her stretching as far as she could go. Her nails missed by a millimeter.

Kali sent a tide of purple sparks in her face temporally blinding her in an attempt to prevent her from transporting to another in between place. "That won't stop her for long. We have to get out of here! You have any suggestions?"

Only one. Touch the computer screen and focus on getting to the fanfiction reality. It's our only hope of survival.

With Killnala ready to bite her in two, she had no choice. Quickly touching the computer screen she was spirited away in a blinding flash of light away from danger.

"NOOOOOOOOOOOO!" Killnala roared angrily as she watched in disbelief as her prey escaped from her clutches again. Glaring angrily at the computer screen she vowed the instant her prey reappeared they would be dead!

Chapter Fourteen

Kali opened her mouth to scream, but no sound came out. She continued to tumble head over heels and twisted around in a swirling vortex of colors. She had no idea where she was or what was going on. Out of the corner of her eye she thought she saw shadows of other people in the vortex, but that didn't make sense to her.

What is going on? Star where are you? Someone help me! Kali screamed in her mind. She was going crazy trying to figure out how to control the vortex around her so she could escape from it.

Suddenly she spied a bright light at the end of the tunnel. Sounds of people could be heard and strange scents filled her nose. A tingling sensation passed through her body as she passed through the light and she landed hard on the ground knocking her out.

A short time later Kali's eye fluttered open and she moaned. "My aching body. Oh I need a massage now. Where in the world am I and why does this place seem so familiar to me?" She stumbled to her feet and looked around trying to figure why this place looked so familiar. "Wait a minute! What about Killnala? Why hasn't she followed us? Star answer me! That fall has rattled my brain. I have no idea what is going on!"

Settle down for a second Kali. Your going to give yourself a heart attack and that won't help either of us. You needn't worry about Killnala, she can't reach us here in this safe haven remember? This reality was created by the creative thoughts, emotions, and energy of thousands of writers. This reality, the Fanfiction.net reality is the one reality where no planes exist. Therefore the Killgonas can't travel here and destroy everything that is found here. That was why I suggested we come here. You are safe here for the time being. Star reassured her. She sent soothing thoughts and energy through her body fixing the damage from the attack.

160

"So you're saying that this is the one place the Killgonas can't get to. That they are completely powerless here because of the imagination? That could be useful information to use against them later. Strange, for such persistent creatures who dream about bloodbaths I didn't think it was possible for them to be stopped by something as simple as that."

You can quit being sarcastic it doesn't suit you. We have other things to deal with right now. We have to locate Kelsey and Nova. If I know my sister she would have thought of getting Kelsey here for safety reasons. I sensed their presences in the vortex. There somewhere nearby and I can't tell if there hurt or no. If she's hurt we can't get back home.

"How are we supposed to find them? I can't sense them and even if we do find them what then? What's going to stop Killnala from destroying the computer effectively trapping us in this world? With me here I can't interfere with her plans. You need to leave my body and help me search. Are you strong enough to do that?" she asked as she walked through the strange, yet familiar brush.

I'm not strong enough to leave just yet. I need to link with Nova if I'm to reenergize my body. Once that's complete I can disengage from your body without leaving any lasting harm. Wait! I sense something. Hurry to the clearing to your left! I think that Kelsey and Nova are about to arrive, Star instructed urgently. Without any further urging Kali took off running for the clearing just as the sky changed.

The air around them became thick and crackled, while the wind whipped around them. The ground was trembling and lighting flashed. Kali struggled to say on her feet, but was blown over landing up against a tree.

"This wouldn't happen to be your doing would it?!"

This isn't my doing! The vortex is opening up again. Someone else is entering the reality and by the way things are acting I think something is wrong! There shouldn't be this much difficulty getting into a reality! Star screamed with such severity Kali couldn't help, but wonder what was happening.

By now the sky was so thick with energy and power it seemed like the world was coming to an end. Kali chocked on the smoky air squinting to see what was happening. The spinning vortex of color reappeared in the sky and with a flash of light three people were thrown clear from it as it disappeared from the sky.

The figures plummeted towards the ground like a ton of rocks. It looked like it was all over for the trio when one of them formed a fist and yelled something. Instantly a black and red sphere surrounded them stopping their rapid descent. The person gently guided the sphere towards the ground where Kali waved them over smiling and laughing. It was Kelsey and she was smiling happily. She gently came to a rest in front of her and her and snapping her fingers, made the sphere vanish. All at once things returned to normal.

The other two forms, two boys, fell collapsed to the ground unconscious. Their clothes were slightly shredded and they appeared uninjured. They also seemed familiar to her for some reason, but she didn't know why.

"Glad to see you're here too. Did you have a wild time getting here to?" Kelsey asked grinning madly.

"Kelsey! Boy I'm glad to see you alive!" Kali shouted in jubilation. She raced over and flung herself into her arms. Both of them were crying and laughing relieved to see each other safe and sound.

Star took control of Kali's voice for a second. There was something that needed to be addressed immediately. "I don't believe my eyes. Nova, how in the name of Entara did you escape from Killroary's clutches unscathed? We barely made it to this reality alive!"

Nova laughed hysterically still trying digests the fact that they were still alive. "You can thank Kelsey and a lot of dumb luck for saving us. Kelsey was in the kitchen making her *third* ham and ketchup sandwich when Killroary struck. He pretty much demolished all the windows and busted down the front door. Glass, wood, and everything that wasn't bolted down went flying. We went crashing into the microwave. That left quite a mark," she said rubbing her back.

"Oh don't remind me. That's when he wrapped his slimy tail around my leg and started dragging me towards his wide open mouth. I was screaming for help, but Dad didn't come bursting out his room to save me. Weird huh?" Kelsey said.

"Not really. I bet he was on another plane of existence at the time. He couldn't help you if he had wanted to. Killroary would have slaughtered him. Please go on with your tale," Kali said.

"Well I had grabbed the doorframe to the computer room with one hand and tried to kick myself free. But he was so stubborn he just wouldn't let go of me. I was inching closer and closer to his jaws and I swear his breath smelled so bad that I wanted to pass out. Instead I tossed my sandwich into his mouth in an attempt to get rid of the bad breath."

"You fed a Killgona a ketchup and ham sandwich? You do know they only eat energy right, right?" Star demanded deadpanned.

"That's the dumb luck part, my dear sister. The moment he swallowed that thing he turned the brightest shade of green you've ever seen. He started to shake uncontrollably and his grip loosened enough for us to scramble free. I had Kelsey incase him in a triangle of injustice so he couldn't pursue us."

"She then ordered me to bring up the fanfic website. The computer was running really slow and Killroary had nearly recovered. He was about to bust down the triangle. Right before he could break free the site came up and we dove in. I saw those two guys over there in the vortex."

"Will deal with them in a minute. Right now I think we should concentrate on getting the Entities out of us. We have a much better chance of getting home alive if Star and Nova weren't limited to our bodies. Surely now their strong enough to link up and free themselves."

"Do we have to? I like having Nova inside me. She's the only real friend I ever had. She actually listens to me." Kelsey whined.

Kali crossed her arms and glared at her. This was hardly the time or place to be selfish.

"Oh fine I'll do it. You always were to the one to spoil my fun."

"Kelsey, I know how you feel, really I do," Kali said empathetically, "But right now we need Star and Nova both at full power. That can't happen while they're inside us. Besides, it wouldn't be fair to them."

"I know you're right. What you're saying is just and good, but I can't help wanting to be a little selfish. Does that make me evil and a bad friend?"

"No, simply human. Now come on sis. Let's do this thing shall we? We have a multiverse to save and a Nameless to kick butt on. Ready Star? Ready Nova?"

Yes!

"Okay then it's up to you to undo what you done."

"Press your palms against each other. Focus on separating your conscience from mine. While you two are doing that, Nova and I will link our minds and fix the last broken connections in our thoughts and energy levels. Once that's over we will be able to exist out on our own."

Doing as they were instructed, they pressed their palms together and relaxed their minds. Both girls started the critical process of disentangling their respective conscience from their Entity counterparts. A little bit at first, but soon more and more of their mind became their own again.

While that was going on the twin Entities had linked minds and were fixing the broken connections. One by one they mended the stray connections and merged stray thoughts back into their collective mind. Finally, they felt themselves completely healed.

They left the girl's bodies the same way they had entered. Emerging from their host in their light form, which looked exactly like their corporal bodies except they wore gowns made of pure white and black light, in a shower of sparkles. Kali and Kelsey had to shield their eyes as they were blinded by the brilliance. The Entities landed and instantly switched to their corporeal bodies. They examined themselves carefully to make sure nothing was amiss. "It's okay. We're back and better then we ever were. Thank you for saving our lives."

"You're welcome. I was scared for a moment that you would fail to reform fully." Kali said.

"Yeah, then we'd be stuck in this strange place with only those guys for company," Kelsey added pointing to the males who still lay unconscious.

"My, God I forgot all about them. Come on we have to wake them up and see if they're okay," Kali said tugging her sister's arm. She knelt down next to both of the boys and examined them. She couldn't shake the feeling that she should somehow know who they were.

"You sense it, too, don't you? This guy feels extremely familiar to me, but the younger one I'm not so sure. Who could they be?" Kelsey asked. Kali shook her head unsure. She looked at the boys again trying to determine where she had seen them before.

One was a Caucasian in his mid twenties with short black hair, gray eyes. He wore a gray sweatshirt and a pair of jeans. He sort of looked like the twin's older brother Kyle except his nose was sharper. The other boy looked like he was in his late teens. He was also white, short length straight blond hair, blue eyes and a few pimples. He was wearing a black shirt and blue jeans and a silver wristwatch. Both were thin, muscular, and looked undamaged from the fall. Suddenly it clicked in her mind where the boys had come from and who they really were. "Ah man!"

"What? You figured out who the idiots are and why there here? Wherever here is exactly in this strange reality. I mean I know we're in the fanfics reality, but in which story?" Kelsey asked propping the boys up.

"It's Agent-G and Slick! I must have accidentally brought them here when I jumped into the computer to escape Killnala. They could have been killed and I would have been responsible!" She replied burying her face in her hands.

"How in the world did you manage that? After all the warnings we received, and your lecture on proper use of their powers, you pick up a bunch of Internet buddies to tag along with you on the trip."

"Hey, I was chatting with them when I was attacked. We were discussing Hellfire and Brimstone and other junk. I think we're in one of the chapters in that story. I was reading it when things got messy."

"I suspect you are correct. In your panic to flee from Killnala's wraith, you inadvertently pulled your friends in here too. Now that has happened, we have to be even more cautious and careful in order to return to your reality safely with these two gentlemen in tow," Star said speaking up for the first time sense returning to her body.

"Good idea, sis; just one tiny problem. Those boys are likely to panic when they wake up. What do we tell them?" Nova pointed out. "It's my experience that men can't handle the truth about such things very well."

"We will tell them the truth and hope for the best. Now be quiet; they're starting to stir," Kali instructed harshly. She only hoped that her friends could accept the truth about what happened to them.

Agent-G's or Gerry's eyes fluttered open slowly. He winced and rubbed the back of his head trying to figure out what had just happened. One minute he'd been chatting with his friend Kali online, the next he was falling through and endless tunnel of color. He glanced around in confusion. "What? How did I end up outside, and why is it daytime?" he muttered confused. Out of the corner of his eye he saw another boy waking up. He looked just as confused as he was. A shadow overlapped him so he looked up and his jaw dropped.

"Hi, Gerry. Hiyah, Slick. Don't be afraid. It's me Kali, and you remember my sister Kelsey don't you? You need to try and remain calm and try not to panic too much. Please listen to what I have to say and keep an open mind to what's going on," she said gently. She held her hands out in a gesture of peace trying to look unthreateningly.

"You want us to remain calm? I think Gerry and I are both far from calm. I'm confused, frightened, and a little weirded out. I mean, I am glad to finally meet you face to face, but could you explain the situation please before I lose what's left of my mind?" Slick begged.

"I hope you two really are as accepting as you say you are. Because what we're about to reveal, only a die hard comic book fan could believe," Kelsey stated evenly.

"I don't have time for a long drawn out, story. So I'll sum up our present situation the best I can. Remember my novel? Well it turns out my characters are real, and I was attacked by Killgonas and escaped into the fanfiction reality where we are currently in one of the chapters in your story, "Hellfire and Brimstone." I'd have to guess chapter fourteen by the looks of things. Oh, and I have no idea how we're getting back home," Kali in a rush.

Gerry and Slick stared at her like she had lost her mind. Kelsey just smiled and tried to stay out of their way. "You're joking, right? This is some kind of dream," Gerry said.

"Trust me on this she's not joking, and you two are certainly not dreaming. What will it take for you to believe us?" Kelsey demanded frustrated by how stubborn they were being.

"How about undeniable proof for one," Slick responded.

"Will we do boys? I'm sure you recognize us. After all Kali's described us perfectly and you Gerry, illustrated us for her," Star said stepping forward with Nova into view. Their auras were in full glow and they were levitating a few inches off the ground.

The boys took a step back shocked by what they were seeing. It couldn't be true; these two couldn't be the fabled Star and Nova. If they accepted this then what other impossibilities were in fact real?

"Hey, sis, I think the boys are in denial. You two really want proof? How's this?" Slick, you've been at the brink of death twice and visited in your sleep by us," Nova said smoothly.

166

"And you Gerry, your friendship with others helps influence you're writing. They helped install in you a moral value that's reflected in your work," Star said calmly.

Both boys were astonished. No one knew about these things. They were convinced because this stuff was of the most private nature. After ten more minutes of talking, hugging, and walking together everyone was on the same page. Now they needed a plan to get home.

They had emerged from the woods near a baseball field in a huge backyard. The group was invisible and intangible to prevent them from accidentally interfering with the reality. In the distance they could see the mansion.

"So, let me see I have this straight. We're in a reality that consists of all the stories on the fanfiction website correct?" Gerry asked as they headed for the mansion.

"Correct. The only way to enter or exit this place is either by the reality bubble or through the computer screen via the vortex. Killroary would have destroyed Kelsey's computer forcing her to join up with Kali. Since Kali was the one that brought you here, she's the one who will send you back to your homes," Star explained as she hovered over the group.

"But since I don't have my powers yet I can't send you home right away. You'll both be sticking around helping me save the world. Sorry."

"This trip just gets better and better. Can't you two Entities use your own powers to find those exits you mentioned earlier?" Slick asked curious.

"Yes, in fact we could leave this reality right now and return to yours this instant if we wanted to. But were not going to," Star replied gently.

"Why in the world not? I mean as cool as it is being in our stories I'd rather be safe at home. Besides, the longer we wait the more time we give those blasted Killgonas to prepare our demises," Kelsey summed up unhappily.

Nova stopped walking and whirled around to face the angry group. Placing her hands on her hips she gave them a look that halted them in their tracks. "I don't believe you four at all. You can all write about great acts of evil, but you don't understand how to fight it? Only one thing can repel a blood lusting assault by those pesky Killgonas at this point. It's the gift of Council Member Emotion entrusted us with. The gift of imagination, friendship, and love is what she gave us to combat against those monsters.

All together the three of them can pack quite a wallop in battle."

"Lets not forget that the Killgonas hate imagination, friendship, and love almost as much as they hate us. This is a perfect solution to our dilemma. If we attack them with the gift you described, they'll go running back home with their tails between their legs," Kelsey yelled enthusiastically pumping her fist in the air.

"What's the catch? If you already know how you're going to handle these creatures why are we still here? What is it that you need us four to do?" Gerry inquired.

"Use your head, Gerry. The gift needs more power then they have. We already have more than enough friendship and love between the six of us, but we need more imagination to use the gift to its fullest extent," Slick surmised.

"Exactly my child. We must hurry and capture the imagination of your stories before it's to late. The longer we remain here, the more time passes on Entara. We can't allow Killnala or her kind to win this fight." Star said firmly.

"We won't, Star I promise. None of us want that crazy dragon to win. How do you suggest we capture the imagination?" Kali asked

"Follow me and I'll show you." Clicking her fingers the group was instantly transported inside the mansion's War Room where Gerry's characters were planning a rescue mission. It seemed they were determined to swarm the enemy's stronghold in order to rescue their trapped friends.

"Whoa, this is amazing. Never in my wildest dreams did I think I would actually meet the cast from my story," Gerry said in awe. He walked around the room touching everything, trying to memorize every last little detail.

"You'll catch flies with your mouth open like that. Star explained everything about this place to me in an earlier conversation. While all character except the ones you made up officially belong to their creators in our reality, in this one they belong to you and Slick because you wrote the story. It's the same all over this place. The imagination and dreams used to create these stories keeps the reality in one piece. Its from here we'll need to collect our prize," Kali informed him as she shut his mouth.

"What do you mean by that? I still don't understand how I'm going to collect the imagination from my story. It's not like I can just touch them and it will flow into me."

"Actually that's exactly what you have to do. Open your mind up and feel the connection between you and your characters. Their conflicts, emotions, and pains are all a part of you. Everything in this story is an extension of your creative mind. When you feel the creative energy at maximum output around you just integrate yourself with the reality fully and seize your prize," Star instructed him. "You have the power to speed this story along to any point you like among other hidden talents you know."

Noticing his blank stare Kelsey chimed in. "She means you two are Crystal Carrier like us. We've always been one, but until now couldn't act on it. That's why each of us needs to get a bit of imagination so we can individually activate our powers."

"What if I don't want any powers? What if I want this to be nothing, but a bad dream?" Gerry demanded. He was clearly frightened by all of this. He never truly believed any of this was real and suddenly finding out it was a bit overwhelming. Being a member of the Canadian Army and training he could handle. Being a Crystal Carrier and protecting the multiverse? That was a completely different story.

"You can't ignore your destiny Gerry anymore then you can forget what you've experience so far. You will have to deal with things as they are and learn to accept the truth. I know you're scared, but being scared is natural. You just have to try and live with it," Star said.

"Yeah and being a Crystal Carrier has a lot of perks. Some of which you're not even aware of yet. We can show all of you later after we settle some old scores," Nova added.

"Look, Gerry, we don't have time to try and work this all out. Right now we're involved in the greatest adventure ever. So use those creative talents, bro, to help us out," Slick appealed to his friend. Gerry sighed in defeat. He knew he had been outvoted.

With a thought the War Room vanished from sight and they found themselves in the enemy stronghold during the rescue part of a new chapter. It wasn't exactly a pleasant scene.

"Get down!" Gerry shouted, dragging the twins to the floor as Slick dove under a table to avoid being shot. Bullets, lasers, and who knew what else, were flying over their heads courtesy of the cyborg mercenaries led by a half human half machine woman. They could hear their motors clearly over the noise, as they got closer and closer.

"This is certainly exhilarating if nothing else. Nothing like a major battle between super powered teams to get the blood pumping and the adrenaline rushing!" Kelsey yelled sarcastically. She winced as another barrage of bullets flew over there head destroying the hallway.

"Shut up, will you? This is not the time to be sarcastic. Star! Nova! Can you keep the two teams relatively away from us while I find someone alone and get what we came here for?" Gerry demanded as they scrambled out of the warpath and down a side passage.

"Can a glishka beast float on air? Never mind we'll handle it. This is what I was born for. Party time!" Nova shouted gaily as she scattered herself all over the place. Star followed close by.

"Come on, you two, and stick close to us. Slick and I wrote this story so we know it better then anyone. I wrote the part we're currently in to be extremely bloody. Be on the lookout for any sign of danger," he said running while at the same time slowly integrating the four of them into the story. So far everyone was to busy fighting to notice their sudden appearance.

"What do we have to worry about? I mean I've only read one chapter!" Kelsey cried as they raced through the halls trying to avoid the battle raging on. Suddenly she was flung into a wall and came crashing down on top of a bust.

"KELSEY!"

"I'm fine just a little banged up. What was that?"

"Apparently that's whom we have to worry about harming us in this story," Kali said nervously pointing at their attacker. It was the Green Knight! Gerry had written that in the story the character, a mutant girl, had become evil and worked for the club as an enforcer. Right now it looked like she wanted to kill them for intruding.

"Uh oh, trouble. Look out!" Slick screamed as an optic blast came their way. They barely managed to avoid it as she kept strutting towards them. Her cape seemed to flow in the non -existent wind and her green lingerie outfits made her look very deadly.

"Gerry, take your imagination from her quick. Otherwise we're all dead meat!" Kelsey screamed as she tried to avoid being ripped apart by telekinesis.

170

"You will pay for intruding," the Green Knight said in monotone as she sent a hexbolt at the small group. It encased them all causing them to wither in pain. They sank to the floor unable to free themselves.

She was about to destroy them when Nova and Star appeared next to her. Quickly they restrained her arms and silenced her mind so she couldn't attack. "Gerry! Come touch her face quickly! Imagine a part of her flowing into you and you will get what you need. Hurry!" Star yelled. It was getting harder to control her.

Gerry rushed over and placed a hand on her cheek. Focusing his scared mind on his deadly creation he let the creative energy flow from her to him. He felt a cool rush of power as a green light entered his body. After a few seconds he let go and the Green Knight tumbled to the floor like a sac of potatoes.

"Let's scat. Reinforcements are coming this way," Gerry said still wheeling from the extraction process.

"Whose story do we got to next? I mean how do we even travel there?" Kali asked hurriedly. She kept glancing around looking for signs of danger.

"We just type in what we want. Here, like this," Slick said as a search engine magically appeared in front of them. Not wasting time wondering were it came from he typed in his info and the six of them were gone.

This time when they reappeared it was outside of a secret weapons facility on the other side of a ridge in the middle of a desert. It was nighttime and everything was eerily silent and still. There was no sounds, no breeze, nothing. Something didn't feel quite right.

One glance around told Kali exactly where and what story they where in. "Sinister Soldiers; right? Five members from the mutant comic universe turned into the perfect soldiers as members of Shadow Cell. This is the chapter with Shadow Cell's last big mission before they start stalking the heroes. Couldn't you have picked a story where we didn't have the chance of being blown up by automatic weapons and nuclear warheads Slick? I think we had enough of that in the last tale we visited."

"Hey, it was my most recent story in my profile and our only option at the time. Personally I thought you be a little more grateful to be out of that mansion. I know this story better then any of my others. There's tons of imagination lying about so we won't be here long, trust me." Slick told her.

"How do you plan to avoid being blown up then? I remember this chapter clearly," Kali replied icily. She wasn't really mad at him just scared. Out of the corner of her eye she saw Gerry whispering explanations to Kelsey who had never read Sinister Soldiers. Her eyes went wide in fear.

"Perhaps it be best if we employ the same method as before to capture the imagination. I'm sure we could secure someone without much difficulty for you to use," Star suggested. Nodding with approval she vanished into the night with Nova.

"Where exactly on Earth are we anyways? I mean I know we're in a desert and I know that you wrote that something bad is going to happen. What I don't get is why you're so tense. I mean its not like we can die in this reality," Kelsey commented bored as usual by the inactivity.

"It's not certain if we can or can't die. The rules of this reality are very different then the ones for ours. As long as we don't fully become part of the story we should be fine," replied Kali. Then under her breath she muttered, "In theory that is, at least."

The boys weren't paying much attention to the girls. They were to mesmerize by the scene. Slick was looking, smelling, and touching everything while Gerry stood over him smiling. He was impressed by every little detail. It matched perfectly with what he had written.

"I can't believe I'm actually here in my story! This place is exactly how I imagined it. Everything I described is perfectly matched. No detail, no matter how small, has been altered the slightest. I don't know about you, but I can't wait to go back home and type the ending the story."

"I know what you mean. This should be quite a chapter. Everything will have to be near perfect because I don't know if you'll be able to convey your feelings of this place accurately," Gerry told him softly. He gazed across the barren landscape looking for signs of danger.

Before he could reply they all heard excessive gunfire followed by the screams of people in tremendous distress. They looked at one another before they hurried over to the ridge to what was going on. They sneaked a peak and it took a lot of effort not to gag in horror at what they saw.

The weapons facility below had been attacked no, more like obliterated. The structure was barely standing, and lying all over the place were the dismembered bodies of men and women. Trucks, tanks, all types of vehicles had been torn in two, craters littered the ground and fires raged all over the facility engulfing what was left of the building. It was a nightmare come to life.

"No way in Hell am I going to forget this in a hundred years," Gerry whispered quietly. He closed his eyes trying to block the horrific sight from entering his mind.

"Well, I think that your computer game and your imagination have created the greatest soldiers ever. Congratulations Slick, you created a monster," Kali said sarcastically still stunned by the horror. Never, in all her life had she seen such bloodshed.

"I never imagined I would actually see this come to life! I just wanted to write a good military/action story is all. I can't help it if Shadow Cell is the perfect unit of soldiers. Its in their DNA!" he shot back at her horrified by what he had created.

"Well, you could have been a little less graphic. I'm going to be sick. Excuse me," Kelsey, who was positively green, said rushing off to puke. A few seconds later they heard the sounds of someone losing their lunch all over the place.

"Maybe I should see if she's doing okay. Besides I think you two could do with some alone time and she's needs company," Gerry volunteered leaving the two friends alone. He didn't want to get involved it want could become a lover's quarrel.

"Well, you have to admit their right about this. While reading about Shadow Cell blowing up weapons facilities and acting like they're not human is fun. In real life it makes the War on Terrorism seem like a school yard fight," Kali told Slick softly. She wanted to tear her eyes away from the massacre, but couldn't do so.

Slick placed his hands on her shoulders and turned her away from the bloody carnage. Maybe he shouldn't have mocked war like this. Seeing his creation come to life had shaken him deeply. And this was the tip of the iceberg if what had been shown them was true. He was about to voice his feelings on the subject when the climax of the chapter occurred. Shadow Cell had planned to blow the facility sky high, only they seem to have used too much dynamite. Instead of a controlled explosion, the place went up everywhere.

Burning chunks of metal rained down from the sky as a blistering heat wave swept through the desert. The wind howled and the stench of burnt flesh filled their noses. Everything went deaf as the explosion rocked the area. Gerry and Kelsey fell to the ground and rolled into a small cave.

A flaming fireball was heading straight at Slick and Kali who where frozen on the top of the ridge by fear. Kali tried to move, but was unable to summon the strength to move. She could hear people yelling at her to move, but her legs wouldn't respond to her commands. She was going to die.

Just before the fireball struck she felt someone shove her hard. She went tumbling head first down the ridge cutting herself up badly as she went. She stopped at the base of the ridge just outside the small cave. When she tried to get up she felt something heavy pin her down. Summoning all her strength, she shoved the weight off. Looking at her hand she was alarmed to see a huge amount of blood all over her, but it wasn't hers. It was Slick's who was lying half dead on the ground. His arms and legs were sticking at all angles, his face was torn up, and his had ribs sticking out of his chest along with several open wounds.

"Slick! God, Slick talk to me! Kelsey! Gerry! Get over here quickly, he's hurt!"

The two raced out of the cave to see if they could help him. One look was enough to convince them that he would die without medical intervention. But who was going to help save him?

Suddenly Nova and Star reappeared next to the fallen boy sides. They looked him over carefully before kneeling next to him. Nova started speaking quickly in the Entity tongue pointing to the boy's injuries. Star nodded and replied in the same language agreeing with her about something. Both placed their hands on Slick's shoulders and started to chant. First a black veil formed surrounded his body. Then a purple mist appeared around him and was absorbed into his skin. Slowly, but surely his injuries magically disappeared. A similar veil and mist surrounded Kali and she gave out a sharp cry as her injuries also disappeared. The veil and mist soon disappeared as the last of Slicks injuries were taken care of. Kali was examining herself impressed by what she saw.

Slick's eyes opened and he sat up, completely healed. He looked over at Kali smiling. "Kali, your okay. I was so sure I lost you. Come here," he said pulling her into a tight embrace. Then slowly the two of them kissed each other full on the lips for a good long time. Gerry and Kelsey watched in stunned disbelief as an imagination ball of yellow light formed between the two of them. "I loved doing that. We should do it more often."

"I'm just glad that you're alive. Thank heavens you're alive and well. I don't know what I would do without you. You mean so much to me and I couldn't live with myself if you died risking your life for me," Kali told him wiping away her tears.

"Hey, were friends and I was hoping to someday become more then just that. Besides I seem to have gotten what we came for," he said indicating the ball in his hands. In the midst of all the confusion he had managed to achieve the objective.

"You two should rest a few minutes after you're near death experiences your bodies need a chance to recover from the shock. My veil to ward off death may have stopped your spirits from leaving your bodies, but it was Star's mist of life that saved you from certain doom," Nova told them gently as she acted as lookout.

"Thank you both. You saved not only our lives, but helped get what we needed. This imagination is very powerful and should help us complete the mission quickly," Kali told them.

"That's the problem you guys. It's taking too long doing it one at a time. We need to get back home before Killnala gets bored and smashed our exit, so Kelsey and Gerry will go with Nova and get her imagination from one of her stories while you two come with me. We'll meet back at the entrance to the vortex in twenty minutes. Move out!"

With a slight pop Kali, Slick, and Star found themselves somewhere else in a new story. The air was stale and it smelled slightly. It took awhile for Kali's eyes to adjust in the dark, and she realized they were in a warehouse or an abandoned building. "I've seen this place somewhere before. Like I've seen it on TV before or wrote about it. It makes me feel, I don't know weird."

"What is it exactly you feel? Do you know were you have seen this place before?" Slick asked, concerned etched in his voice. He was also getting the strangest feelings about this place. It was different than the last story they'd been in. The emotions he had been feeling previously couldn't explain the ones he had now. It was a mixture of fear, worry, and concern instead of joy and pleasure mixed with excitement.

Star pressed a finger to her lips indicating they should be silent. Motioning to them to follow behind her as quietly as possible, she crept forward slowly through the building stealthily. Shrugging their shoulders, they followed her lead knowing she was right. As they crept forward they could make out the sounds of people yelling and the distinct sounds of a fight. Flashes of light spurred them on to hurry. They had to know what was going.

The closer they got to the noises, the more Kali felt strange and stranger. Her head was throbbing like crazy and her body was shaking. Her link with Star was becoming extremely muddled. She kept getting mixed images and thoughts in her mind. Star's voice seemed to be magnified by a hundred times. She clutched her head and squeezed her eyes shut and started humming in an attempt to block out the mixed messages. She took several deep breaths and let them out. She started to walk forward when the pain overwhelmed her and she fainted from the mental overload.

"Kali! Come on, Kali wake up. Wake up Kali, everything is okay. What's wrong with her? People don't faint for no reason. There has to be something that's hurting her," Slick said panicking as he checked her vitals. They seemed fine; there was no reason for her to have loss consciousness.

"I feared this would happen if we came here. Her link with me has been interrupted by another signal on the same frequency. Her brain simply couldn't process the two signals through one link all at once so it shut her body down for the time being in order to keep her alive. She'll be fine in a few minutes. If you'll carry her, we can collect our prize," Star informed him unconcerned. Her face only betrayed a hint of worry.

"Two signals? Interrupted link? What are you talking about? How could Kali possibly pick up another Entity's signal when she's exclusively linked to you?" Slick demanded as he carried Kali through the darkness.

He turned to face to the Entity. "Stop being cryptic it's annoying. I deserve a straight answer to what's going on here?" Star merely pointed and Slick let out a small gasp of amazement at what he saw.

There was a reason this place felt familiar to Kali. They were in the first season hideout of a one eyed mercenary watching Kali's rewrite of her favorite cartoon first season ending. Slick knew Kali had thought that ending to it could have been better, so she had written a spectacular extension entitled, "Dark Robin" which was the first in her three-part trilogy. The reason for Kali's condition was apparent to him at once. Hovering above the fighting oblivious to everyone was a past version of Star herself.

"As you can see that's the source of our problems. The same mental signal coming from the same person, only from two different time periods. My past self is completely unaware of the harm she is inadvertently causing Kali here. I never taught Kali how to deal with two completely different sets of memories at once. She is greatly confused by it and the best medicine for this would be for us to leave as quickly as possible."

"Then let's get what we came here for. What do we need to do in this story to collect the proper amount of imagination?"

"Nothing drastic if that's what's concerning you. Just let her feel her OC and we can be on our way. Follow me and stick close. I can't protect you from harm if we get separated in this mess," Star told him as she walked into the frenzy, completely oblivious to the danger around her. She didn't seem bothered by any of the fighting going on.

Slick took a deep breath and hefted Kali into a more comfortable position before plunging into the foray. It was extremely hard to match Star's brisk pace while carrying his heavy load. He was nearly plowed over by two of the teenage superheroes and had to jump out of the way quickly as a piece of metal came flying his way. He tightened his grip and continued to keep pace with Star. "This is madness. Do they have any idea that we're here?"

"No, the characters in the story are completely oblivious to our presence here. They will only become aware of us if we chose to become part of the story. Ah there's are target."

In the center of the room two teenage boys were fighting. Slick instantly knew who they were. The one on the right in the tattered red and green costume w and the one on the left who was wearing body armor and had glowing red eyes was Kali's character OC. Both boys were in a life and death battle.

Using her powers Star guided the evil OC towards Slick. When the boy stumbled backwards he left behind enough imaginative energy to light an entire stadium. "We have what we came for let's go."

They reappeared next to the entrance to the vortex in time to hear Kelsey talking up a storm about her encounters in her story, "The Princess and Me." They had no problems gathering any imagination and were startled by Kali's condition. Kelsey quickly took measures to wake her sister up by pinching her hard.

"Oww! That hurt! Why did you do that? What, Slick why are you carrying me? Put me down at once!"

Well it was fun while it lasted. Slick thought unhappily.

"Alright we are returning to your reality now. Everybody make sure you have your imagination at hand. When Star and I give the signal release it into the air and focus on joining it all together for one last attack. Hopefully it will be enough to send the Killgonas straight back home," Nova said as she activated the vortex.

Back in the regular reality Killnala was getting ready to destroy the computer and tear it to shreds. She was beyond furious, beyond rage at this point. When Killroary had returned to her empty handed it had taken all her self-control not to strangle him to death.

At the moment both of the Entity Eaters were standing ready to gobble up whatever came out of the computer screen. "They better come back through this contraption within the next two minutes or I'm going upstairs to kill the mother. I am not leaving this apartment without some type of kill," Killnala vowed angrily smashing the futon.

"I'll help you with that. I never should have left the father breathing back at the other house. We've been humiliated more then enough times during this mission. We deserve something for our troubles. If those Entities and the brats don't show soon we're going to have a real tough time explaining this mess to our Master. You know how the Nameless feels about failure."

Before she could reply to that, a blinding flash of light filled the small living room. The two foul creatures shielded their eyes against the intense brightness. Finally the brightness faded and in its place stood six people surrounding them.

One of the boys, the one with gray eyes took one look at them and let out a long whistle, "Man, you two weren't lying about these two. I have to admit they look a lot scarier then any design I could come up with."

Killnala growled at the comment. She sniffed the air trying to figure out who the interlopers were and how they came to be. What she smelled wasn't encouraging. "Your from Canada! That country is infested with too much flora and fauna! Your no better coming from the mountains of Virginia and smelling like education. But the worst smell is the one proofing your both soon to be Crystal Carriers! Its really sweet and touching if you think about it. Our Master was only expecting the bodies and energy of the Entities and the Chosen One. Now we get to bring back an entire smorgasbord!"

"Dream on that's never going to happen. Once you return back to your master empty handed it's the end of the line for you two. You go tell that black shroud of yours to go eat itself because the six of us aren't going to let you win this fight!" The other boy said spitting at them.

"Yeah, the two of you have over stayed your welcome. Get lost and never come back before we give you the boot!" Kelsey informed them picking up an empty soda can and hurling it at them. It smacked Killroary right in the nose.

Killroary's eyes changed from blue to red and he snarled at them angrily. How dare these pathetic life forms insult them and try and stand up to them. It was unheard of. Who did these people think they were? "No one insults us or the Nameless and lives to tell the tale. I don't care who you even think you are, but you're going to regret your actions and your words!" he told them as he leapt for Slick's neck.

Killnala hissed and whipped her entire body around. She flipped over the couch and slashing her claws as she aimed for the girls. "I'm going to enjoy killing you and drinking your blood!"

"I don't think so Killnala! This time you lose!" Nova shouted.

"Now! Concentrate with all your might on the things that inspire you and the love and joy from your stories. Let them build up and when they reach their peak combine them with Nova and mines gift!" Star shouted as she sent a wave of positive energy at Killnala halting her in her tracks.

The six friends held their hands in front of them letting them change from a soft white to a dark purple in color. Holding the balls above them, they let fly six balls of imagination joined together as one. The combined power of the imagination plus the friendship and love felt between the six friends, was more then enough to blow the Killgonas right out the door.

"NO! The love, the friendship, and that disgusting imagination it burns! I can't hold my form! Make it stop!" Killroary shrieked as he changed back. Next to him Killnala withered on the ground in pain. Her skin fell off in pieces revealing her blue scales underneath. With her remaining strength she transported the two of them back to the extinct reality.

Killana and Killarthur had been discussing the progress of their leaders when they heard a thump behind them. Turning around they let out a cry and rushed over to aid their fallen leaders. Both of them kept asking a dozen questions and demanding for details about everything as they used their metamorphic powers to heal their leaders. Finally Killnala yelled at them to be silent which they immediately.

"Thank you both for taking care of things while we were gone. You've done a wonderful job and both of you will be handsomely rewarded. Right now we need time to recover from our mission and discuss our opinions. Now is their anything that we need to take care of right away?" Killnala asked tiredly.

"Ye..ss. Yes there i.s is. The the Ma.. Mas... Master wishes to to speak with... you. It sounded extremely... angry," Killana stammered. She was frightened by whatever news the Nameless wanted to speak with their leader about.

Killnala's face paled and she shuddered at the prospect of her meeting. She knew that whatever happened next wouldn't be good for her. Determined to not look weak and keep some sense of dignity around her she reared up to full height. "Continue to update Killroary on what's been going on. Try and keep the moral up as well. I will be speaking with our Master in my private chambers. I don't want any interruptions."

Approaching the meeting area she could barely contain her fear. For the second time in her lifetime of service to the Nameless she had failed it and brought shame to herself. What would it do to her? Quickly she created a soundproof barrier around her so no one could interrupt her. She kneeled the best she could and spoke. *Master, it's your humble servant Killnala. I've returned from my mission to capture the Chosen One and getting rid of Star. I'm sorry to report I have failed in my duty to eliminate the girl or the Entity.*

Don't forget that you missed killing another Entity and three other soon to be Crystal Carriers! I trusted you to bring me the energy I needed to regain my strength and you failed! A girl with no powers and an injured Entity beat you several times during this mission! The Nameless shouted at her, its voice echoing loudly inside its servant's head.

Killnala felt an intense pain run through her body. She screamed in agony as she was twisted and nearly ripped in two by her Master's anger. *Please stop, Master I beg of you. I promise to do better next time!*

I will spare your miserable excuse for a life for now only because you succeeded in preventing the girl from gaining her powers. Your unique talents are needed in our final assault on Entara. Can I count on you to get the energy I require to be freed or will you fail again?

Of course, Master. I swear to you I will not fail a third time. Those Entities are as good as dead. The multiverse will be crushed. This time you will succeed in returning everything to a complete state of nothingness and nothing will prevent your victory, Killnala promised it.

Good. Be ready for my signal. Once I'm free I will be able to create a portal through the anti-universe and bring you straight to Entara. You and your brethren be ready to aid me in my victory.

We will be, Master. We strike tomorrow!

Back in Kali's living room, the group was discussing their options, which weren't many. The boys couldn't return home, the Entities had no idea how to deal with the Killgonas retreat, and Kali still needed to get her powers.

"Enough arguing! We are trying to avoid the truth and we don't have time for it. We have only one choice. If I am to gain my powers and save the entire multiverse, the four of us will accompany Star and Nova back to Entara."

"Back to Entara? But only Entities have ever been there before!" Kelsey exclaimed.

"Then we will be the first humans there. Time has run out. The time for the final battle is upon us and we need to be ready to bring the fight to them," Kali prophesized.

Chapter Fifteen

Kali was upstairs in her bedroom stuffing her bookbag full of items that would be essential to them in the final fight. Star hovered nearby wringing her hands, anxious to get going. Kelsey was downstairs with the rest of the gang preparing for final departure.

"I still don't know if this plan of yours is such a good idea. The Council was very adamant about you remaining here to receive your powers. They believed it was the only way to stop the Killgonas plan from happening."

"Star, please stop trying to persuade me to stay here because it won't work. We've done everything humanly and Entity possible to awaken my latent abilities, but nothing has resulted from it. Your techniques, healing the bond with Kelsey, and being united for the first time ever with Gerry and Slick hasn't helped in the slightest. We both know we only have hours left until the energy output occurs and if the Killgonas get that energy we're all doomed. Our best chance in saving the multiverse and Entara lies with the Council of Four. Hopefully they know something to help activate my powers," Kali told her as she put her jean jacket on over her purple long sleeve shirt and grapping a belt to tighten her jeans so they wouldn't fall. She looked up at her Entity counterpart waiting for an answer.

"But you intend to go to Entara! No one, but an Entity, has ever been there before. The idea of a mere Crystal Carrier going there is laughable! You can't even comprehend my true form. How in the world do you expect to deal with an entire world that's beyond your brains ability to comprehend?"

"Don't know and at the moment I don't really care. Right now the important thing is to get to Entara and try to prevent the Killgonas from taking the prime realities energy output. And if we fail to do that, prepare for the fight of our lives."

"Sometimes you are too stubborn for your own good. You remind me of myself; always willing to do whatever it takes to ensure that good wins. If we never unlock your Crystal Carrier powers at least we've unlocked the power of your loving heart."

"Thanks Star it means a lot to hear you say that."

"We mustn't waste anymore time then. If we want to meet with the Council about your Crystal Carrier powers we must leave at once. The Killgonas won't wait much longer to attack."

Hefting the heavy bag onto her shoulders she brushed back a stray hair from her face. She smiled confidently at her friend and showed no trace of fear at all. "Go join the others downstairs; I'll be right down. I just need to say goodbye to Mom."

Star understood her need for privacy and glided down the stairs and out of sight. Screwing up her courage Kali tiptoed into her Mom's bedroom to give her Mom what could be her final hug and kiss goodbye.

Her mom was sleeping peacefully unaware of the danger going on around her. Oso was resting comfortably at the foot of the bed making sure nothing disturbed his mistress. Picking her way across the room, she finally made it to the bed.

"Goodbye, Mom, be safe. Know that I love you no matter what and I'll be back as soon as possible. I promise I won't stay out to late or get in any trouble. Kelsey, Gerry, Slick, and I just have help Star and Nova save the entire multiverse from destruction and send the Nameless back to the anti-universe. Don't worry your head off I'll be fine. I love you," she whispered into her ear. She gave her a quick hug and kiss and left the room.

When Kali rejoined the others they were sitting on the futon waiting impatiently for her. "What took you so long? I was getting bored talking to these two," Kelsey chastised her.

"I'm sorry. I had something I needed to take care of. Okay, last chance to stay here. Where I'm heading it isn't safe at all. There is every chance I'm going to die so unless your willing to risk your life for a great cause get out of this room," Kali informed them. She looked at each of them one by one making sure they understood the danger they were putting themselves in. She was scared to death, but she couldn't admit that to them. She hoped at least one of them would come with her.

"Are you kidding? Me, not going on the adventure of lifetime and see the places you've described? You're out of your mind to think we would let you go alone. Besides, you're my ticket home and I'm not letting you out of my sight," Gerry told her grinning.

"Besides, you need all the help you can get to keep this Nameless creature locked up tight as a steel drum," Slick added. He was determined not to let her or the others down.

"So quit stalling already. We have a multiverse to save and a planet to visit," Kelsey cheered.

"Thank you, all of you. I don't think I could've done this alone. No matter what happens, I'm glad the four of us finally got to meet," Kali told them happily. "It's up to you two get us where we need to be. Think you have enough power for this?"

"Girlfriend, we have more than enough for something as simple as this. Hold tightly to one another and don't let go until I tell you to. Entity Reality Travels is taking off in five," joked Nova pleased to be going home.

They all took each other's hands and hung on tightly to one another. The twin Entities auras became more visible to the naked eye as their powers merged together to open the reality bubble. The bubble swallowed them up and they were gone. The trip only lasted for a second, but it was incredible. They were traveling at lightspeed to a place that didn't exist within normal time and space. What would they discover once they got there?

Guardian and his family had been standing guard over the reality bubble for weeks. They had attempted numerous times to contact either Star or Nova, but to no avail. They all feared the girls had been destroyed. The lack of any evidence otherwise didn't calm the storm of their minds.

"Why do we stand here waiting for two people who aren't coming home? We have to be practical here, they're dead!" Jasmine stated angrily swishing her robes around. The past few weeks had been nothing, but agonizing torture. Even with Asteroid's help the children of Entara were nowhere near ready to face the onslaught of the Killgonas or the Nameless.

"We don't know that for certain, my dear child. Aren't you the one who said we shouldn't be giving up on hope only weeks ago? Trust me, everything will be fine I can feel it. Star and Nova have never let us down and they aren't about to start now," her father said holding her tightly. He too, was near a panic. In his entire lifetime never had he felt this much fear as he did now. Not even the first time they had faced down their foes.

Before she could reply, the reality bubble began to pulsate like crazy. The room began to shake uncontrollably and the three Acolytes fell flat on their faces. Something or someone had activated the reality bubble and was coming through.

"I've never seen a reality bubble react like this before. Something strange is happening and I don't know if it's a good thing," Sapphire said out loud. She shielded her eyes as a brilliant light bathed the young family and the entire room as the reality bubble continued to act up.

With one final pulse the bubble split open and out tumbled four humans and two Entities into a heap on the floor. The Acolytes got up and ran over to see if everyone was okay and who the newcomers were. They were shocked to discover they were human beings. It was unthinkable to imagine mere mortals coming to Entara, let alone being sane!

"You're back! Thank the Celestial Gods your both back and in one piece. I feared that the danger had proven too much for you two and that you had died. Did you complete your mission? Is Entara safe once more?" Jasmine asked anxious for an answer. Her eyes searched for reassurance, but found none.

"Not exactly I'm afraid. We ran into some difficulties along the way that shorten the amount of time we had. Not to mention our little run in with the Killgonas that nearly cost us our lives," Nova explained to her. The Entity of Evil looked her friend over wondering what had caused Jazz's state of ill health.

"We did bring the Chosen One, her two friends and sister here. That's them over there with your folks. I'm stunned that they're not suffering brain damage from being here," Star said gazing at the humans in disbelief. She was astonished by how easily they reacted to Entara. It went against everything she'd been taught.

"Your human companions are fine. I believe it is a combination of their own will and crystal energy that is allowing them to exist here without problems. Remarkable indeed. But to be on the safe side I'll alter their minds perception so they can comprehend the world around them without suffering any ill effects to their bodies or minds," Sapphire informed them.

"May I ask what happened that made you desperate enough for you to risk the lives of the Chosen One and three other soon to be Crystal Carriers? It's not like you to gamble with lives Star," Guardian asked her.

"Believe us we had no other choice in the matter. It would take too long to explain everything to you. Time that we unfortunately don't have. Suffice it to say we need to talk to the Council like yesterday. And don't give us the runaround because we're running low on patience as well as time," Nova said hurriedly.

They got no argument from the three Acolytes. They took the six of them straight to the Council's Sanctuary. The Council was in the midst of making final battle plans for the eventual confrontation with their ancient foes. They were surprised to see the girls and shocked by their guests.

"Star! Nova! I'm shocked to see you two here. I hoped by your prolong absence you had completed your task. Have you?" Time asked hopefully. He looked tired like he hadn't slept in days and his brilliance had faded considerably. He was nearly unrecognizable as the Master of all Time.

"No, sir I'm sorry to report we haven't. We've run into a lot of unforeseen difficulties on this mission. We have failed in our quest to awaken Kali's powers. However if you hear us out, Kali, her friends and family, and myself included, I think there's still a chance to save the mission," Star began.

"Then tell us your story as quickly as possible, child. Don't keep us in suspense," Emotion prompted. Her freckles had dulled since the last time Star had seen her. She looked like she had undergone a major depression depleting her of her emotional powers.

It took the better part of an hour to get through the entire story from start to finish. Nova couldn't resist adding her own input while Slick, Kelsey, and even Gerry put their two cents in about the events. Only Kali remained silent throughout the tale never moving.

"And that's when we sent Killnala and her boyfriend back to where they came from. After that it was a simple matter of coming here hoping for your help," Star said wrapping up the story.

"You both performed splendidly under circumstances. Your never once abandoned your mission and kept your heads on straight during a life and death situation. I am willing to forgo your final exams and instate both of you as fully graduate Entities. After the crisis is dealt with of course," Wisdom informed pleased by the two. But even the pleasure in his voice couldn't hide the fact that his clothes weren't on straight and his scales were peeling off right in front of them.

"That certainly explains the presence of these non Entities here in our Sanctuary. But I'm unsure how were going to get the backup seal now," Nature confessed. She looked the worst surrounded by dead plants.

That's when Kali stepped forward and bowed respectfully to each member of the Council. "Honorable Council Members', I ask that you listen to me and ponder carefully what I have to say. It could mean the difference between life and death for all of us. I have no idea why my powers haven't emerged. Nothing seems to work at all. I came here in the hopes the four you might be able to solve this little problem. After all you're the ones who chose me for the job as your champion, your Chosen One. Your plan to have me create a power surge by working in conjunction with Star so that we reset the energy barrier thus producing the backup seal is still the best plan available. However we must stall for time by using the backup plan that you devised until my powers emerge. I can vouch for my sister and friends here, that while their powers may be small compared to my supposed ones their hearts aren't. Allow them to help in the coming battle. They will not disappoint you. Truth is, you can't turn them down. You need all the help you can get for this fight."

"Kali speaks the truth honorable Councilmen. We may not understand everything that is happening, but we don't need to. We are willing to fight with you to protect the lives of everyone in the multiverse. Allow us to fight, the Nameless can't be freed," Gerry stated eloquently stepping forward ready to fight.

"Its our duty as almost recognized Crystal Carriers to help protect the delicate balance between good and evil. Without that balance everything else in the multiverse will cease to exist," Slick added catching on to the momentum.

"We can hold our own in a battle. We stood up to two Killgonas and survived to tell the tale. That must tell you something about our courage and bravery. The time to end this conflict once and for all is now," Kelsey said finishing for their proposal.

The four friends grabbed each other's hands firmly. Smiling at one another they looked at the Council with hope in their eyes. They were ready to complete their duty. Never before in their lives have any of them been so sure about something as they were now. They had embraced their destiny whole-heartedly.

"We thank you for both your honesty, and your willingness to help. Your loyalty is equal to that of one of us. Your ability to stand here before us proves beyond a shadow of a doubt that you are Crystal Carriers of the highest caliber. Since we do need all the help we can get and time is running short, we have no choice, but to accept your generous offer," Emotion told them kindly. The four of them cheered with delight.

"I hope that the four of you understand the seriousness of your request. By taking up the call of duty today you are risking your immortal souls," Wisdom pointed out.

"If we die today it won't matter what happens to our immortal soul. Everyone's soul is in jeopardy with the Nameless loose. By fighting along side you we know that we are dieing doing what is right," Kali said firmly. The others echoed her words unafraid by the news.

"If I may say so Council, if you are so concerned about them helping us the why not give them an edge? Bestow upon them a blessing of sorts to aid them in the coming battle. I know from personal experience your gifts are quite powerful," Star suggested humbly.

"Besides their going to need every advantage if they're going up against a swarm of bloodthirsty monsters," Nova added.

The Council of Four looked at one another and nodded. They raised their symbols above their heads and each cast their powers over a separate individual bestowing upon them a small fraction of their power. Hopefully this would protect the four humans from great harm.

After they were done they sent for a messenger. The messenger arrived and escorted the boys to the front lines to help command the troops. Gerry had been selected to help lead the adults to victory and should he fail, Slick was ready with the children to defend the Grand Meeting Hall. Only the girls remained behind to provide a final defense for the Council.

"Child, we have thought long and hard about your predicament and it still an enigma to us. Our symbols have never lied to us before. If they prophesied you as the Chosen One selected to save us you are. We keep coming back to the grand design of our original plan. When two beings become one the multiverse will be saved and apparently that hasn't occurred. Its most puzzling," Nature mused.

"But I don't understand that. How can two beings become one? I was bonded to Star for a week and nothing happened! If that isn't two as one I don't know what is," Kali said frustrated. She had been agonizing over this stupid prophecy for days and still the answer eluded her! What was she missing? What clue would unravel this mystery?

"I know my dear. It's frustrating for all of us. But you must try to remain calm." Wisdom told her patiently. He too was frustrated, but he couldn't let his fears override his logic. That would only make the situation worse.

"Maybe you aren't supposed to take what they're saying literally. Maybe it means something else entirely," Kelsey suggested helpfully. Abstract thinking wasn't her strong suit, but she was trying to assist the best she could.

"But what else could it possibly mean?" Nova wondered.

Before anyone could respond an alarm went off throughout the entire building. Lights began to flicker and sirens were blaring. Outside the rainbow colored sky went pure black and it became very cold. Throughout the capital and the rest of the planet everything shut down. Entara seemed to be dying. It could only mean one thing; their time was up.

In the cosmic plane that divided the multiverse and Entara from one another strange things were beginning to happen. The prime realities were reaching critical energy output causing the energy barrier to go nuts. Throughout the realities the protectors felt a sudden sense of dread as their crystals went dark for the first time in their lives.

The prime realities crackled and strain under the pressure. The energy that had been building up for so long was released in a mighty wave. It went crashing through the rest of the energy barrier leaving a wake of destruction in its path as it headed towards Entara. The Killgonas were ready and waiting to intercept the energy wave. All two hundred attack dogs were position right between the last reality and Entara. They had their jaws wide-open ready for the feast of a lifetime. Centuries of planning all came down to this.

"Hold steady. Wait for it. NOW!" Killnala ordered sending her brethren to collect the energy they had waited for so long.

The entire group rushed forward as if shot from a cannon. They enveloped themselves in the glorious, bountiful, sweet tasting energy swallowing every last drop of it. They let out screams of delight as they felt themselves be recharged to full fighting strength. Then they began to transmit the remaining energy to the Master.

The Nameless was waiting with great anticipation for this moment in the anti-universe. Slowly at first, but soon faster and faster the energy poured into its body revitalizing it. Within moments it had regain all of its former power. Using its newfound navigational abilities it headed straight for the doors to its prison. It was time for revenge against those wretched Entities!

On the other side of the door the three hundred Acolytes stood ready for anything that came bursting into the chamber. Already the door was showing signs of strain. Huge cracks had formed in it as something pounded against it. Pieces of the stone wall came crashing down. The lights flickered on and off and the entire Temple shook as tremors racked the ancient structure.

"Stand ready! Remember to use all you have in this fight, because no matter what we can't let the Nameless escape. Nor can we allow it to form a portal between the anti-universe and the multiverse, which would unleash the Killgonas upon Entara. Do what you must to protect our home!" Guardian ordered. He looked at each member of his Congregation knowing in his heart they would do what was necessary. He gazed lovingly at his own family and swallowed hard. He prayed to the Celestial Gods everywhere that this wasn't the end. He wanted to save the multiverse, Entara, and his race, but most importantly he wanted to save his precious wife and his little girl.

Sapphire looked longingly at her loving husband and precious daughter. Nothing in their long-lived lives could prepare them for this. If they lost here, the Nameless and its Killgonas would win sealing the fate of the entire multiverse forever. As she gave her husband one last reassuring look she prayed that this wouldn't be their last night together.

Jasmine was ready to fight despite her own fears of what they were about to face. She didn't know if her powers would make much of a difference, but she was going to try her hardest to keep everything she held dear safe from harm. She would rather die then allow the Temple and its contents to be eaten. She was concentrating so hard; she nearly missed what happened next.

The doors glowed brilliantly as the weakened seal tried to contain the monstrosity behind it. The chains were stretched to their limits. With one final shove they broke apart and fell to the floor in a clatter. The seal deteriorated completely causing the door to lose its glow. The doors were flung open and standing in the doorway was the most feared being ever. The Nameless floated out swiftly followed by the Killgonas, who came rushing out the portal behind it.

"Kill them, kill them all. Destroy everything you come across, but leave the Council of Four to me!" The Nameless said simply, its red brain pulsating. Finally after all this time, after eons of its tortures existence, it would finally have its revenge!

"ATTACK!" roared Killnala to her brethren. "The time for bloodshed and revenge is upon us! Destroy every last stinking Entity! Leave no one breathing!" With those words the brethren of Killgonas launched themselves at the Congregation.

"Acolytes defend yourself!" Guardian shouted letting loose a powerful burst of raw power right into the heart of the swarming mass. His powers over protection and guarding were intensified by the situation. It was just the edge he needed in this type of situation.

Within minutes everyone was in a life a death struggle. One Killgona attacking at least two Acolytes at once in a life and death showdown. Each Acolyte giving it all they had to stop the threat. They were attempting to force them back into the portal with little luck.

The Nameless was already on its way out when the one hundred eldest Acolytes attacked it. Guardian and Sapphire led the attack hoping that their combined attack would be enough to stop the threat, but The Nameless just ignored them as it headed for the exit.

"You will not leave this chamber!" Guardian shouted rearranging space in order to bar the exit. His eyes blazed with barely contained anger. How dare this creature try to destroy his home? The entire multiverse just so it could die! It was totally selfish! "Your new reign of terror will not come to pass!"

The Nameless spread its shroud around him. Guardian sank to the floor coughing as the darkness surrounded him. He could feel the Nameless attempting to erase him from existence. He struggled to summon his powers to free himself, but his powers were to weak. It was the end for him.

Suddenly the darkness was driven away and he heard the distant echo of something in pain. He took a deep breath of fresh air. He was trembling all over and he had been slightly blinded from his encounter he couldn't tell who his savior was until they spoke.

"STAY AWAY FROM MY HUSBAND!" Sapphire shouted sending a massive wave of energy at the anti creature. It backed off for a moment recovering its strength. Sapphire rushed over to her fallen husband. "My love, are you okay?"

Before he could respond some else did. "He's fine, but neither of you will be for long." Killana said acidly. With a flick of her claw, she impaled both of them releasing her poison. She smiled as they fell to ground in a heap. They'd be dead within minutes. But why wait? Why not eat them now?

Killana opened her jaws wide to bite them in half when Killarthur smacked her hard with his tail. She growled at him annoyed and snapped her jaws at him. "Why did you stop me from finishing them off?" she demanded.

Killarthur didn't even flinch. It took more then her snapping at him and threatening to break him into two to scare him. Without missing a beat he transformed into his humanoid form. "Have you lost your senses? Stick to the plan. The Congregation has been incapacitated. Right now the two of us, plus ninety eight others must secure the Temple for the next phase in our plan."

"I know, I know! Once the Temple has been secure we blow it sky high so the Entities can't escape to the multiverse or seal the Master back into the anti-universe. But why can't we be on Killnala and Killroary's strike team," she whined turning into her humanoid form for easy mobility.

"Because I ordered it so. Now if you two are done blathering, get to work! I will be searching for the Council," The Nameless said as it left the chamber. Shrugging their shoulders they got to work securing the Temple along with the rest of their small group.

Jasmine had been gravely injured in the fight, but wasn't dead yet. She moaned at the sight of seeing the Congregation strewn across the chamber all of them near death. She crawled over to her parent and put her hands over their wounds. "Heal, please heal," she whispered but nothing happened. All she saw were her blood soaked hands. "Mom, Dad, please hang on. I'm sure that the Council will be victorious and they'll be able to cure you. Don't give up just yet," she whispered to them, but even she didn't believe what she said.

Killnala marched her troops through the halls diligently as her Master led the way. Already the next phase in the plan had begun. The Temple's glory was vanishing from sight as the Nameless turned it into nothing. She smiled pleased that victory was in their grasp. "I can hardly believe that we're finally on Entara! After all this time and all the probes we sent I expected something grander then this dump. This world of theirs is too innocent and fragile. What a major let down."

"Don't worry about the planet, worry about its people. They are probably waiting for us outside this place. This time around the Killgonas will be the ones singing in triumph. Nothing can stop us from destroying Entara. No Crystal Carrier, no Entity, and certainly not some mystical Chosen One!" Killroary laughed.

Laughing along with him Killnala strolled up to the front doors and flung them wide open. She smirked at what she saw waiting for them at the foot of the steps. Standing there was every adult Entity plus Gerry.

Gerry had gotten a major makeover. He was wearing custom fit silver body armor with timepieces etched all over it. On his waist hung a multiweapon utility belt. He was carrying a samurai sword, which was pointed straight at her. "This is as far as you, your brethren, and your master goes! Surrender now, and no one has to get hurt!" Gerry commanded.

"So this is who they send to lead the ultimate battle? A kid whose mind is too absorbed with make believe to notice the real world. Pitiful," Killnala replied shaking her head in amusement. What was the Council thinking? Sending an unrecognized Crystal Carrier to fight their battle was a sign of desperation.

"Looks can be deceiving, Killnala. I ask you and your kind one more time. Stand down and return to your own reality!"

"Forget it! We've waited three eons for this moment. Now that we're so close to the end of our quest, nothing shall prevent us from bringing the end to everything in existence! Master, let us continue on our way. My team of females shall protect you. Killroary, dispose these do gooder interlopers with your males once and for all."

"Right, go now my love and be victorious," Killroary told her giving her a farewell kiss. With tremendous leap the females and the Nameless vaulted over the adults and continued on their way towards the Grand Meeting Hall.

"Don't worry about them. Worry about my brothers and me. You may outnumber us greatly, but we shall overwhelm you with our power. Get them!" he ordered as his brothers descend upon the group. The Killgonas shifted into a dozen deadly forms in mid air before jumping into the frenzy. All hell broke lose as everything and everyone was separated in the chaotic mess of battle.

Sun found herself cornered next to her favorite art gallery. She glared up at her opponent who had shifted into a giant razor beast. He was twenty feet tall with razor sharp spikes all over his brown body and had six-inch long tusks pointing out at her.

"You think you can invade our home and destroy us along with it? I don't think so. Take this!" She shouted igniting a solar flare beneath her attackers feet causing him to jump around in pain.

"You're all the same. You Entities think you're so self-righteous and honorable. Well, I think you're nothing, but a bunch of selfish brats!" growled the Killgona as he sent a barrage of spikes at her.

Sun sprang out of the way and launched another well-timed attack. This time she released the full fury of a newborn star. Most creatures would have been incinerated, but instead he *ate* it. Sun stumbled backwards in astonishment.

"Did you think we were to stupid to have learned some new tricks? This isn't three eons ago lady. Your attacks are to predictable so is it any wonder that your doomed?"

Suddenly a small moon hit him in the back of the head. "Step away from her, now!" Moon commanded. Several moons still orbited around him. His entire focus was on protecting his wife from harm.

"Bring it on old timer. I'm not afraid of you or any of your kind. Your stupid parlor tricks can't harm my form," the Killgona boasted proudly as he licked his lips in anticipation.

Moon paid him no heed as he reversed the orbit of the moons sending them back at the beast. This time he was ready for the attack. The creature morphed its body till its arms became chutes, which sent the moons shooting back at Moon. They pelted him in the stomach and a well place spike sent him crashing into the museum located next to the gallery.

"Too bad. Better luck next time," the Killgona said changing into his true form so he could gloat.

"Forget about little old me?" Sun shouted hurling a massive energy amount at him, which he narrowly dodged.

He kicked off the side of the building and came back at her for another attempt. "Time for you to die once and for all!"

Sun quickly teleported out of the way and reappeared next her husband side. She helped him up. "Come on lets double team him. There's no way he can take two of us."

"Your right, lets do it," he said. Together they flew into the air and attacked with a double eclipse attack. Their adversary screamed in pain as he absorbed the full impact of the attack. He crumbled to the ground in a withering heap.

"I really hope that Gerry is doing a better job then we are," Sun muttered under her breath. This fight was worse then any battle she had ever fought in the war and it was only going to get worse from here on in.

"We can only hope my dear. Time to get back to work," Moon replied as they hurried back into the battle.

Gerry was holding his own up against Killroary himself in a one on one fight to the finish. Killroary kept his normal head and tail, but had his human body. Round and round the two of them circled looking for an opening to attack.

"You're the poorest excuse for a warrior I've ever laid eyes on. I'll bet you've never even used a weapon before in your life. I know your type. You never like to risk anything. Destroying you will be pitifully easy," Killroary said as he tried to mess with his mind.

Gerry wasn't even fazed by him. This guy was a big pushover who had a big ego. His collage roommate had been scarier then him. "You going to talk all day or what? Come on Killroary show me you can fight!"

"You seem very eager to die. I was going to give you a quick and painless death, but after you banished me and getting my love in trouble, I'll think I'll make you suffer," he growled. Then without warning he launched himself at his throat.

Gerry brought his sword up just in time to block him. He pushed him back and punched him in the side followed by a spinning kick that sent Killroary into a store window. "Want more, tough guy?"

Killroary brushed off the broken shards of glass and looked at his wounded body. Gerry approached him cautiously waiting to see what he would do.

Without warning Killroary lashed out his tail and it snaked it's way around Gerry's body bringing him down. Gerry tried to grab something as he was dragged across the road, but couldn't find a hold. Soon he was in front of Killroary who looked ticked off. Without a word he began to ravage the armor as he attempt to get to his soft flesh underneath. "AHH! Someone help me!"

Right before he was about to be decapitated he felt one of the etchings on the armor come to life. A huge hourglass appeared in the air and trapped the Killgona inside. "No! I will not be contained!" Killroary roared as he pounded on the glass.

Gerry took no notice as something extraordinary was happening with his armor. The silver armor was repairing itself at lighting fast speeds. His wounds had also healed. He smiled at his prisoner. "It seems as Time's champion I have a certain advantage over you."

"Time can't protect you from everything boy! My poison is lethal!"

But to both their surprise the poison wasn't affecting Gerry at all. Instead Gerry's heart was glowing a brilliant blue color. In a flash of light his crystal necklace appeared around his neck revitalizing him and granting him new fantastic powers. "Seems I'm finally a full fledge Crystal Carrier. That means you and the rest of your kind can't touch me anymore."

"Guess again boy! We're at war so the ancient rules don't apply anymore," Killroary informed him, as he broke free.

Gerry quickly touched his crystal and let its warmth spread through his body. With a snap of his fingers every piece of art he had ever drawn came to life in front of him. "If you want me you'll have to get through my army. To the death!"

At the same time Gerry's forces were fighting the male Killgonas, Killnala's own forces had run into their own opposition just outside the Grand Meeting Hall. While Killnala and the Nameless slipped through the gates to get to the Council, her troops stayed behind to battle Slick's and Asteroid's troops. It was pandemonium as the kids tried their hardest to protect the most sacred spot in all of Entara. But the female Killgonas were equally determined to get rid of them and the structure behind them.

Faith flew in the air her hands clasped in a praying position. "Perhaps you ladies need to channel your energies into something more positive. Might I suggest Buddhism?" From the sky rained down statues of Buddha. The Entity of Faith and Religion smiled as her bombs hit their targets.

"Keep your filthy religion to yourself!" One particular Killgona with a scar over her right eye shouted. She picked up a fallen statue and chucked it at Faith damaging one of her wings. Faith came crashing down like a ton of bricks.

"Nobody hurts my friends like that! Hope you guys like hover ball because I'm a pro!" Sporty shouted using a black racket to hit a hovering sphere into the crowd. Her ball bounced off several targets before returning to her. "Bulls eye!" Sporty didn't see the building collapse on her. Animal and Gem rushed over to help her each using their own powers to clear a path. They cleared the rubble and found Sporty shaken, but still alive. After helping her and Faith the four friends rushed back into battle determined to keep their home alive.

Asteroid was using all the power he could muster to pen in the Killgonas. He sent meteor showers and asteroid belts into the crowd, but was having little success. Training children to fight in battle had been tough, but leading them into battle was even harder. He was grateful for the assistance Slick gave him.

Slick was all over the place helping out wherever he could. His green body armor shone brightly and you could make out the plant designs coming to life on it. He used a blowgun to defend himself as well as his new crystal necklace. "Report Asteroid. What's the situation?" he asked as he jumped down next the boy.

"We can't hold out much longer Slick. We're being overwhelmed at all fronts. As long as the Nameless roams free through Entara our powers will be weakened," Asteroid replied wiping blood off his face.

"We have to keep going! The Council, your sisters, and the twins need more time. We have to try to end this fight now and prevent the Nameless from reaching them. Look out!" Slick shouted extending his force field to protect the young boy from a powerful blast of energy from the Killgonas.

"Man, I really hope the girls have better luck then us," Asteroid stated as he readied himself for another onslaught.

Killnala blasted the doors apart and strode up the stairs towards the Inner Sanctuary. "We must hurry, Master. I sense that our forces are weakening. Apparently the Entities have more fight in them then we originally thought. Even with their world dying around them they continue to fight simply amazing. If we don't take the Council's powers soon it won't matter if we destroy the Temple at all," she warned her Master.

"I understand. They're not that far away I can sense their presences. With Entara dying they are far too weak to hold me off for long. You just handle anything and anyone who gets in the way," The Nameless instructed her as they flung open the doors to the Sanctuary.

"Hey, punk princess. I hope you like playing with balls because here's a bunch of them!" A voice called out from the shadows. Out of nowhere the two of them were pelted by kickballs, basketballs, and even stress balls. Stepping out of the shadows was Kelsey wearing magenta colored armor. Every emotion there was beautifully engraved on it. In her hands she held a knife, which she pointed at them. Standing behind her in a protective space was the Council of Four. "Can I help you two with anything?"

Killnala looked at as if she was a joke. "You're the last line of defense? I must say this is easier then I expected. Oww!" Killnala yelled as a novaburst hit her in the side. She pressed her wound closed and looked around for the source of the attack. She didn't have to search long. Nova dropped down from the ceiling and back flipped next to Kelsey. "She's not alone in protecting the Council from you and your evil master."

"Nova, I should have guessed. Pity you're not your sister. She's the one I have a problem with."

"I don't care about your petty thirst for vengeance. Kill them both so I may erase the Council for good. After I have done that nothing will stand in my way of completing my quest."

"Except for maybe me and Star! You will not succeed, Nameless. You and your forces will lose and I will put you back where you belong, which is in the anti-universe," Kali stated solemnly stepping into sight. Her blue body armor glisten as her book designs caught the light. She carried no weapons all she had with her was her book bag.

The Nameless turned its attention to Kali. This was the major threat to its plan? The Council's powers must be weaker then it thought. This girl wasn't any trouble at all. "I shall enjoy turning your remains to nothing. Killnala, don't fail me this time. Take care of them."

"With pleasure, my Master. You won't be disappointed," she purred extending her nails and opening her jaws wide. Her blue tendrils pulsated with life. "I've waited three eons for this moment, Star. You will finally meet your demise."

"Bring it on Killnala. Its about time we end this conflict between us," Star said calmly.

Killnala flipped into the air and spun around fast whipping her nails around attempting to tear open Star's chest. Star back flipped out of the way and fired a starburst at her opponent.

The attack went right through Killnala's body. She stood on her hands and spin kicked all four of them in the chest. Flipping to her feet she grabbed Nova's arm and hurled her over her shoulders. With a flick of her wrist she sent Kelsey crashing into the video wall. She then flipped over and got Star into a headlock. "Can you feel your pitiful existence ending?" she asked licking Star's face with her long, wet, tongue. "I can taste your fear."

"Get a breath mint why don't you!" Star coughed elbowing her in the ribs. Killnala merely grunted and held on tighter. She wasn't about to let her prey go now. A sudden flash of light blinded her causing her to release her prey. Growling she looked to see Kali smiling as she snapped more photos of her blinding her with the light from the flash. "Never underestimate your opponent! You never know what they will come up with!"

"Like, take this ordinary clothes hanger for instance. It does a lot more then hold your garments up," Kelsey informed her as she used the hooks to trip the Killgona up.

Killnala rolled over and pinned Kelsey to the ground. She was in a full-blown rage as she attempted to tear the armor off. But her anger just fed the armors natural defenses making it stronger and more resistant to damage. "Why won't this stuff come off?!" she screamed. Suddenly the sound of music at maximum volume filled the air. She clutched her ears in pain and stood up. "What is that horrible racket?" she wailed.

"Creativity at full blast. I know your strengths and your weaknesses, Killnala. You thrive on cold, bloodshed, and destruction. Your cruelty knows no limits. But you can't stand creativity, load noises, and friendship because you were created from dead star matter in the cold, dark, depths of space! I guess a bit of Wisdom's knowledge rubbed off on me huh?" Kali said holding the CD player high above her head. She was grinning widely at her own ingenuity.

"That does it! I'm sick to death of you four interfering with my plans! You've embarrassed me in front of my Master for the last time. I don't care what it takes, but I will kill you all and tear you up into a hundred tiny pieces!" Killnala replied in full-blown rage. She then grew and grew until she was twelve feet tall. "Nothing you do can stop me now!"

"Maybe she can't stop you, but Nova and I can! Sis, lets combine our powers together. Maybe we can finally get rid of her!" Star cried out firing all her power at the monster before her.

"Right back at you sis!" Nova yelled as she sent all her power at the evil being. She focused on giving all she had to defeat Killnala once and for all.

Black and red power combined with blue and purple to form a brilliant white beam of light. The beam shot straight for Killnala who didn't seem concerned.

Killnala extended her own hands pouring all her power into a single dark gray beam, which she aimed at the twin's white one. "You'll never defeat me!"

The two beams of power met and there was a huge explosion. Neither one was gaining ground in the fight. Kali and Kelsey could only watch helplessly as the gray beam started to eat up the white one.

"The end is near. You've lost. Your world, your friends and family, and your precious home gone! Give up and accept your fate!"

"Never!" the girls said in unison. With renewed strength they tripled the beams power. It obliterated the gray beam and hit Killnala square in the chest sending her crashing through the windows.

"NOOO! I won't be defeated!" she screamed as she fell. She hit the ground nearly impaling herself on the gate. She reverted to her normal body and twitched once before lying still on the ground knocked out. She was defeated.

The feeling of triumph didn't last long. Screams alerted them to the Council's peril. Whirling around they saw the Nameless was almost through the protective barrier. Their fight with Killnala had given the Nameless ample time to strike.

"Leave them alone you beast!" Star commanded tossing the thrones at it. She then used her elemental powers to create a huge fire, which engulfed it.

The Nameless extended its shroud and reverted the fire and thrones into nothing. "You are powerless to stop me. And for the record, you're the monster not me."

"Let me try something, sis. Let's see how he handles some transmogrification," Nova stated changing the broken shards of glass to hot metal. Picking up a good size piece, she hurled it at the anti-creature pinning it to the ground. "Yes! What?"

The Nameless had freed itself and went back to its task of ignoring them. Kelsey touched two emotions on her armor, bravery and love. They glowed and their energy filled her knife. She took a swipe at the Nameless depositing the emotions inside it with no effect at all on it. Kali let the texts on her armor come to life. She read several pages out of them using the words to block the Nameless progress. She too was defeated when it ate her right through her powerful words. Was there no stopping this creature?

"That's enough! Leave me alone now!" It commanded them as the four girls rushed it. It let them attack it futility for a few moment before tying them up with fragments of itself. "Now to complete my quest," it said just as the barrier disappeared.

"No! Council Members fight! Use your symbols to protect yourself!" Star screamed in a panic.

Time stepped forward and pointed his scepter at the heart of the Nameless. "This has gone on long enough. Time for you to go extinct!" he shouted sending a wave of time at the anti-creature. Time held on to his scepter tightly as he turn the hands of time back. Soon he collapsed to the ground to tired to fight on.

"Foolish Time. You can't get rid of me with your powers because I am nothing!"

"Try this on for size. Plants grow and entrap this intruder!" Nature ordered squeezing her globe tightly. Out of nowhere hundreds of tiny trees sprouted entangling the Nameless. Nature kept the plants growing until she couldn't stand up anymore. She fainted and with her went her plants.

"Nature! My turn. You've messed with the wrong Entity. Hope you like knowledge because you're about to get a mind full," Wisdoms said unwrapping his scroll and he began to read the ancient text. Instantly the Nameless was pinned to the ground by the ancient wisdom.

With a great heave it sent the knowledge back to Wisdom. He tried to stand up through the surge of power, but it was too much. He fell to the ground out of the fight.

"No! I guess its up to me then. I won't let you take us. I hope you can handle raw emotion!" Emotion screamed firing the full rainbow of emotions at the Nameless. It faulted and fell backwards. She kept pressing her advantage trying to drive it back.

That's when the Nameless sent out tendrils from its shroud and grabbed her. She screamed and tried to break free. It held her tighter and tighter until she passed out. The Council of Four had been defeated. It was all over.

"NO! Council Members get up and fight! Leave them alone!" Star and Nova screamed together. But it did no good. The Nameless floated above their bodies and enveloped them. Once that was done the anti-creature sped out of the room and headed towards the sky.

The four girls finally broke their bonds and ran towards the broken windows. They watched helplessly as the world below started to die at an accelerated rate. The fighting forces below had stopped. They to saw the Nameless in the sky and knew what it meant.

"Its all over then. The Council was the only thing that could stop the Nameless from fulfilling its plans. Now that they're gone there's no hope at all," Star admitted sadly. She was crying her heart out.

"They're not dead yet! I can still feel them in my mind and I know you can to. There's still time to save the day," Kali urged.

"How do you propose we do that? This isn't your stupid novel! What you write doesn't always come true in real life!" Nova told her harshly. In her mind there was nothing that could stop the total annihilation of the multiverse and Entara now.

"My novel? That's it! Kelsey bring my bag here. I left the story in there. Thanks. Okay look here everyone. According to my story we win the fight, but the part of how we do it is missing."

"So? What good does that do us then? If we don't know how to beat them what good is your story?" Nova asked.

"Because this highlighted text here answers the question to the prophecy the Council told us about. When you two combined your powers, you combined two opposing forces as one creating one new thing of great power. The four of us, two Entities and two humans, make two people because of the link between us. Working together we're one person. We can do this if we work as on now come on! There isn't much time," Kali told them taking off with the others close to her heels.

The Nameless hovered over the planet waiting patiently for its servants in the Temple to give the signal. Once Entara was destroyed it could use the reality bubbles and eliminate one reality at a time. After returning the Killgonas to their normal state it would finally complete its mission. With the Council trapped inside its body and slowly fading there was nothing to stop it. "Soon I will return to my beautiful lifelessness. The end of all life is upon us!"

"Keep dreaming, Nameless. The multiverse is going to continue to produce life and Entara will continue to exist. You and your Killgonas are going to the anti-universe for all eternity!" Kali shouted as she appeared in space right in front of it surrounded by a brilliant glow. Around her neck hung a crystal necklace.

"So you finally got your crystal. Do you think I'm frightened of you?"

"You should be! Because I'm going to get rid of you with a little help from my new friends and family. Say hello guys," she said as Kelsey, Star, and Nova popped into existence next her. Kelsey also had her crystal and the twin Entities auras were off the chart.

The Nameless looked upon the four girls in front of it and felt real fear. The four of them formed a pincer by linking hands and it got ready for their attack by firing a gigantic burst of power at them. They didn't hesitate a second. Within moments the four girls unleashed their full force of power. A power that was fueled by love, friendship, and imagination unlike anything the Nameless or its forces had seen before.

"You can't destroy me without harming the Council. Give up before someone gets hurt otherwise my forces will obliterate you," The Nameless warned them as it used some of the Council's own power to force them back.

"Not going to happen. I have my own backup," Kali replied. *Entities, Crystal Carriers, and Champions of Entara. Lend me your power so I can defeat this thing and its minions once and for all. Think of what gives you the greatest pleasure and your power will double. Only by working together as one can the Nameless truly be defeated.*

Through out the multiverse and Entara everyone heard the Kali's telepathic cry. The Crystal Carriers touched their crystals and concentrated hard on their pleasures. The Entities stopped fighting and each one of them sent a concentrated burst of power to Kali and her friends.

The effect was amazing. The entire color spectrum surrounded the girls as the energy passed through the girls and into Kali's body. Once inside she acted like a catalyst magnifying the power a thousand fold. Holding her hands high above her head she formed a huge ball of energy. With a great amount of effort they sent the ball at the Nameless, which screamed as it absorbed the anti creature. Its body twisted and contorted as it released the Council. Down below the Killgonas, who were connected to their Master, also withered in pain. The ball engulfed the Nameless and all the Killgonas weakening then as it sped back into the anti-universe were it deposited them. It then created a thick layer of pure imagination trapping the Killgonas inside permanently.

Once gone the energy ball headed for the sky were it exploded releasing a wave of healing energy all over Entara. Almost at once the damage was repaired and the injured healed. The remaining energy headed into the multiverse where it attached itself to the energy barrier. A surge of power rippled through all the realties until it produced a brand new seal. The seal attached itself to the door in the Temple closing it forever. It was finally over. The battle had been won. Entara, the multiverse, and even the anti-universe were safe once more.

Everyone was cheering and celebrating their hard earned victory. Slick and Gerry were congratulating each other on a job well done. A huge cheer went up when the Council reappeared, but an even louder one went up for the quartet.

"Congrats, Kali. You did it! You saved the entire multiverse!" Kelsey shouted

"We did it together, all of us!"

"Hey girls look like your okay. And you found your powers that's awesome," Gerry commented.

"Yeah I just had to look harder."

"Guess what? There's going to be a huge celebration and were invited as the guest of honor!" Slick told them excitedly.

"Then what are we standing here for? Its party time!" Kelsey shouted.

Epilogue

That night everyone was celebrating the greatest triumph sense the war ended three eons ago. There were fireworks, music and dancing, tons of decorations from hundreds of worlds, and a huge feast. Everybody was having a good time enjoying a well earned victory celebration.

There was a huge wooden table set up that was covered with all sorts of dishes. Fresh fruit and veggies, lots of meat, all sorts of things to drink and to top it all off a humongous chocolate cake. Seated at the head of the table was the Council of Four fully recovered from their ordeal. On their right were Star, Nova, and the rest of their family who were happy to be back together. On their left were the Four Champions as they were being called. Further down were Guardian and his family.

Currently everyone was watching a power demonstration by Faith, Sporty, Animal, and Gem. Faith had created a bunch of halos that Animal had a giga beast job through while Sporty had the little guy chase a ball that Gem had coated with crystals. It was a pretty amazing sight and an excellent source of entertainment.

"As you can see Council Members our recent crises has taught us a lot about working together," Faith told them as she retrieved her halos. Her powers had increased greatly since the battle and she was looking forward to testing them out.

"That's right no matter what you can always count on your friends to help you out," Sporty added picking up her ball. This battle had been the greatest challenge of her life and she couldn't wait to see what was next.

"Even if that help comes in the form of lending a helping hand out and not complaining," Animal said petting his giga beast, which looked like a cross between a kitten and a puppy. This battle had only increased his desire to protect all animal life and spend more time with his girl.

"Yeah, it took us twenty minutes to clear the rubble off of these two and what do we get? Not even a thank you. Standards are falling let me tell you," Gem said. He was laughing and smiling knowing that nothing could, not even exams, could be worse then what he had just faced.

"Were not that bad!" protested Sporty, but the other's drowned her out.

"Its nice to see that everything is returning to normal so quickly. I guess everything did work out in the end." Jasmine admitted to her family. She was pleased to have finally left the Temple and be outside. It was a wonderful feeling.

"It sure did dear. Your father and I are very proud of how you handle yourself today in the fight. Even when the chips were down you kept believing that things would work out," Sapphire said hugging her daughter tightly.

"Its because of that belief that the Temple is still safe. You must have done something to keep the reality bubbles safe while the rest of us were incapacitated because the Killgonas in the Temple couldn't get into the chambers. What did you do exactly?" Guardian asked curiously.

"I just let my natural powers take over. I was so intent on protecting you two from harm my ability to control herbs and spices must have activated delaying the Killgonas in taking over the Temple. You know how sensitive their noses are. They must have been chocking in all those sweet scents," Jasmine simply told her folks.

On the other side of the table Asteroid was talking about the fight with his parents. "I have to admit I was scared to death. I've never had to fight that hard in my life before. Still I know we did the right thing in helping with the fight. Hey it even helped me get control of my powers."

"That it did son that it did. I'm just pleased none of our kind are dead and Entara is safe again," Moon informed him.

"I'm just glad my two daughters are safe at home where they belong. Although now their adults I probably won't be seeing them as much," Sun sniffed

"Were not adults yet Mom, just graduated students," Nova told her.

"Yeah, now we can help out more often in the multiverse and be with you so you don't have to worry about us so much," Star added.

"Somehow I think that's impossible," Kali told her.

"Yeah from what we've seen your Mom is super protective. How you ever survive?" Kelsey asked as she ate some ice cream.

Before she could reply the Council cleared their throats and stood up. Everyone stopped talking, the boys quit playing poker, and calmness settled upon the world. It was time to hear exactly what the Council thought of their champions.

"Thank you all for the tremendous courage and bravery you have shown today. Three eons ago we thought we seen the last of the Nameless and that its Killgonas weren't a major threat. For three eons we lived in peace and added in the reconstruction of the multiverse with the help of Crystal Carriers never dreaming of a possible threat." Time began.

"But one did arise and we didn't trust you enough to see how you handled it. Instead we ignored it and delayed taking action. Finally we sent two teenagers on a journey through the stars on an impossible mission. To find the one person who could add us in the fight against the Nameless." Nature continued.

"But even we couldn't foresee them returning with four crystal carriers or the power they demonstrated. Working together they helped save everything we hold dear and for that they have our eternal gratitude. But more importantly you have your Crystal Carrier necklaces, which will add you in your mission once you go home," Wisdom told them.

"Even though you live in a normal reality you can still help with the balance between good and evil. The crystal shows that you are a representative of good and protected by us. Your powers include; the power to use one of our own, double your own, create a force field, heal, transform you clothes, teleportation, location, lie detector, energy manipulation, it can contain a piece of your soul, summon Star and when you join them together unlimited power. Also your aging will slow down so you can help out longer. Lastly you will be able to move through time and space through short distances. I hope you will use it wisely and remember if you ever get lost in the dark hold the crystal to find the light," Emotion said finishing up.

The four look at one another and nodded their heads. They understood what they were getting into and gladly accepted their new responsibilities. Kali stood up and spoke for all of them. "Thank you Council and thank you everyone. The four of us have shared a spectacular adventure, which we won't soon forget. I only hope that we can perform in our own world as good as we did here."

"I have no doubt you will. Now let's go dance!" Star said dragging her friends to the dance area. Everyone followed laughing and having a good time knowing soon they have to say goodbye.

No one noticed Kali's book bag glowing. Inside her novel finished writing itself. Perhaps there'll be more tales, but no one knew for sure. One could only hope.

LaVergne, TN USA
28 November 2010
206511LV00003B/100/P

9 781606 726587